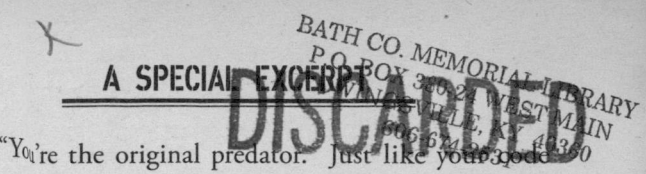

"You're the original predator. Just like your code name says. Cain. History's first assassin. And you more than honored your predecessor's legacy. No one lived for the kill more than you."

Collins stood in the doorway and watched Lucas drive off into the night. A good man, Lucas White. Always had been, always would be. No field soldier could ask for a better man to have calling the shots during crisis time. And this was crisis time. A man like Lucas White didn't come out of retirement unless something big was going down. Of course, he hadn't laid all his cards on the table. He knew more than he was telling. But that's the way it should be. Information, especially early on, shouldn't be dispensed too soon. Too many chances that it might be inaccurate, too many opportunities for leaks. Occasional whispers are better than loud screams during the early stages of any mission. Lucas would fill in the blanks when the time was right.

Hell, man, you're a psycho.

Collins smiled.

The killing never ends, does it, my boy? It just goes on and on.

The smile widened.

You're the original preda

Goddamn right.

HEIRS OF CAIN

TOM WALLACE

MEDALLION

P R E S S

Medallion Press, Inc.

Printed in USA

HEIRS OF CAIN

TOM WALLACE

DEDICATION:

For Julie Watson:
No brother could have a better sister.

Published 2010 by Medallion Press, Inc.

The MEDALLION PRESS LOGO
is a registered trademark of Medallion Press, Inc.

Typeset in Adobe Garamond Pro
Printed in the United States of America

ISBN: 978-160542102-5

10 9 8 7 6 5 4 3 2 1
First Edition

ACKNOWLEDGMENTS:

The author wishes to thank Kerry Estevez, an early and ferocious champion of the book. Also, two superb and enlightening books by Joseph J. Trento—*The Secret History of the CIA* and *Prelude to Terror: The Rogue CIA and the Legacy of America's Private Intelligence Network*—provided valuable insight into the darker involvement of the CIA during the Vietnam War. Thanks to Brooks Downing for guiding me through Florida. And a big thanks to the usual suspects, Amy Reynolds, Sarah Small, Wanda Underwood, Ed Watson, and Denny Slinker. And, always, Marilyn Underwood, my companion and confidante. Thanks to my editors, Emily Steele and Helen Rosburg, for smoothing out the wrinkles and pushing me to go the extra mile.

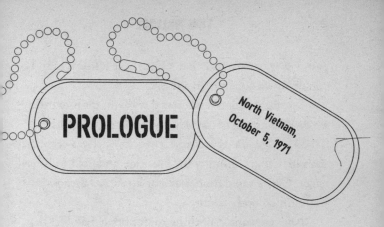

PROLOGUE

North Vietnam,
October 5, 1971

Nguyen Van Luc stood on the riverbank, shifting nervously from one foot to the other, watching intently as the small boat silently cut through the murky water. In the darkness, with the dense jungle at his back and a cold moon overhead, Nguyen, a notorious Vietnamese operative and black marketer, had but two things on his mind: pass along the message, and get away as quickly as possible.

He didn't care for these men. Didn't trust them. Most of all, though, he feared them.

Especially the leader, the one called Cain.

All Vietnamese, North or South, friend or foe, feared him.

Cain.

The fuckin' man was a legend on both sides of the DMZ. A stone-cold assassin known for killing with his bare hands. A "Cain kill" was rumored to be so quick, so perfectly executed that the victim seldom experienced pain. It was also said that Cain never killed a man he couldn't look squarely in the eyes.

Skeptics questioned whether this was the truth, or merely another fabrication of the U.S. mythmaking apparatus.

Not Nguyen. He knew it was true. He'd seen the man in action, killing with precision and cold indifference. Cain's reputation was not built on falsehoods; it was built on body count.

Nguyen wanted nothing to do with a man like that.

With the boat only a few yards from shore, Nguyen lit a cigarette, took two deep drags, and then tossed it into the water. Rubbing his hands together, he squinted into the darkness, silently counting the men in the boat. Five. *Oh, shit.* Fear stabbed at his heart. *That many here this time. Even that crazy goddamned Indian, the one called Seneca. This must be big.*

He plucked another cigarette from the pack and tried to light it. He couldn't. His shaking hands wouldn't cooperate. Frustrated, he threw the cigarette into the water and watched it float away. As the boat finally slid into the bank and the men came into focus, Nguyen's fear overwhelmed him. He felt the warm piss stream down his legs.

Nguyen forced a smile, stepped back, and watched as the men silently climbed out of the boat. They were dressed in dark pajamas, and their faces were painted black. Each one carried an M16, a machete—and a knife.

Together, Nguyen thought, they looked like five

faces of death.

When all five men were on the bank, Nguyen quickly pulled the boat behind a mango tree and covered it with bamboo and grass. His task completed, he took a deep breath, tried to steady his nerves, and then turned to face the five assassins.

The one called Snake, wiry and wild-eyed, put a hand on Nguyen's shoulder. Nguyen spun around, terrified, heart beating rapid-fire.

"Lucky, my man," Snake said. "Good to see you. We had our doubts about the fidelity of your commitment to our side."

"Not to worry. Lucky always on side of money."

Snake snickered. "A true patriot, huh, Lucky?"

"Patriot, yes. Lucky a patriot for sure."

Cain moved forward. "Did Houdini give you the map?"

"No need map." He shook his head. "Lucky born near here. Village less than three kilometers away."

"There's supposed to be a map," Cain said.

"Map in Lucky's head."

"Forget this shit, Cain," Seneca said, stepping forward. "This ain't playin' out like we planned."

"Yeah, Seneca's right, man," Deke said. "If this sorry slopehead is lyin', we're screwed. I may be just a dumb nigger from Chicago, but I ain't stupid. No way we should go in blind."

Holding up both hands, Lucky said, "I no lie.

Village three kilometers west. Meeting in school building. Wife's cousin work there. I know this area good."

Nguyen looked into the faces of all five men, his eyes finally coming to rest on the one man who had remained silent, the only one who exhibited any degree of understanding or sympathy—the one called Cardinal. Nguyen's scared eyes pleaded for a friend.

"What do you think, Cain?" Cardinal said, sensing Nguyen's silent plea. "You trust him?"

"Trust him? No. Believe him? Yes. He has no reason to lie. He hates the North Vietnamese more than we do."

"Yeah, and he hates us even more," Seneca said. "I say, no way we go in. Houdini scrounged us a map. We use it, or we pull the plug."

"We're too close to pull out," Cain said.

"Maybe we should have brought Rafe and Moon," Deke said. "Maybe we're travelin' light."

"We don't need them," Cain responded. "We're going in."

"No fuckin' way," Seneca said.

Gray eyes narrowing, Cain moved two steps toward Seneca.

"With the gooks, you've got a chance," he said, looking hard at Seneca. "With me, you don't. Your call."

The two men glared at each other for almost a minute. Seneca's right hand touched his knife, his fingers dancing up and down the handle. The other four men watched, barely breathing, paralyzed, as though they stood in a minefield.

After several more seconds of thick silence, Seneca grinned slightly and then backed away. "Have it your way, Cain. You have the most stripes. And as we all know, stripes rule."

"Don't challenge me, Seneca. Ever."

The Indian sneered, "Yes, sir, Captain."

Cain grabbed Lucky by the arm and pulled him close.

"If one of my men dies—one—I'll hunt you down like a dog. And when I find you—and I *will* find you—I'll cut your gook heart out and feed it to your children. Then I'll kill them. Understand?"

Trembling, Lucky nodded and backed away. "General White speak to me this morning. Say give message to you."

"Lucas? What message?"

Lucky dug into his shirt pocket, took out a piece of wadded paper, unfolded it, and handed it to Cain.

Cain read it silently, then out loud. "*Tuez le messager.*"

He carefully folded the note, looked at Seneca, and gave a slight nod. Seneca pulled Lucky forward, flashed a quicksilver smile, and then plunged his knife into Lucky's chest. Eyes wide and registering total and absolute terror, Lucky staggered toward the water, dropped to his knees, looked around quizzically, and then collapsed into a spreading pool of his own blood.

"Dumb little slant-eyed bastard wasn't so lucky after

all," Seneca said, wiping blood from his knife.

"Wonder what's in his head now," Snake said, laughing. "Wonder if that map will guide him into gook heaven."

"You believe gooks got their own heaven?" Deke asked.

"Nah, not really, 'cause they ain't got a soul."

"All God's children got a soul, Snake," Deke said. "Even the gooks."

"Yeah, and all rats have fleas," Snake answered.

Deke bent down and began rummaging through Lucky's pockets. He stood up, holding a wad of U.S. money. Most of the bills were hundreds.

"Goddamn. Look at this," Deke said. "Must be ten grand here. Where'd a little dink monkey like him come up with this kind of scratch?"

"War's a profitable enterprise," Snake said. "Everybody knows that."

"Yeah, profitable for everybody but the killers," Cardinal answered.

"Here. Take some," Deke said, offering a handful of bills to Snake.

"Money's not what I want," Snake said, moving toward the river's edge. "What I want is to waste every dink in this fuckin' shit-hole country. Every fuckin' dink, regardless of what side he's on. They're all useless, chickenshit, untrustworthy slopeheads. I wouldn't give you a drop of spit for any of them."

Snake yanked Lucky's body into a sitting position

and, with a single swing of his machete, separated head from torso. He held up Lucky's head, kissed his cheek, and then tossed the head into the river.

"Rest in pieces, Charles."

The head hit the water and rolled over, eyes open and looking toward the night sky.

Deke said, "You is one cold motherfucker, Snake. One hard-hearted white dude."

"Don't pay to have a heart in this place," Snake said.

"Pocket the money, Deke," Cain ordered. "We need to move. It's blood time."

"My favorite time," Deke said, stuffing the cash into his pocket.

Snake rolled Lucky's body into the water. "One down. A million to go."

Their destination: an old school building in the North Vietnamese village of Hoa Binh.
Their mission: kill nine high-level ARVN generals and two Russian advisers.
Operation Nightcrawlers.
The final test; a preview of coming attractions.

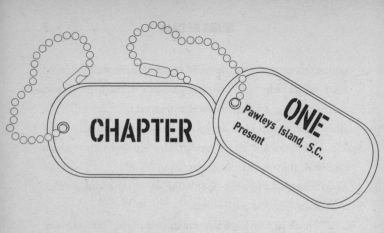

CHAPTER ONE

Arnie Moss cursed out loud. The phone was going to ring. Don't ask him how he knew; he just did. And he was seldom wrong. Knowing when the blasted phone would ring was a special knack he'd had since he was a kid. His mom always told him his intuition was a blessing from God. He wasn't so sure. A true gift, he felt, should extend beyond knowing when the phone would ring. If he only had the same ability with picking ponies at the racetrack or the Lotto numbers, he wouldn't be stuck in this crappy job. He'd be on the inside looking out.

He especially didn't want a phone call now. Not while he was watching a recording of Jack Nicklaus winning the 1986 Masters championship. Moss considered Jack the most incredible friggin' golfer to ever stride down a fairway—Bobby Jones, Ben Hogan, Sam Snead, or Arnie notwithstanding. What the Golden Bear accomplished during his career swamped by a mile anything any of his

8

predecessors had ever done. Or ever dreamed of doing. Sure, those other guys were great, but there is great and there is *great*. And Jack was the greatest of them all, even at age forty-six, when he won the Masters for the sixth time. The Golden Bear had the goods, which was all that counted. Jack Nicklaus was Michael friggin' Jordan in golf shoes. The best of the best.

Ever.

But at this particular moment, Jack was in deep trouble. His second shot lay hidden behind a tree, his view of the green obstructed. Moss took some comfort in Jack's predicament, in knowing the greatest golfer of all time could produce a hacker's result. Right now Moss knew exactly how Jack felt.

Jack's third shot, which he somehow managed to curve around the tree, landed on the edge of the green and rolled to within four feet of the cup. Quickly, Moss's connection to the Golden Bear was broken. Watching, he could only shake his head in amazement, awe, and wonder. *Jesus, how can one human body possess such extraordinary ability? Incredible. Simply incredible.*

Ten seconds later, the phone rang.

Well, at least the caller had the decency to wait until after the Golden Bear's latest bit of magic.

"Pinewood Estates. Moss speaking." He pulled the phone away from his ear and eyed the TV screen again. "What can I do for you?" he asked, hoping the answer would be short and sweet. He didn't want to miss Jack's hard-earned birdie putt.

What Moss heard wasn't an answer. Indeed, what rattled his eardrum and caused him to flinch barely qualified as a man's voice. It was shrill, high-pitched, and extremely loud. Obviously panicked, the caller threw out words in bunches, making absolutely no sense. In the background was hysterical screaming. Probably a woman's, Moss guessed, although he wouldn't swear to it. It could just as easily have been coming from a mortally wounded animal.

"Bungalow nine, hurry, the man's been shot, looks like he's dead, hurry, God, please hurry!"

Moss put the phone directly against his ear. "Slow down a little, willya? I can't make out a word of what you're saying."

"He's dead, been shot in the head, hurry!"

"Who's dead?" A feeling of dread began to work its way up Moss's spine. Jack's golfing adventures had faded into the distance.

"Bungalow nine, please hurry!"

Moss could barely hear the man's words above the woman's screaming. "You said nine?"

"Yes. Oh, God, hurry!"

Moss processed the information. "Nine. That's Taylor. And you say he's dead?"

"Dead . . . yes."

"Have you called 911?"

"No."

"Well . . . hell . . . I guess I'd better do it."

"Please, just hurry."

"I'm on my way. Don't touch or disturb anything. Hear me?"

"No, we won't. Please hurry."

Moss placed the phone back on the receiver. Considering what he'd just been told, he was surprisingly calm—no fear, no panic at all. Fear, for him, was little more than an imposter once the unknown was revealed. Death he could handle. Death he had seen. Death he understood. But the unknown—that's a different ball game. It was spooky and unsettling.

He dialed the police, gave them the details of what he'd been told, hung up, gave a nod as Jack sank his putt, then jumped into his battered red Pontiac.

Two minutes later, he walked into bungalow nine.

Three people were waiting in the living room. Two men stood on either end of the couch on which a woman sat and sobbed into a Kleenex. Moss noticed the woman's raven black hair, the apparent result of a recent dye job. With her head down and eyes covered by tinted glasses, she looked to Moss like Roy Orbison.

Not exactly a compliment, Moss knew, but . . . the truth is the truth. When she looked up, Moss found himself staring into the face of a woman who had seen her share of summers and was making one last attempt at outrunning the clock. It was a race, Moss decided, that she had lost long ago.

The two men stood still as statues, flanking her like a pair of gargoyles. They were similarly dressed, wearing khaki shorts, loose-fitting flowery shirts, sandals, black socks that stretched to their knees, and grim looks. Not natives of the South, Moss concluded—not with those threads and that chalky, pale skin. These were big city folks all the way. Quintessential snowbirds, retired, vacationing in the sun, living the easy life.

"He's in the upstairs bathroom," the man nearest Moss said, his voice quivering and barely audible. He started to say something else but hesitated, instead putting a hand on the woman's shoulder.

She burst into louder sobs, sending a fresh stream of black mascara tears racing down her cheeks.

Moss hurried up the stairs and went straight to the bedroom. It was no trouble finding it; all of these bungalows had practically the same design. Connected to the master bedroom, the bathroom was to the left as he entered. He looked around the room. The bed was still made, the curtain closed. He noticed a dark spot he guessed to be a bloodstain on the comforter. The television was on,

its volume turned all the way down. Moss glanced indifferently at the TV screen. Golden Bear Jack had pulled
off another miraculous shot. This time, however, Moss
wasn't interested in Jack's magic act.

Moss opened the bathroom door and looked down
at the body lying on the floor. It was Taylor, all right,
and he was a goner. He was on his back, eyes open, head
ringed by a ghastly scarlet halo. Moss knelt down and felt
for a pulse. For an instant he thought he detected one, but
there was no way. He'd seen plenty of dead men in Korea,
and he wasn't mistaking this. Taylor was history, done in
by the bullet that had crashed into the side of his head.

Moss stood, careful not to touch anything, and
began looking around the bathroom for a gun. He
couldn't find one, and that bothered him. He had auto-
matically leaped to the conclusion that this was a suicide.
But how could there be a gunshot suicide without a gun?
There couldn't be, which meant it had to be something
else. But what?

Murder? No way. A murderer would have to come
through the front gate, past him—and that damn sure
didn't happen.

Of course, there was a second possibility: the murderer could be one of the residents living at Pinewood
Estates. *No, that's an even more ridiculous notion,* Moss
thought. *The folks here may be old, wealthy, and somewhat cantankerous, but they aren't killers.*

Had to be a suicide, Moss finally concluded. *Definitely. Okay, so where's the damn gun?*

As Moss turned and started to walk out, he heard a groan. Pivoting, he looked behind him and then down at the body on the floor. Several seconds passed before he realized Taylor wasn't dead. He knelt down next to the wounded man, whose groaning had given way to a rattling sound deep in his chest.

"Taylor, it's me—Moss. You're gonna be all right. You gotta hang on. Hear me? I'm going for help."

Moss tried to rise but felt a violent tug from Taylor. The grip was surprisingly strong for a man who was only seconds away from death.

Moss drew close enough to feel Taylor's breath on his face. Blood began to trickle from Taylor's nostrils and the corner of his mouth. The groaning was now a hollow, gurgling sound.

Death may not have arrived, but it hovered close by.

"Fallen," Taylor managed to whisper.

"Don't try to talk. I'm going for help." Moss tried to stand, but Taylor again drew him closer.

"Fallen angels," Taylor said, his voice fading.

"What's that?"

"Fallen angels," Taylor repeated, this time sending the word *angels* into eternity on the winds of his final breath.

All signs of imminent death vanished. The rattling and gurgling ceased; the eyes, fixed and dilated, stared straight into nothingness. The dark angel had descended. There was no mistaking it this time. Taylor was gone.

Two uniformed police officers rushed into the room with weapons drawn. Close behind was a plainclothes detective. Moss looked at them and then stood. *They needn't hurry*, he thought. *Hurrying ain't gonna do nobody any good.* No one was going to be saved tonight.

"Dead?" one of the officers asked, seemingly to no one in particular. He had to repeat the one-word question before Moss responded.

"Afraid so."

"Who are you?" the detective asked, stepping between the two officers.

"Arnie Moss. The night watchman."

"You find the body?"

"No."

"Who did?"

"One of the clowns downstairs."

The older of the two officers knelt beside the body, felt for a pulse, briefly examined the wound, and then looked up at the detective. "Gunshot. Pretty heavy duty, from the looks of it. Body's still warm, too. Couldn't have happened much more than an hour, hour and a half ago."

The detective's eyes scanned the room. "Where's the gun?"

"Didn't find one," Moss answered.

"Really? That's interesting." The detective motioned

to the two officers. "Start a canvass of the neighborhood. Maybe somebody heard something. And when CSU gets here, make sure they go over this place with a fine-tooth comb. I mean, scour the place. You ever been printed, Moss?"

"Yeah. When I was in the Army. Why?"

"We'll need to eliminate your prints from any others we might find."

"You sayin' I'm a suspect?"

"You and everyone else who wasn't with me the past two hours."

Moss immediately disliked the detective. The smugness, the arrogance, the better-than-thou demeanor. Moss saw enough of that from the folks living at Pinewood Estates. Old farts with fat bank accounts, healthy stock portfolios, and overblown opinions of themselves. He tolerated it, barely, because he had to. It went with the job. But seeing the same attitude in this jerk detective almost made him sick to his stomach. There was no excuse for behaving in such a disrespectful way.

The detective, whose name was Randy McIntosh, walked over to the bed and looked down at the small dark stain. He stood perfectly still for a moment, then abruptly started out the door, signaling for Moss to follow.

Moss seethed inside with anger.

"Which one of you found the body?" McIntosh asked before reaching the bottom of the steps.

"I did."

"And who are you?"

"Clyde Bennett." The man paused, then looked at the other man and the sniffling woman. "That's Landon Walker, and the lady is Loretta Young." Again he paused, before adding, "Just like the movie star."

"Never heard of her."

"She was before your time."

"Tell me about it," McIntosh said, removing a notepad from his coat pocket. "Why are you folks here?"

"Taylor is . . . was . . . a friend of ours from the old days," Clyde Bennett said. "Sometimes the four of us got together and played cards. Gin rummy, you know? Penny a point. Nothing serious. That's what we were going to do tonight."

"I take it you're not from around here," McIntosh asked.

"New York. Syracuse. Not the City, which everyone assumes when you tell them you're from New York. We come down to Pawleys Island three, four times a year. Have for more than twenty years. When we do, we always make it a point to see Taylor."

McIntosh looked at Moss. "You verify that?"

"Yeah." McIntosh's question fired Moss's anger. "What do you think? That I let strangers pass through the gate?"

McIntosh glared at Moss for several hard seconds, then turned back toward Clyde Bennett. "How long since you found the body?"

"What? Twenty, twenty-five minutes now? I don't know exactly. As soon as I did, I called the guard shack. Mr. Moss was here almost before I hung up."

"Did you see a gun or weapon of any type?"

Clyde Bennett looked puzzled. "No, sir. Come to think of it, I didn't. But I have to confess I didn't spend much time up there. When I saw Taylor on the floor, I ran straight down here and called Mr. Moss."

"How'd you get in?" McIntosh asked. "You have your own key?"

"The door was unlocked. I called out several times, and when there was no answer, we figured Taylor was out by the pool and simply couldn't hear us. When I saw he wasn't out there, Landon suggested I check upstairs, that maybe he'd fallen asleep. I went up there. That's when—"

"He was dead when you found him, right?" McIntosh asked.

"Yes, sir."

"No, he wasn't," Moss interrupted. All eyes quickly shifted to him. "He was still alive when I got to him. Barely, but still alive."

McIntosh moved closer to Moss, who was leaning against a bookcase. "You're positive of that?"

"I'm positive. He tried to tell me something before he died."

"What?"

"He muttered something about fallen angels."

"Fallen angels? You sure about that?"

"Yeah, I'm sure," hissed Moss through clenched teeth. "Fallen angels."

McIntosh wrote something in his notepad, then looked around at the other three. "*Fallen angels* mean anything to any of you?"

McIntosh's question was met with silence. Finally, after a few seconds, Clyde Bennett said, "Means nothing to me. How about you, Landon?"

An ashen Landon Walker shook his head and looked down at the floor.

"You said you've been coming down here"—McIntosh looked at his notes—"more than twenty years. How did you know Taylor?"

"Through Loretta," Clyde Bennett said. "She and Taylor went to high school together."

"In St. Louis," Loretta Young whispered. "A long time ago."

"Landon and I first met Taylor right after he got back from his last tour in Vietnam," Clyde Bennett said. "That was sometime in the early seventies."

"When was the last time you saw Taylor?" McIntosh asked.

"About four months ago," Clyde Bennett said. "That's right, isn't it, Landon?"

"Yes."

"Did he know you would be here tonight?" McIntosh asked.

"Oh, sure, I spoke with him last night," Clyde Bennett said. "Just after eight. Told him to expect us sometime around five thirty or six."

"Anyone else know you were coming?"

"Not that I'm aware of."

McIntosh turned to Moss. "Anybody been here to see Taylor lately? Say, within the past week?"

"No."

"I'll need to speak with the three of you again tomorrow at headquarters," McIntosh said. "Around ten. To take your statements and get fingerprints. That includes you, Moss. It would also be helpful if you folks could stick around these parts for a few days. That pose any problem?"

"No, no problem at all," Clyde Bennett answered. "We'll do anything you ask of us."

McIntosh closed his notepad and crammed it into his coat pocket. He walked toward the door, stopping along the way to check his appearance in the oval mirror hanging on the wall. After deciding his hair needed combing, he continued toward the door.

"Fallen angels." Rhetorically, he asked, "What was the guy? Some kind of a damn poet?"

CHAPTER TWO

Dark clouds were beginning to drift in from behind the fine arts building, a sure sign heavy rains were on the way. The area forecast had called for a pleasant, sunny weekend, with almost no humidity and temperatures in the mid-70s. However, the reality was proving to be something quite different. The clouds now heading for the campus looked like they were coming from the skies of hell. The folks analyzing the weather data really blew it this time around.

So much for all that super radar, Dual Doppler nonsense.

Michael Collins turned his chair toward the window and watched the rain begin to come down, slowly at first, then in windblown sheets. It never failed: Friday, only a few more papers to grade, a big weekend planned, then seemingly out of nowhere, a three-day deluge. As one colleague said, "When tennis or golf calls, rain falls." It was God's eleventh plague, sent to vex teachers. Collins was convinced that educators were the latest recipient's of God's wrath. Ramses only happened to be first.

Collins picked up a blue exam book and began reading. The exam, which covered Eliot's *Four Quartets*, wasn't a final, but it did carry heavy weight. With finals less than two weeks away, the eight grad students in this seminar had undoubtedly put forth their best effort. Better to enter finals week with room for slippage than to have a mountain to climb. Collins used this bit of logic to lessen the disappointment of another dreary weekend. He'd stay inside and give the students his best effort rather than fight this downpour.

He was well into an examination of *Burnt Norton* when Kate Marshall came into his office, walked up behind him, and kissed him on the cheek. She leaned over and kissed his lips.

"Passion inside the hallowed halls of academia," he remarked. "What would the chancellor say if he knew such hanky-panky was going on behind closed doors? He's a Republican, you know. And Republicans aren't big on pleasures of the flesh."

"He'd say, 'Damn, Collins, you're one lucky dude,'" Kate answered, laughing. "'Where can I find someone as lovely, intelligent, sexy, and charming as Miz Marshall?'"

"No, what he'd do is tell you to forget about tenure."

"Yeah, you got that right." She kissed him again, more playfully this time. "I have a theory. Want to hear it?"

"Do I have a choice?"

"Not really," she said, sitting on the edge of his desk. "Shoot."

"Well, I suspect if some of these stuffy, staid old professor types, our beloved chancellor included, would only get laid a little more often—say, once every two weeks instead of every six months—things would be a damn sight better around here. It would relieve all the unwanted pressure and stress that builds up. Make them all a little more pleasant, more agreeable."

"What you're saying borders on treason," Collins said. "And you know the penalty for treason."

"The penalty for horniness is far more severe."

She stood and straightened her skirt. Kate Marshall was medium height with dark hair, hazel eyes, and the figure of a Ford Agency model. Slender legs, nice breasts, killer lips. In male parlance, the total package. But what Collins liked most about her—and had from the first time he'd met her four years before—was her quick, agile mind, her fearlessness and her wonderful sense of humor. Kate Marshall could hang with anyone, male or female.

And yet . . . there was a twenty-year age difference, which he saw as a problem. He'd brought it up on several occasions, hoping for a frank discussion, but she'd quickly dismissed it. Age, she said, simply wasn't important. Not when it involved two slightly weathered adults. It was a viewpoint he didn't entirely agree with.

"Why are you still hanging around this late on a Friday?" he asked.

"Same reason you are—grading papers." She went to the door. "What about tonight? We still on?"

"Can we make it a little later? Maybe nine? I'd really like to get most of these papers finished."

She nodded. "Oh, yes, dedicated educator. I will wait for you until the last *A* is awarded."

"But not past 9:30, right?"

"Right. A girl has to set limits or she risks being labeled a pushover. And . . . I'm no pushover." She started out, then turned back to him. "Oh, I almost forgot. There's a gentleman here to see you. Says it's extremely important. He was rather insistent about it, too. No, actually, he was downright rude."

"Have any idea who he is?"

"No, but his name tag says Nichols."

"Name tag?"

"Yeah, on his uniform."

"What kind of uniform?"

"Army or Marines. I don't know. Military."

"Wonder why some military guy wants to see me."

Kate smiled. "Maybe you flunked his beautiful little daughter."

"I never flunk the beautiful ones," Collins said. "Oh, well, show him in."

He closed the exam book and laid it on top of the

others. Too bad he couldn't finish it now. Spillage from the keen mind of young Bradley R. Alexander III was just getting interesting, and now it had to be put on hold. *What the hell,* Collins reasoned, *if it took old T.S. five years to write the* Quartets, *surely young B. R. Alexander's promising interpretation could wait a few more minutes.*

Kate led the man into the office, but he quickly brushed past her and extended his right hand to Collins. He was stocky-going-on-pudgy, maybe five foot ten, and dressed in full military uniform (Army), complete with a multicolored jigsaw puzzle of commendations pinned to the front of his jacket. On his collar, a single star glistened.

"It's a pleasure to meet you, Professor," he said. "I'm General David Nichols."

Collins shook the general's hand, then motioned for him to take a seat across from the desk. As Nichols found his way into the chair, Collins winked at Kate. "Nine, right?"

Before she could answer, the general said, "And please see that we're not disturbed."

Kate backed out of the office without acknowledging his command.

Collins picked up a can of orange juice and took a sip, letting his eyes examine more closely the cluster of medals on the general's jacket. At first glance they were impressive. But to someone familiar with such matters, there was nothing of real consequence, nothing of genuine merit, nothing that would distinguish the general as an exemplary soldier, like a Combat Infantryman's Badge, Silver Star, or Purple Heart. This was dime store jewelry. Junk. Obligatory gifts for time wasted. Collins's term for such commendations: chest candy.

"What can I do for you, General?" he said. "Sign you up for one of my classes?"

"Not today."

"We're studying the Beat writers next term. Ginsberg, Kerouac, Burroughs. Sure you're not interested?"

The general paused—a little too dramatically, Collins thought—while lighting his pipe. He sucked in a couple of times, exhaled a white circle of smoke, and smiled. "You don't fit the image I had of you. But then, shadows can be deceptive, can't they?"

"Depends on the shadow."

"I hadn't been in Nam more than a week when I first heard of you. I wasn't infantry--just a clean-faced second lieutenant assigned to an ordnance and supply outfit in Qui Nhon. Fairly safe gig, all things considered. Primarily, I was responsible for making sure supplies made it to various parts of the country. And everywhere I went, your name was mentioned. *Cain*. Strange how the men always whispered your name. Like they were praying."

He leaned back, the pipe in his right hand.

"It was all hush-hush, of course," he continued. "The Phoenix Project, Armageddon, Silent Night. No one was supposed to have any knowledge of those ops. But you know the military grapevine. Things have a way of filtering down. Secrets, even top secrets, are seldom well kept. Especially ones that deal with a legend."

Collins finished the orange juice, crushed the can in his right hand, and tossed it into the wastebasket. His eyes remained fixed on the general. "I'm afraid you have me at a disadvantage, General. I have no idea what you're talking about."

The general smiled one of those fraternal smiles that says, *Sure, let's keep this between brothers, between confidants*. His eyes gleamed; his smile widened. "You know, stories about you were passed around like an opium pipe. Everybody wanted some. Give us a fix. Shoot us up with the exploits of the great Cain. Tell us what you've heard about him lately. We couldn't wait to hear about the midnight missions, the kills. You were the rage, I must say."

"Opium pipe, shooting up, fix—terrific imagery, General. Sure I can't interest you in that Beat writers class? I think you would enjoy it. Especially Burroughs."

"No."

"Then I'm afraid you're wasting my time. And yours. You see, I don't know what in the hell you're talking about."

"That's precisely the response I expected," Nichols said. "Indeed, I would have been terribly disappointed had you responded otherwise."

The general reached into his coat pocket and pulled out a piece of paper. He studied it closely for several seconds, folded it, and put it back in his pocket. "Major Collins." He paused, a look of betrayal in his eyes. "Do you mind if I call you Major?"

Expression unchanged, Collins said nothing.

"Major," Nichols continued, "an old friend of yours, Anthony Taylor, was killed sometime yesterday afternoon. Make that *murdered* yesterday afternoon. Before—"

"General, I don't know anyone named Anthony Taylor," Collins said, his expression still stony.

The general nodded slightly, again offering his fraternal smile. "Before Taylor died, he said something I'm sure will be of interest to you."

"If I don't know Taylor, how can anything he said interest me?"

"What Taylor said before he died was 'fallen angels.'"

"Fallen angels? Very poetic. This Taylor—perhaps he was a former student of mine. I've had so many; maybe I've forgotten him."

Collins leaned his chair back against the chalkboard, keeping his icy stare directly on Nichols. He could tell the general was becoming unsettled, unsure of his next move. Things weren't going as expected, as rehearsed. The general's primary plan was crumbling like a melting icecap, and apparently there was no plan B to fall back on. Collins could see the panic gather like storm clouds in the general's eyes.

Silence is a great weapon against the arrogant and phony tough. It's an unwanted burden capable of identifying and crushing imposters. Collins knew it would be only a few more seconds before the general became an emotional casualty.

Collins was wrong. It didn't take that long. Nichols stood and began pacing the room. His cool, confident attitude was gone, replaced by a rising sense of uncertainty.

"Fallen angels," Nichols repeated. "You are familiar with that, aren't you?"

"Don't have a clue what you're talking about, General."

"I'm fully aware of your disdain for someone like me, Major," Nichols said. "Your feelings of superiority. I can't change that. Nor do I care to. The reality is, you have every right to feel superior to me. But you are making a mistake by not talking to me. I'm not the enemy. I'm on your side."

"Can't help you, General. Sorry."

"If this is how you choose to play it, that's your business," Nichols said. "Obviously, I can't make you talk to me. But you'd be well advised to hear me out, to be more cooperative. This is an urgent matter of grave importance. I can't stress this point enough."

"You've got the wrong man."

"Okay, I've got the wrong man." Nichols opened the door. "You'll be hearing from Lucas White within the next twenty-four hours. Maybe he'll have better luck than I had. Good evening, Major."

Collins sat at his desk for almost two minutes after Nichols left. Finally, he stood and scooped up the eight blue exam books. As he reached out to open the door, he looked over his shoulder and caught a glimpse of his own reflection in the darkened window.

He smiled.

Taylor, Phoenix Project, Armageddon, Fallen Angels, Lucas White.

Ghosts reborn.

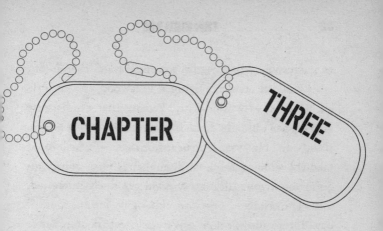

CHAPTER THREE

Moss opened a can of Coors, grabbed a bag of Doritos, flopped down in the reclining chair, and stared blankly at the television screen. Seldom did he drink this early in the day, but last night hadn't been a typical night. Truth was, if he had some bourbon in the apartment he wouldn't waste his time with the Coors.

He had spent the past two hours at the police station, answering basically the same questions he had last night. Why it had taken so long was a mystery to him. What he had to say hadn't taken more than ten minutes. There was one consolation, however. He hadn't needed to deal with that asshole McIntosh. Moss had told his story to a Detective Connors, who was, all things considered, a nice enough young fellow.

Moss looked at the TV screen—Judge Judy was scolding some poor mutt for damaging his neighbor's car—but the images and sounds failed to make much of an impression. His thoughts were on Taylor. *Poor Taylor.*

Of all the residents living at Pinewood Estates, Taylor had been Moss's favorite. Perhaps that was because Taylor wasn't like the rest. Not spoiled or selfish or self-absorbed. He wasn't arrogant, either. Taylor would take the time to talk, ask how things were going, inquire about your life. He seemed genuinely interested, too. The others . . . they wouldn't give you the time of day. If they did speak, it was usually to bark an order or complain about some petty annoyance disrupting their tranquil universe. In their eyes, a poor night watchman didn't exist. It's hard for a person to speak when his nose is aimed straight up in the air, and upturned noses were a fact of life at Pinewood Estates.

Perhaps loneliness was another reason Taylor acted so friendly. Not counting the widows and widowers, he was the only single resident, and unmistakably the most solitary. There were no women in his life, or at least none Moss was aware of. Seldom did he entertain visitors. Save for the two or three times Taylor had his card-playing group over, Moss couldn't remember ever seeing anyone visit the bungalow.

Moss smiled sadly.

Fallen angels. He wondered what that could possibly mean. It meant something important: this much he was sure of. A dying man's final words always mean something important.

Poor Taylor. Poor friggin' Taylor.

Moss flashed back to a morning last fall, to the day when Taylor unexpectedly appeared at the guard shack dressed in shorts, a tank top, and tennis shoes. Moss remembered thinking how Taylor, who was sixty-three at the time, had held up so well physically. Wide shoulders, trim waist, not an ounce of fat or flab on him. And strong-looking, too, like a former athlete who hadn't let himself go. But what really caught Moss's attention were Taylor's arms. Big, powerful arms easing down into hands that looked equally powerful. Moss had seen his share of tough men in his lifetime, and Taylor was a tough man. It didn't take Sherlock Holmes to deduce that Taylor was not someone to tangle with.

Taylor had stopped at the guard shack that morning and asked Moss if he'd be interested in joining him for a walk along the beach. It was the first time anyone at Pinewood Estates included him in anything. Moss, who had finished his shift, quickly said yes. The two men walked for nearly an hour as the reddish-orange sun sprang from the ocean with majesty and splendor.

Only now did Moss realize how little was said during that walk. A couple of times Taylor had remarked about how much he loved the ocean. "It's so free," he'd said. "So restless and free. Not even God himself can tame the ocean." But beyond that, there were few exchanges between the two men. Only silence.

During their walk, Taylor did make a couple of re-
marks that perhaps provided a glimpse into his past.
One, in particular, had stayed with Moss. Taylor said he
had spent a great deal of time in the military doing some
things that were "nasty but necessary." The phrase had
haunted Moss like a bad dream.

"Nasty but necessary." *What the hell could it mean?*
Moss now wondered.

At police headquarters, Moss had asked Detective
Connors for permission to look through Taylor's file.
Connors gave his okay, adding almost apologetically
that there really wasn't much to see and wouldn't be until
Taylor's full military records arrived later in the day.

Moss learned Taylor had been born and raised in
St. Louis, joined the Army at age eighteen, served three
hitches in Vietnam, earned a battlefield promotion to
first lieutenant, and eventually risen to the rank of captain. He retired in 1990 after twenty-seven years of
active duty.

Connors had said there wasn't much to discern from
the file. Moss frowned. *How wrong. How very wrong.*
The one page detailing Taylor's military career spoke
volumes about a man who had dedicated his entire adult
life to serving his country. Connors, a cop, should have
seen that. He should also appreciate it better than most.
If he couldn't, then maybe he should take another look
at the section detailing the awards and commendations

Taylor had earned along the way. Silver Star, Bronze Star, Purple Heart (three times), Medal of Freedom, special citations from Presidents Johnson, Nixon, and Ford, etc., etc. Connors had to be blind to miss all that.

"Looks to me like Taylor was a helluva soldier," Moss had said. "A real warrior."

"Yeah, looks like it," Connors answered, not turning his attention away from the form he was filling out.

Now, as Judge Judy laid down her ruling, Moss sat sipping beer, thinking how little he knew about Taylor and how he wished he'd taken the time to really get to know him. But isn't that the standard lament when someone dies? We wait too long, and then it's too late and we end up racked with regrets for what wasn't done or said. *How sad,* Moss thought. *How very sad.*

Of one thing Moss felt certain: when Connors and that asshole McIntosh did finally receive the full military records, they would see that what was written on the single sheet of paper wouldn't qualify as much more than the tip of the iceberg.

They would learn Taylor—Captain Anthony Leon Taylor, United States Army (Ret.)—had been in deeper shit than most of us could begin to imagine.

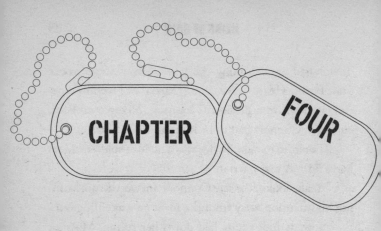

CHAPTER FOUR

Frances Casey was nervous.

She wasn't used to having foreign dignitaries in her restaurant. For that matter, she wasn't used to having dignitaries from anywhere outside the D.C. area in her restaurant. And most of the D.C. crowd? Well, she didn't consider them to be all that dignified, despite the high opinion they had of themselves. But this . . . this situation, with real foreigners and big-shot government folks—well, it wasn't her cup of tea.

Frances went to the front window and looked outside, the rising sun hitting her directly in the eyes. She lowered the blinds and closed them. Turning, she looked at the clock: 7:45. Her guests were scheduled to arrive in less than four hours.

She'd already been at it for two hours despite the promise she'd made to herself to keep things simple, as always, and to basically stick with the regular menu.

The food that had earned her place its great reputation. Lasagna and veal parmesan and those big Caesar salads. Those were her specialties. Still, she felt the need to do something out of the ordinary. But what? What do people from Saudi Arabia eat? She couldn't serve someone from that country a hamburger and french fries. And she certainly didn't want to risk offending them by serving something that went against their religious beliefs. Again she looked up at the big clock: 7:50. "Come on, girl," she muttered under her breath, "get your ass in gear."

Frances went into the kitchen, filled three huge pans with water, and put them on the stove. She opened the walk-in freezer and was about to go inside when she heard the bell above the front door ring. It startled her. She was positive she had locked the door when she'd arrived that morning. The restaurant didn't open for business until promptly at ten, and she never unlocked the front door until she heard the chimes from the old grandfather clock in the corner. That was a tradition her late husband, Harold, had followed for more than thirty years. And Frances believed in upholding tradition.

Feeling somewhat apprehensive, she peered over the swinging door separating the dining area from the kitchen. Standing just inside the front door was a well-built man of medium height with coal black hair and deeply tanned skin. He was dressed in an expensive, blue pin-striped suit, white shirt, red tie, and black shoes. In his right hand, he held a black attaché case. His eyes, which Frances guessed would be as dark as his hair, were hidden behind Armani sunglasses. Her quick inventory revealed one final detail: in her sixty-four years, she had never laid eyes on a more handsome or distinguished-looking man.

"You're a little on the early side. We don't open for another two hours." She moved behind the counter. "Wasn't the front door locked? I'm sure it was."

"No, it was unlocked," he said, his voice deep yet soft.

"Well, I must be slipping in my old age." She came out from behind the counter and extended her right hand. "I'm Frances Casey. I own the place."

"And I'm—"

"Oh, I know who you are," she interrupted. "From the way you're dressed, you're either a lawyer or a government man of some sort. My guess is government."

"Very good. My name is George Armstrong. I'm with the FBI, and I'm here to—"

"Check out the security," Frances said. She held up both hands in a forgive-me gesture. "That's twice I've interrupted you. How ill-mannered. If my daddy were here, he'd swat my behind real hard. I'm truly sorry."

"No problem."

"Now, go on. You're here to do what? Make sure everything is safe for our guests?"

"An excellent observation. You should be in my line of work."

"No, thanks. It's all I can do to come up with something decent enough for those folks to eat."

"From what I hear, you do that just fine."

Frances smiled. She liked this man. And not only because he was quick with a smile or a compliment. There was something genuine about him. Something real, solid. He certainly didn't seem to be at all like the legions of standard-issue government officials and Yuppie lawyers she usually came in contact with. This one was a different breed altogether—a breed she much preferred.

"Whatever it is you have to do, you just go right ahead," she said. "Consider the place yours. I'll do my best to stay out of your way. If you do have any questions or need any help, give me a yell."

"Thanks."

"Would you care for a cup of coffee before you get started?"

"No, thank you. Never drink the stuff."

"My God, man, I don't see how anyone can function without a minimum of two cups of coffee first thing in the morning."

"Coffee just isn't my cup of tea."

"Now, that's clever." She laughed.

Frances occasionally cast a discreet glance at the man as he went about his business. He was thorough; that was for sure—much more so than the men who were in there the day before. He inspected every corner,

every crevice, every forgotten cranny, including several
she would rather he left alone. As Frances watched him,
she reminded herself to give the kitchen area an extra-
good cleaning on Sunday.

"It's a good thing you're not from the health department," she said, laughing. "You've looked into some places
I didn't know existed. I apologize for any mess you find."

The man removed his Armanis, revealing eyes even
darker than she suspected. He was, she surmised, a Native American and, most likely, a full-blooded one at
that. Also, she judged him to be even more handsome
without the glasses.

"No problem at all," he said, looking behind the
oven. "Actually, the place appears to be in tip-top shape
from a security standpoint." He folded his sunglasses
and put them into his shirt pocket. "Where are your
restrooms? Better not forget them."

"Right this way," Frances said, leading him back into
the dining area and down a small hallway. "Would you
like me to tidy up the ladies' room a little before you go in?"

"That won't be necessary."

Frances returned to the kitchen, leaving the handsome, dark-eyed man alone to do his business. She
simply had to get on with her cooking. Time was fleeting; the big shots would be here before she knew it. She
had to get hopping.

More than thirty minutes passed before it dawned

on Frances that she hadn't heard a peep from the man. She put down the knife she was using to peel potatoes and went into the dining area, then on to the restrooms.

Tapping on the door to the ladies' room, Frances said, "Mr. Armstrong, you in there?" No answer. She opened the door and looked inside. Empty. She repeated the same routine at the men's room, again getting the same results. The man was gone. *Peculiar,* Frances thought, *him leaving without saying goodbye.*

She walked to the front door. It was locked. Nice gesture on his part. No, he wasn't at all like the usual self-absorbed, always-in-a-hurry hot shots who are too busy to show kindness or gratitude. *And what a damn fine-looking man. Handsome in every sense of the word. A real hunk.* Frances smiled. *Oh, to be a few years younger.*

Standing alone, Frances was struck by a strange sensation, a feeling that the past hour had been a dream, the Indian hadn't really been there, and the front door had been locked from the beginning.

She frowned and shook her head. "You're going bananas, girl; that's all there is to it."

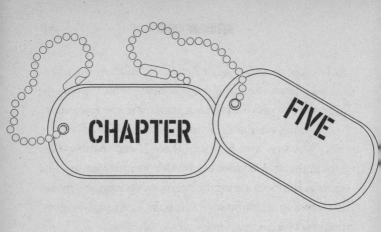

CHAPTER FIVE

Everything had gone smoothly, perhaps a little too smoothly, and that had Frances worried. She didn't trust good times any more than she trusted a used car salesman. That was especially true when the situation presented so many possibilities for disaster. But so far, knock on wood, there hadn't even been the slightest hint of trouble, of the disaster she feared.

Two things stood out: how much her guests appeared to be enjoying the food and how little they appeared to be concerned about security. The last part probably surprised her the most. After all, the guest list was heavy-duty: Sheik Abdul-Nahir, the number two man in Saudi Arabia; Ambassador Richard Froning; two U.S. Army generals; and a deputy chief of staff. For all this combined importance, they were behaving like regular folks out for an afternoon picnic.

Frances Casey was worried. Something just had to

go wrong.

"My dear, this food is absolutely splendid," one of the generals said to Frances's niece Cynthia. "Simply marvelous."

"Thank you, sir," Cynthia said.

"Don't let him fool you, young lady," Ambassador Froning said in a voice heavy with Texas twang. "The general has been eating Army chow so long, he thinks McDonald's is gourmet. He has no idea just how good this food is."

Cynthia smiled awkwardly and walked back into the kitchen.

"Everything going okay?" Frances asked.

"So far, so good," Cynthia answered.

"Well, keep on your toes." Frances carried a pitcher of iced tea through the swinging door. "Anyone need a refill?"

"I could use another shot," Froning said. "How about you, Abdul? Care for more tea?"

"I'm fine, thank you."

His perfect English surprised Frances. "How did you learn to speak our language so well?" she asked.

"I've spent a great deal of time in this country," Abdul said. "Most of it during my college days."

"Oh, so you went to school in the United States?"

"Yes, I did."

"Mind if I ask where?"

"I earned degrees from Georgetown and Princeton. After that, I worked for several years at the United Nations."

"Well, little wonder you speak English better than I do." Frances finished filling the ambassador's glass. "I'm surprised there isn't more security."

"There's more than you might guess," the ambassador said, looking around. "You simply don't see it. Here but not here, if you know what I mean."

Frances nodded. "I guarantee you one thing—if your people here now are half as thorough as the man who was here this morning, then you have no reason for concern."

The ambassador put his fork down. "What man?"

"Oh, George something or other. Let me think for a minute and maybe his last name will come to me. I'm just terrible with names."

"What time was he here?"

"Before eight."

"Can you describe him?"

"Oh, medium height, dark, very handsome. He looked Native American."

"General Marshall, did you have someone in here at that hour?" Froning asked.

"We had no one here until ten hundred hours. And no one fitting that description."

The ambassador looked at Frances. "Did the man specifically say he was with the government? That he was here to inspect the security?"

"Yes, sir, he did. Said he was with the FBI. He sure gave the place a good going over, too."

Froning's expression hardened. "You're positive he said he was with the FBI?"

"FBI . . . yes, that's what he said."

"And you can't recall his name?"

"No. Sorry."

Froning stood and said, "General, why don't you have a couple of your men come in and take a look around? Just to be on the safe side."

"I think that's a good idea." General Marshall rose and walked outside. He returned seconds later, followed by two military policemen.

Frances looked at the grandfather clock: 12:28. Now she was more than worried; she was anxious, tired, frazzled. What she wanted most at this point was for the ambassador and his entourage to finish up and move on. This business of playing host to government leaders and foreign big wigs was for someone else. Her blood pressure was high enough without the added stress and strain that went hand in hand with entertaining a group like this.

One of the MPs asked Frances to show him the way to the alley out back. She forced a weary smile and led him through the kitchen. While he made his way outside, Frances went into the walk-in freezer to get some steaks that needed thawing for tonight's customers. The coolness of the freezer felt good. Finding an upturned Coke case, she pulled it beneath her and sat down, deciding her frazzled nerves needed a rest and the goings on out in the restaurant could proceed for a few minutes without her. She leaned back and closed her eyes.

At least, thank God, the disaster she feared had not come about.

Frances Casey couldn't have been more wrong.

The explosion was so violent it blew Frances off the Coke case and backward into the steel wall. Fortunately for her, a stack of empty cardboard boxes served to soften the impact. As she rolled to the floor, she was acutely aware of the ringing sound in her head, a sound that intensified with each heartbeat. She was equally aware of the pain gripping her body, especially the sharper pain in her left leg and left shoulder.

Feelings are good at a time like this, she reminded herself, *because it means everything is still alive, still functioning.* She tried to roll over but couldn't. Lifting her head, she looked outside the freezer door. A thick cloud of black smoke casually drifted by. Frances again made an effort to stand, only to fall back against the boxes. Although the pain was becoming more and more intense, she was certain of two facts: she was going to live, and she was going to pass out. There was yet another fact, one final truth, and it filled her with great sorrow.

She was the only survivor.

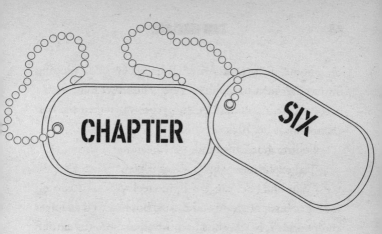

CHAPTER SIX

The shapely redhead paused to check the hem of her skirt. During her inspection, she lifted her eyes and smiled at Collins as he entered Pete's Bar. "Damn thing is forever coming loose," she said.

"Need some help? I have killer hands."

"I'm sure you do." She motioned to an empty chair at the table. "Care for some company?"

"I'm waiting for someone. Sorry."

"Lucky girl." She touched his arm. "I assume it is a woman you're waiting for?"

Collins nodded.

"You can never be too sure these days," she said. "Oh, well, if things don't work out, give me a buzz. Amy Brandenburg. I'm in the book. I'd love to meet you for a drink sometime."

Yeah, me and the rest of the first infantry, Collins thought as he watched her walk away.

"Some dish, that Amy," Pete Daley said, slipping into a chair next to Collins. Pete, a heavyset man with a perpetual grin and dark bushy eyebrows, owned the bar. "Know what her nickname is?"

Collins shook his head.

"Target. Know why?"

"Why?"

"Because everybody takes a shot at her." He laughed loudly. "Hell, Mick, she's been invaded more times than France."

"You could get sued for a line like that, Pete. Better watch your tongue. We live in PC times."

"You know, I'm surprised you haven't had a sample of that," Pete said. "Big man on campus like you. How come you haven't given her a ride?"

"Too much competition; that's why. Besides, I'm getting too old for the chase."

"That's some crappy philosophy you have. If every guy adopted that line of thinking, we'd never get any nookie. We'd all be sitting at home playin' with ourselves."

"There's worse things than not having sex."

"Oh, yeah? Name one. Other than dying, of course."

"Let me think about it," Collins said.

"Think all you want, Mick, but you won't come up with a satisfactory answer. Know why you won't? 'Cause there ain't nothing better than sex. Nothing, I'm telling you."

"What about the absence of art in the world?"

Pete frowned. "You're putting me on, right?"

"No, I'm dead serious. Think about it. No Michelangelo, da Vinci, Shakespeare, T. S. Eliot, Emily Dickinson, Citizen Kane. That would make for a pretty grim world."

"Maybe for you, but for this old infantryman-turned-bartender, not being able to score a little snatch would make my world a whole lot grimmer. You keep Citizen Kane. I'll take the dames."

"Rosebud."

"Huh? Rose who?" Pete leaned forward and pointed a finger at his own face. "See this mug, Mick? It ain't no threat to George Clooney, right? Women don't break down walls to hang out with me. Never have, never will. I'll do whatever it takes to score, anytime, anywhere. I have no shame."

"I never thought you did, Pete."

"Know what your problem is, Mick? You've been sitting behind a desk too long. You need to come down out of that ivory tower, get to know the common folks. Forget all that theory bullshit, and spend some time in the trenches. See what warfare is like in the real world."

"Like I said, Pete, I'm too old for any more wars."

"You're only too old when they put you in the ground or when you can't get it up anymore. Otherwise, you gotta keep pluggin' on."

"And now with Viagra, one of those concerns has

been put to rest. Right?"

"Tell you one thing, Mick. If I ever get a hard-on—
I mean, an *erection*—that lasts more than four hours, I
ain't goin' to see no doctor."

"I would hope not."

"I'm takin' full advantage of those four hours; that I
can promise you. I'd have me some serious fun."

"And make the dames smile, right?"

Pete quickly bounded out of his chair. "Would
you look at that?" He began walking toward the end of
the bar, where a tall, bony man was violently shaking a
woman. "Hey, asshole, leave the lady alone."

The man, his slender arms covered with cheap tat-
toos, pushed the girl away and began moving toward
Pete. "Who you callin' an asshole?" he shouted.

"Who am I looking at, genius?" Pete retorted. The
two men stood face to face in the center of the dance area.
Pete reached out, grabbed the man's arm, and began leading him toward the front door. "Put 'em on the pavement,
pal. I'm not so desperate that I need your business."

The man jerked free of Pete's grasp. "Bad mistake,
tubby. No one lays hands on me 'less I want them to."

"Tough guy—is that it? Well, let's see how tough
you really are."

The man backed away several steps, dug into his
pants pocket, brought out a switchblade knife, and
flicked the blade open. "Keep your fuckin' hands off

me or I'll carve my name on your fat ass." He spit out the words with venomous anger. Then, emitting a loud, primal scream, he jabbed the knife forward, making contact. Having inflicted damage, the man, now even more wired and fanatical, brought the blade to his mouth and licked away the blood.

Pete clutched his forearm, stepped back, and saw the blood begin to ooze through his fingers. "You lousy cocksucker."

The wild-eyed man drew the knife back, prepared to strike again, when he suddenly realized Pete was no longer his primary concern. Someone else was about to enter the equation; someone closing in rapidly from his left—a blurry figure moving at blinding speed. He whirled toward this new threat, cognizant of a terrifying reality: this was a challenger of a different sort.

"You want some of it, too?" he snarled, lunging forward in the general direction of the new threat.

But the man's attacking movement amounted to nothing, his strike coming two full seconds after his target had disappeared. As the knife sliced through empty space, and long before he could comprehend what was happening, he felt his legs begin to buckle, the result of a sweeping kick. He struggled to keep from tumbling backward, but a second blow—he couldn't tell if it had been administered by hand or foot—ended those hopes. He crashed to the floor, and it wasn't until three seconds later that he realized two things: first, he had dropped the knife; second, it didn't really matter.

His kneecaps, both of them, were shattered beyond repair. It took only a second after those messages hit his information center for him to feel the unbearable pain shooting through his body.

"Oh, goddammit, my legs! They're broke! They're broke!" he screamed. "Help me, please! Somebody help me!"

Pete, wide-eyed and holding his bleeding arm, looked down at the screaming man writhing on the floor, then up at the man who had expertly inflicted such damage. His brain circuits were overloaded with a mixture of excitement and disbelief.

"Damn, Mick, you made scrambled eggs out of that poor bastard's knees," he said, his voice filled with awe. "He'll be lucky to ever walk again."

No answer.

Pete continued to shake his head. "You didn't learn shit like that sitting behind a desk. No way." He looked down at the man on the floor, then up at Collins. "Where *did* you learn that?"

"High school judo class."

"High school was a long time ago."

"It's amazing how quickly some things come back to you."

It *was* amazing how quickly things came back. Amazing and exciting. Perhaps even mystical. Things never forgotten: riding a bicycle, kissing, easily dismantling a knife-wielding attacker. How long had it been now? How long since he had executed a serious martial arts move, especially one against an armed and dangerous opponent?

He couldn't remember.

And yet—

All the critical elements were still present: the instincts, the quickness, the maximum use of energy and space, the look in his eyes.

The look.

That's what Pete zeroed in on after the initial rush of excitement had abated. "Goddamn, Mick, you should have seen the look in your eyes," Pete said, shaking his head. "You looked like one cold-blooded killer, man, like some kind of icy-eyed executioner. I've never seen you look like that before."

After wrapping a towel around his wounded arm, voice still filled with excitement, Pete again said, "Damn, Mick, you should have seen the look in your eyes."

Collins didn't have to be told. He'd seen the look— *been* the look—more times than Pete could ever know. Or ever begin to suspect.

The look was crucial. Without it, all the other skills

somehow didn't matter, regardless of how sharp they might be. He understood this perhaps better than any living man. The look, he knew, was why he had survived. Anyone in the killing business would tell you an assassin without the look is destined to become a victim.

Funny thing about the look—it can't be taught. You either have it or you don't. Some of his finest pupils, top-of-the-line talents, though in possession of great killing skills, simply didn't have the look. Without it, they had no chance of succeeding. Not in this business. And he couldn't tell them to go work on it, to sharpen it like a physical skill. It didn't work that way. It was in your DNA, or it wasn't. And without the look, reassignment was the only alternative.

Collins left Pete's place a little past midnight and drove home. Turning onto the darkened, narrow street that led to his house, he recalled how one of his most talented students, code name Cobra—Collins never forgot a code name—had reacted upon learning he was a washout: "What the fuck do you mean, I'm out? I'm as good as anyone in the house, and you know it." It was the standard response, one Collins had heard countless times.

"Sorry, Cobra, you don't have what it takes. You think you do, but trust me, you're badly mistaken. You can't cut it when it counts the most—when it's blood time."

That's really what it all comes down to: how you react at the last split second. When it's your life or the other guy's.

Blood time, as it was known inside the Shop.

Collins looked in the rearview mirror. A thin smile danced across his face. Pete had remarked how Collins's eyes looked like gray shadows. An excellent observation on Pete's part, much keener than he could ever imagine. For in those gray shadows, Pete had seen the very essence of what Collins and others like him were all about.

Every assassin's eyes are gray at the moment of the kill.

But now, at this moment, Collins's eyes narrowed, his smile faded. Thoughts flashed forward, past bled into present. Something wasn't right. He knew it, could sense it, even though he was still several hundred feet from his driveway. It wasn't the yellow taxi turning around at the end of the street that caused concern; rather, the black sedan parked across from his house set off the warning signals.

Collins pulled over to the curb, turned off the lights, and cut the engine. He sat in the darkness until the taxi passed and turned onto the freeway ramp. After exiting the car, he quickly moved to within twenty feet of the house. A light in the living room flickered briefly, then went out.

Who turned on that light? Who was this intruder? What nameless fool had been dispatched to take him out? There was no way he could answer that. His list of enemies was long, going back decades. Two countries—Russia and North Vietnam—were reputed to have put a two million-dollar bounty on his head. There was never a shortage of takers when that kind of money was involved.

But the *who* was irrelevant. All that mattered was that someone had finally come to collect.

He smiled. These were the moments he coveted and appreciated, the minutes and seconds of uncertainty, when plans and contingencies were open to endless possibilities. The moments before actual confrontation, before fates and outcomes were decided.

Before blood time.

Bullshit.

He loved nothing better than the combat, the killing.

Blood time.

His time.

How long had it been?

Too long.

Collins sprinted toward the back door, staying low to the ground, a shadow among shadows. He felt good . . . confident. The intruder, whoever he might be, wasn't a foe of equal stature. Too sloppy, too indifferent to details to be considered a worthy foe.

And yet, one never takes a foe lightly. Never. Regardless of the situation.

In his world, that was the first commandment.

Collins opened the back door wide enough to slide through. Once inside, he crawled to the end of the hallway, reached up to a table, and took down a crystal decanter. He removed the lid. Running his fingers gently across the rim, he felt the serrated edges. Sharpened by endless hours of meticulous, patient work, they were more deadly than a hundred razor blades.

He eased down the hallway like a rat staying close to the wall, the decanter in his right hand. As he crept forward, he realized that at no time did he consider the intruder to be anything other than an opponent. The realization pleased him. The killer's instincts, like *the look*, were alive and well.

What more did he need?

Nothing.

Once he reached the door to the living room, he rose to a kneeling position and peered into the darkness. He couldn't see ten inches in front of him, yet he knew precisely where the intruder was—standing next to the oak bookcase in the right corner of the room.

But this was too easy, too much like a setup. A trap. Probably more than one person waited. That was fine with him. The more, the merrier. In the end, it wouldn't matter.

The critical element was speed. The opponent by the bookcase had to be exterminated swiftly. That would be easily accomplished; sharpened crystal twisted against the jugular is messy but remarkably efficient. Then his attention could be shifted to any other foes who might come at him. For them, he would use his best weapon: his hands.

Under cover of perfect darkness, ready to move,

Collins suddenly felt young again—quick, alert. *Check it out now, Pete. No ivory towers, no desks. This is the real me, the man you've never known.* Memories of countless similar situations flooded his brain. Memories connected to a dark and bloody past. Back to those times when he was poised on the edge of a kill. Or possible death.

It seemed like a lifetime ago.

Like yesterday.

The look; the cold, gray eyes—they were here, now. The past had become the present.

But this was blood time—he wouldn't have expected anything less. Neither should the fool, or fools, waiting in the darkness. By his calculations it would be over for them in less than ten seconds, regardless of how many lay in wait. Numbers were irrelevant. There could be one or five—it didn't matter. He had often taken care of that many at one time, and he could do it again. It was simply a matter of doing the things that needed to be done.

Now.

But only milliseconds before he moved, before the deadly dynamics were set in motion, the stillness was broken by an old and familiar voice.

"Hello, Cain."

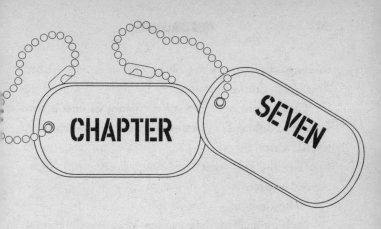

CHAPTER SEVEN

Collins turned on the light. "That's not the smartest thing you've ever done, Lucas. Coming in here like that."

Lucas White nodded but didn't answer. He was in his late seventies, tall, slender, with closely cropped hair, a white mustache, slate blue eyes, and the bearing of a proper English gentleman. Indeed, most people meeting him for the first time mistakenly assumed he was English. And for good reason. Lucas had always looked more like a character in a Noel Coward play than a four-star general from Davenport, Iowa.

"Men have been killed for much less," Collins said.

"No doubt." Lucas took the decanter from Collins and inspected it closely. "But it had to be done. As a sort of test." The tension in his face softened; his narrow lips relaxed into a smile. "I see you've not lost your touch."

"A test? For what?"

"Are all of your decanters empty?" Lucas asked,

handing the piece back to Collins. "I'm dry as the Sahara. Any Scotch on the premises?"

Collins motioned toward the liquor cabinet across from the bookcase. "You didn't answer my question. A test for what?"

"Clearly, the years have not lessened your impatience. Any ice?"

"The kitchen."

"What kind of a host fails to keep ice close to the booze?"

"A surprised host."

"Jolly good answer, my boy. It's a pleasure to see that you have retained your sardonic sense of humor. I always treasured that aspect of your personality."

Lucas brushed past Collins and went into the kitchen. Collins could hear the sound of ice clinking against glass. Moments later, Lucas reentered the room, carrying a glass of Scotch and a bucket of ice. He sat on the sofa, took a drink, and smiled at Collins. "Why so tough on General Nichols?"

"Why send a second-rate amateur?"

"Nichols isn't second rate. He's a desk wizard, a paper pusher; that's all. Even the mightiest military power on Earth requires office lackeys."

"He's a joke."

"Now, now, my boy, be kind. He's no joke. Furthermore, he worships the ground you walk on."

"So I gathered." Collins sat in the leather chair across from Lucas. "You should have come, Lucas. I'd like to think I still deserve the best."

"I concur wholeheartedly, my boy. But urgent matters prevented it." Lucas took a drink before continuing. "I'd apologize, but such a hollow act is beneath both of us."

"Those 'urgent matters' have anything to do with Cardinal's death?"

"And with his final words." Lucas sipped. "What do you make of that?"

Collins shrugged.

Lucas swirled his glass. "Cardinal lived alone, seldom went out, entertained on few occasions. He was, it would seem, merely playing out the string. Then this . . ." He took another drink. "You knew Cardinal. Why would he say 'fallen angels' unless he was trying to tell us something?"

"Who knows what thoughts go through a dying man's head?"

"That's wonderfully philosophical, but not very helpful."

"It's the best I've got."

"There's another matter you need to be aware of," Lucas said. "Last week an explosion in an Arlington restaurant killed twelve people, including—"

"I still read the papers, Lucas. I know about Arlington. How does what happened there connect with Cardinal's death?"

Lucas lifted himself off the sofa and shuffled to the liquor cabinet. He refilled the glass with Chivas Regal.

"I'm not sure there is a connection," he said.

"Then why are you here?"

"Oh, caution, I guess."

"Come on, Lucas. You can do better than that."

Lucas sipped at the Scotch before returning to the sofa. "There was a survivor in Arlington. The lady who owned the place had the good fortune to be in the freezer when the blast went off."

"And?"

"She told the investigators a man claiming to work for the FBI had been there earlier that morning. He apparently stayed about an hour, then disappeared. She also said Froning and his people were awfully concerned when they heard about him."

Lucas fell silent.

"What is it you're not telling me, Lucas?"

"How she described the man."

"Dammit, Lucas, cut the melodrama. What did she say about the man?"

"That he looked like a full-blooded Native American."

"And he told her his name was George Armstrong, right?"

"Yes."

"Seneca."

Lucas nodded. "It's comforting to know we continue to think alike."

"Look, the lady's probably right, but . . ."

"What's troubling you, my boy?"

"The use of explosives—that's just enough of a worm in the salad to cast a cloud of doubt. Seneca prefers more intimate methods of killing."

"The use of a knife, if memory serves."

"Arlington is a question mark, but one thing is for certain: Seneca didn't waste Cardinal."

"What makes you so sure?"

"Careless work. Seneca never went one on one with a target and left him breathing. Never. No, Lucas, someone else took out Cardinal."

"Maybe he's slipping."

Collins eyed Lucas hard and laughed.

"Do those marvelous instincts of yours detect a connection between Seneca, Cardinal, and the bombing in Arlington?" Lucas asked.

"You can wager those four stars and your pension on it," Collins answered. "And since Seneca didn't take out Cardinal, that means he's not working solo."

"My, my, what is one to make of such nasty business?"

"Fallen angels. Our mission into North Vietnam. Into Hanoi."

"And a dying man's last words."

"Cardinal was obviously telling us someone has been targeted for a hit."

"Yes," Lucas said. "And if Seneca is involved, that someone must be big."

Collins briefly stared at the decanter, then set it on the

table. After several seconds of silence, he looked at Lucas.

"I tried to warn you people about Seneca, but you wouldn't listen. Tried to tell you he was a time bomb waiting to go off. I begged you to let me cut him loose, but you said no. The only time in all those years that you bucked me, and now this."

"Seneca had the tools, the skills. He was a useful, effective soldier. You know that."

"He was a psycho."

Lucas set his glass on the table and leaned forward. He smiled a weary smile. "Hell, man, *you're* a psycho. You had to be a psycho to do the things you did. It was one of the job qualifications."

Collins knew that what Lucas said was both right and wrong, but at the moment he was in no mood to debate the distinction. He suddenly felt overwhelmed by fatigue.

"Why have you come to me?" he asked, leaning back, waiting for an answer he already knew.

"Because it's time for Cain to be born again."

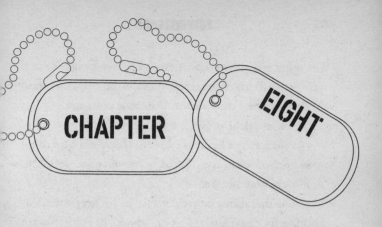

CHAPTER EIGHT

Lucas White picked up the leather briefcase, opened it, pulled out a swollen folder, and handed it to Collins. "This is only a refresher course," he said. "There's nothing in it you don't already know."

Collins placed the unopened folder on the table, walked to the liquor cabinet, took a piece of ice, and popped it into his mouth. "Your timing couldn't have been worse," he said. "I still have a week before the semester is over. I can't just up and leave."

"A week shouldn't be a major problem," Lucas said, "although time is of the essence. There's no chance you can finish early?"

"No."

Lucas took a drink. "Seneca will be a problem, won't he?"

"Seneca will be a problem."

Collins stood next to the window and looked outside.

The night was darker now than it had been when he was racing toward his house, toward blood time. Darker than the first night he met Seneca. All those years ago.

All those deaths.

Collins felt a hand on his shoulder. "The killing never ends, does it, my boy?" Lucas's voice was soft, sad. "It just goes on and on."

"Tell me about Seneca. The last I heard, he was working for the Russians as an adviser in Afghanistan. But that was twenty, twenty-five years ago. What's he been up to lately?"

"It's all in the file. At least as much as we know, which isn't considerable."

"To hell with the file, Lucas. Tell me."

"Fact is, no one knows for sure. Afghanistan, Libya—we've heard rumors, but nothing we could nail down. There had been previous intel connecting him to bin Laden, back when Osama was fighting the Russians. Back when he was on our side. The most persistent rumor had him married to a KGB agent and living in Moscow. Personally, I have my doubts about that one. It doesn't fit with Seneca and, hell, if he was working against the Russians, like we suspect, he certainly wouldn't have been in Moscow. He could be anywhere. We just don't know. Hell, we don't even know if he's behind Taylor's death or the bombing in Arlington."

"He's behind it."

"Then the question begs, who's he working for? And why?"

"*Why* is the easy one, Lucas. Because he lives for the kill. For a high body count. Seneca's a predator. He's not alive unless he's cutting some poor slob's heart out. As for who's calling the shots, that's your concern. It means nothing to me."

"Naturally, we'll give you all the support you need," Lucas said. "That includes manpower. I'll assign Nichols to you, along with a young captain I'm impressed with, a kid named Raymond Fuller. I believe you knew his father, Thomas Fuller. Anyway . . ."

Collins began to laugh.

"What's so amusing, my boy?" Lucas asked.

"No excess baggage, Lucas. It would only slow me down. Keep your desk jockeys. I don't need them."

"Always the loner, right?"

"I travel best when I travel alone."

"Have it your way. But the support will be available if you need it."

"Same rules as before. I'll work directly with you and no one else. All communications will be strictly between us."

"My boy, these are different times we live in," Lucas said. "A post–Twin Towers world. The CIA, Homeland Security, FBI . . . they'll want their voices heard, and they will demand to be involved. I'll do everything in my power to limit their involvement, but that won't be easy to do. My challenge will be to keep them in the loop, but only on my terms. There's a lot we don't know, so the fewer people involved, the better. At least for now."

Lucas lifted a card and a pen from the briefcase. He scribbled something on the card and handed it to Collins. "You can reach me at this number. Night or day. I'm on twenty-four-hour call. Just like the good old days."

"I've got a bulletin for you, Lucas. The good old days weren't all that good."

"What's this I'm hearing? A reluctant warrior?"

"I like the peace."

"My boy, peace is the one enemy you can't handle."

"You're wrong about that."

Lucas closed the briefcase, looked at Collins, and smiled. "No, I'm not. You see, you're overlooking one crucial factor, my boy. You're the original predator. Just like your code name says. Cain. History's first assassin. And you more than honored your predecessor's legacy. No one lived for the kill more than you."

Collins stood in the doorway and watched Lucas drive off into the night. A good man, Lucas White. Always had been, always would be. No field soldier could ask for a better man to have calling the shots during crisis time. And this was crisis time. A man like Lucas White didn't come out of retirement unless something big was going down. Of course, he hadn't laid all his cards on the table. He knew more than he was telling. But that's the way it should be. Information, especially early on, shouldn't be dispensed too soon. Too many chances that it might be inaccurate, too many opportunities for leaks. Occasional whispers are better than loud screams during the early stages of any mission. Lucas would fill in the blanks when the time was right.

Hell, man, you're a psycho.

Collins smiled.

The killing never ends, does it, my boy? It just goes on and on.

The smile widened.

You're the original predator.

Goddamn right.

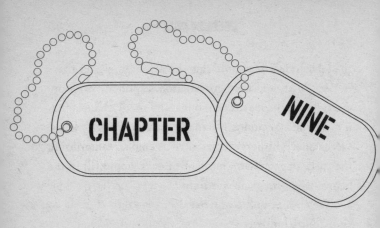

CHAPTER NINE

The summer was going to be a scorcher. Only the second week in May and the temperatures had settled in at the mid-80s. Forecasters were already warning that a hot, dry, uncomfortable summer lay ahead. If this was any indication, it looked like they might be right on the money.

Collins loosened his tie and unbuttoned the top button of his shirt. He'd just dispatched his grad assistant to the registrar's office with the final grades. After she left, he opened a bottle of orange juice, picked up the phone, and dialed Lucas White's number. Lucas answered on the first ring.

"All done with the dirty work," Collins said.

"My boy, I'm afraid the dirty work is only beginning."

Collins said nothing.

"Is it safe to assume you took time out from dispensing great works of literature to study the contents of the file I left with you?" Lucas asked.

"Haven't opened it."

"Why am I not surprised?" Lucas muttered.

"Because you know me."

Such a response would have provoked an outburst from most military commanders. But Lucas White wasn't like most commanders. He was unique, wise as an owl, pragmatic. He did what the situation demanded, always. His theory: whatever it takes is what you do. That pragmatism enabled him to understand and tolerate what others often referred to as "Cain's fucking unorthodox ways."

"Should you get a couple of free minutes, you might give it a quick glance," Lucas said. "If for no other reason than to justify the expense and effort involved. And to please an old man. Will you do that for me?"

"I trained Seneca. There's nothing about him I don't already know."

"I'm aware. But, please, humor me. Who knows? Even someone as omniscient as you might eventually stumble upon a hidden kernel of information. Stranger things have happened."

"Enough, already, Lucas. I'll look at the damn file."

Such verbal sparring was old hat between the two men, and given their respective personalities, it was perhaps inevitable. It was their way of communicating, of bridging the wide gap separating them, of overcoming their many differences.

And there were many.

Lucas White was a by-the-book soldier, but one who could, when times dictated, bend enough to offer a certain amount of latitude. He could handle those soldiers who drove his fellow officers to early retirement, alcoholism, or both. Soldiers like Collins, who detested everything associated with by-the-book restrictions. The rebels, the hard cases.

There was another reason Lucas could be lenient toward this particular rebel: rebellion was typical for a career soldier's children. Collins's father, like Lucas, had been a thirty-five-year military man. Historically, military brats either followed closely in their father's footsteps or rebelled completely. Seldom was there a middle ground when it came to children raised on military posts around the world. With them, it was either West Point or Haight Ashbury.

Collins rebelled. At least, initially. Later, drawn by some inexplicable pull—perhaps an ironic manifestation of his rebellious nature, Lucas concluded—he broke from his anti-war comrades and, at age seventeen, with his father's blessing, signed up for a three-year hitch in the Army. The war in Vietnam was heating up, and within eight months after enlisting, Collins was sent into those jungles. It was there, during the final weeks of his first tour of duty in Nam, that his special "talent" became apparent.

The talent for killing.

A talent so enormous, so expert, that any command-ing officer with the least bit of wisdom would gladly accommodate it, even if it meant accepting unmilitary behavior. Whatever it takes is what you do. After all, Lucas reasoned, men with such rare gifts are exempt from certain rules that apply to the mediocre among us.

"Jolly good," said Lucas. "When you finish slogging your way through it, call if you have any questions."

Collins was silent.

"Advise me as to your planned course of action," Lucas added. "Most of all, be careful. And may God grant you his blessings."

"Does God grant his blessings to killers, Lucas?"

This time it was Lucas who was silent.

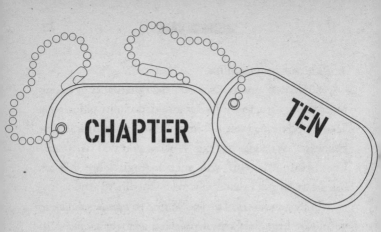

CHAPTER TEN

Lucas White was lenient for reasons beyond peaceful coexistence with Collins. Lucas cared deeply for the younger man. Loved him, really. He regarded Collins as the son he never had. It was a feeling he'd had almost from the beginning.

They first met when Lucas and the boy's father were stationed together at Fort Benning, Georgia. The two men, both full-bird colonels at the time, had known each other in Korea, but it wasn't until they were at Fort Benning that they became close friends. Collins was fourteen at the time and a source of great concern to his father, who naturally assumed his son would choose a career in the military. Three generations of Collins men had been career soldiers, and young Michael—the elder Collins refused to call his son Mickey—was expected to follow in their footsteps. At the time, and given Michael's anti-establishment leanings, neither his father nor Lucas White could see that happening.

"Richard, you may as well get that notion out of your head," Lucas said to the elder Collins during a lengthy drinking bout. "The more you push him in that direction, the wider the gap between you will become."

The elder Collins had only nodded. He knew his friend was right.

Lucas, not bound by the chains of family tradition, recognized from the beginning that a career in the military would serve only to waste a near-genius intellect.

Here was a boy barely fourteen who already had a staggering grasp of philosophy, history, music and literature. Condemned to the life of a nomad by his father's frequent transfers, Michael Collins found friends not in the various military outposts, but in the books he read. Friends as diverse as Socrates and Spinoza, Kierkegaard and Kafka, Thomas Aquinas and T. S. Eliot. Ask him about music, be it Mozart or Dylan, and you could expect a discourse lasting long into the night. Here, Lucas knew, was a mind more fertile than any he'd ever encountered, a mind rich with potential.

More than anything, though, Lucas loved the boy's audacity. How else can you describe someone who, at the tender age of fifteen, dared to take a graduate class on Nietzsche at the University of Heidelberg? Taking on the great German philosopher on his home turf. How could Lucas not be fond of this child?

Lucas also recognized in Collins an almost total isolation. The boy either didn't need or didn't want contact with other human beings, using his books and music to lock them out of his world. Lucas had seen this behavior in other military brats. Indeed, it was a common defense mechanism. To a child who might have to move at a moment's notice, friendships were heartbreaks waiting to happen. After enough sudden good-byes, a child learned to isolate himself, to back away from making friends. To build walls for protection. But never had Lucas seen this behavior taken to such extremes. With Michael Collins, the isolation was total.

Never in a million years would Lucas have imagined this boy in the military. Yet, it happened. Without warning and completely out of the blue, like a bolt of lightning.

Given the clarity of hindsight, Lucas should have predicted it.

The hint came during a dinner party. One of those informal and boisterous affairs where old warriors discuss past battles through the haze of too many years gone by and too much alcohol consumed. During the course of the evening, when the discussion turned to the Battle of the Bulge, one of the men—Lucas could never recall which one—praised the brilliance of a bit of strategy employed by a certain Army colonel. Upon hearing the comment, young Collins flew into a rage, accusing the officer of a serious tactical blunder that had, only because of a series of outside variables, worked out in his favor. Collins then proceeded to lay out the plan as he would have implemented it, demonstrating with forks, knives, and salt and pepper shakers exactly how his plan would have looked, why it was the proper course to follow, and why it would have succeeded.

Lucas was spellbound by what he was hearing, not only by the boy's understanding and passion, but by the correctness of what he was saying. Lucas had studied that particular battle and was familiar with the officer in question. Lucas knew that in the early hours after the battle, Eisenhower had recognized the serious nature of the blunder and the great good fortune that followed. Had it not been for luck or divine providence, many GIs would have died needlessly. Lucas also learned that only a handful of officers in high command had this knowledge. The blunder had been well covered up. Or so Lucas assumed until he sat and listened to a fourteen-year-old give a remarkably accurate view of what did happen, what should have happened, and why.

Here was a boy who professed his distaste for anything military yet had a profound knowledge and understanding of military history and strategy.

Lucas should have seen it then. He should have looked beyond the anti-military rhetoric, the rebellion, the screw-all-authority attitude. Perhaps if he'd only dug a little deeper, gotten further inside that iron curtain, he wouldn't have been so surprised by Michael's decision to enlist in the Army.

But hindsight isn't always 20/20. Some things simply are beyond seeing, regardless of the situation. This was one of those instances when perfect vision wouldn't have been good enough. For nothing, no amount of digging or psychological probing, not even the highest level of imagination, could have prepared Lucas for the way things turned out.

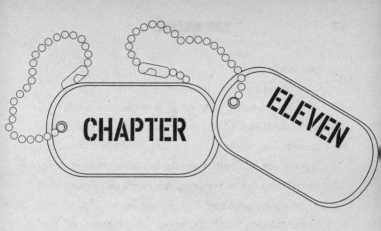

CHAPTER ELEVEN

Pete's place was really jamming, even by the usual Saturday night standards. College kids and professors, thankful for having survived another semester of mutual mental warfare, celebrated together on an almost-equal footing. The curtain of separation had been lowered—at least until next semester. "A temporary détente," one professor termed it.

Collins spied an empty booth in the corner and led Kate in that direction. The waitress was there before they settled in.

"Pepsi for me," Collins said, "and a vodka and cranberry juice for the lady."

Kate reached under the table and squeezed his thigh. He smiled; she winked. "Just a Pepsi?" she said. "You're being awfully conservative."

"Conservative is my middle name."

"Since when?"

"Since always."

"You couldn't prove it by me."

"Perhaps you don't recognize it when you see it."

Kate laughed. "If you were conservative, I wouldn't be with you."

"I don't see you as the all-out left-wing radical type. You don't strike me as someone who stirs the shit."

"How do you see me?"

"A middle-of-the-road centrist. A pragmatist. You may lean a little left, but not much."

"Ouch. What a nasty assessment."

Collins laughed. "Not really. Radicalism, in either direction, is not usually a good thing. Being in the middle may resonate like an uneventful roll of the dice, but it is generally the best bet to make."

Kate eyed him hard. "You've never been a centrist in your life. I see you as nothing but a lifelong rebel."

"There are plenty of folks who would heartily concur."

The waitress brought their drinks, told them to wave if they needed anything else, then walked away.

Kate stirred her drink. "Rumor has it that you're taking a sabbatical next term. True or false?"

"It's possible. Depends on how some things play out this summer."

"Came rather suddenly, didn't it?"

"Yeah."

"Anything serious going on that I should know about?"

"Not really. I only need a break; that's all. Too much T. S. Eliot can wear a person down."

"T.S. would be hurt to hear you say that."

"Good. It'll give him something to whine about to his old buddy Ezra Pound."

"What about the Beats? Don't you have them on tap next term?"

"They'll still be here when I get back."

"Are you sticking around here, or are you planning on leaving town?"

"Leaving town."

"Anywhere in particular?"

"Not sure yet."

"Sounds mysterious."

"More uncertain than mysterious."

"That man, the one dressed in the Army uniform—it has something to do with him, doesn't it?"

Collins leaned back against the wall. "You didn't like General Nichols very much, did you?"

She shook her head. "Too arrogant, too pushy for my taste."

"He's a small man who's spent his life doing secondary jobs. He tries to give an impression of authority, of being important. It's his way of feeling necessary."

"How come you know so much about a man like that?"

"I've known a thousand men like him."

"You haven't always been a teacher, have you?"

"No."

"What were you before you became a teacher?"

"What do you think I was?"

Kate took a drink, leaned back, and sized him up. "A business executive . . . a salesman of some sort."

"Now, that's a nasty assessment."

"Okay, what were you, then?"

"An infamous mass murderer."

"So, I'm dating Jeffrey Dahmer?"

"Just call me J.D."

"Be serious."

"Seriously, I've always been a teacher. Different subject; that's all."

Pete broke through a crowd of dancers, spotted Collins and Kate, and walked quickly to their booth. A mile-wide smile crossed his face.

"Just the fella I've been looking for," Pete said.

"How's the wound?" Collins asked, pointing to the bandage covering most of Pete's left forearm.

"Few stitches, but otherwise it's fine. No permanent damage, praise the Lord. But you know what? That bastard is threatening to file suit against both of us. Some beady-eyed shyster was in here two days ago talkin' it up pretty good. I took about three minutes of his jabberin' then ran his ass outta here. I told him to do what he had to do; just get outta my face or I'd give him a reason to file his own damn suit."

"I wouldn't worry about him, Pete. He doesn't have a case. Too many witnesses saw what happened."

"That scumbag don't worry me none." Pete nodded to Kate. "Little lady, you're runnin' with a questionable character, hangin' around with the likes of Michael James Collins."

Kate shifted her eyes to Collins. "He's all bluff, Pete. A piece of cake."

"Mind if I join you for a few seconds?" He squeezed into the booth next to Kate. "I need to take a load off. Old Arthur has about got the best of these knees."

Collins spied his old redheaded friend standing in front of a table, talking with two men. The conversation, whatever the subject, didn't appear to be cordial. She was spitting fire at the younger man sitting to her left.

"Amy looks pretty upset, doesn't she?" Pete asked. "Not to worry; it's all an act. That's her standard M.O. She acts real ticked off at some guy, makes him feel like shit, then turns it all around and takes the guy for a ride. Hell, before the night's over, that bum will be eating out of her palm. She's some worker, that Amy."

Kate looked over her shoulder. "A hooker?"

"Hooker, schmooker," Pete said. "No, I wouldn't classify Amy as a hooker. A hooker takes the offer. Amy offers the take. That make any sense?"

"None."

"Ah, hell, you're too young to know about such things."

"I'm not sure I want to know," Kate said.

"Good for you." Pete shifted his attention to Collins. "By the way, Professor Cake. About the other night— how long you been doin' that stuff?"

"What stuff?"

"That chink stuff. You know . . . judo, karate, whatever you call it."

"Since I was about five."

"Who'd you learn it from?"

"You really interested?"

Pete nodded his head eagerly. "Damn straight. Hell, man, I was impressed. I mean, I've seen that shit on TV and in the movies, but that's the first time I've actually seen it for real."

"I learned it from a man named Chin."

"A chink. Figures."

"He was only half Oriental. His mother was an American, the daughter of a Marine colonel."

"You get a black belt?"

Collins laughed. "Yeah, Pete, I got a black belt."

"Well, after what you did to the poor bum, I can believe it."

Pete struggled out of the booth and hitched up his pants. "Well, better get back to the wars. Plenty of drachmas to be taken in tonight." He put a hand on Collins's shoulder. "God, how I love to make a buck."

Kate watched Pete shuffle back to the bar. "What's

he talking about? Were you involved in a fight?"

"Not really. Some drunk cut Pete with a knife. I helped break it up. No big deal."

"Knife? That sounds serious."

"It wasn't."

She took another drink. "Mind if I ask you a question?"

"Go for it."

"It's kinda personal."

"Is there any other kind?"

"You've never been married, right?" she finally said.

"Right."

"How come?"

"That's two questions."

"Sorry."

Collins ran his hand through his hair. "It simply wasn't in the cards, I guess. Anyway, it wouldn't have worked out." He looked away. "My work wasn't conducive to married life."

Kate started to ask another question, caught herself in mid-sentence, let it go unfinished. Something in his eyes said she had intruded into territory best left uncharted.

Those eyes—

"Well, if you ever change your mind, I know an excellent prospect."

She smiled.

He didn't.

An hour later, after dropping Kate off at her apartment and making a quick stop at a 24-hour grocery store, Collins walked into his house. He stood motionless in the darkness, letting several minutes pass before turning on a light.

This time there were no tricky shadows, no plans and contingencies. No Lucas White.

But he wasn't alone. Ever. The ghosts were forever with him.

Waiting. Always.

He sat on the couch and reached for the brown folder marked "Eyes Only." In it was a history of his prize pupil, his oldest adversary.

Seneca.

CHAPTER TWELVE

The breeze was soft, the sun blazing like the fires of hell. *Perfect,* Hannah Buckman thought, as she loosened the bikini strap and removed the top. Her breasts, free from their confines, seemed to defy gravity. She liked her breasts. Always had. The best thing about her body. Large but not too large, firm, round, and, most important, created by Mother Nature herself, with brown nipples forever erect. Men continually raved about her Hollywood looks or her long, toned legs or her firm butt or her thick, pouty lips. But to Hannah, her breasts were the only part of her anatomy that rated a ten.

After five minutes of carefully applying sunscreen, she lay down on the lounge chair, lowered her sunglasses, and began reading the latest Danielle Steele novel. She had concluded by the end of the second chapter that this wasn't one of Danielle's better efforts. About a B minus up to now. But with five chapters remaining, who knew?

Maybe it would improve. It was getting more interesting, no doubt about that.

Hannah made a mental note to keep an eye on the time and not forget to turn over. Her breasts were easy prey to a quick sunburn. Ten minutes at a time were about all they could handle, sunscreen or not. Any longer and they would be cooked. That had happened a couple of times before, and it was damn painful.

Hannah finished a chapter, the best one thus far, when she felt her breasts begin to sizzle. Time for more lotion. As she sat up and reached for the bottle, she saw the two men who were about to board the yacht. They were an odd-looking couple, the medium-built dark-skinned man wearing shades and the mammoth, round-faced black man walking on unsteady legs. She lowered her glasses and peered over the top. The man with the shades was so strikingly handsome she had to get a better look at him. As they approached, she realized he was an American Indian. She also realized her uncovered nipples were fully erect and it wasn't from the sun.

"Hello, I'm Hannah Buckman," she said, offering a well-manicured hand. "I assume you're here to see Simon."

"That's correct," the Indian said.

"He's below, in the cabin."

The Indian squeezed her hand, gently. She couldn't see his eyes through the dark lenses, but she knew he was staring at her breasts. The black man, clearly embarrassed, looked away.

"Simon's expecting you," she said. "And he's not a man who likes to be kept waiting."

The Indian released her hand and grinned. She followed him with her eyes until he and the black man disappeared down the steps. When they were out of sight, she sighed and went back to reading Danielle.

Below, Simon Buckman lay sprawled on an oversized couch, his face covered by a sailor's cap. He was sixty-ish, bald, and not nearly tall enough to accommodate his weight, which long ago had surpassed three hundred pounds. Simon was a man suffocating in the quicksand of his own flesh, a man whose every breath was labored, whose every movement was a struggle. Even the task of lifting himself to a sitting position to meet his two guests was accomplished only by using a cane to hoist himself up.

"Come in, come in," he said. His accent was clearly old South. Alabama, maybe Mississippi. The words escaped through a reptilian slit barely visible within the mounds of fat. "Did you meet Hannah?"

"Yes," the black man said. "Your daughter is very beautiful, very . . . uninhibited."

Simon convulsed in laughter, his flesh shaking like a vat of Jell-O.

"What's so funny?" the black man asked.

Pounding the cane on the floor, Simon bellowed,

"She's not my daughter; she's my wife."

"Your wife?"

"Pretty amazing, isn't it?" Simon said. "It just goes to show you: if you've got money, you can marry anything you want. Women are drawn to money like my old grandpappy to a Klan rally." He looked at the two men, his eyes gleaming. "I know what you're thinking: how does a fat SOB like him service a young kitten like that? Hell, I don't. It'd kill me if I tried. But it's goddamned impressive to walk into someplace with her hanging on my arm. Makes me the envy of every young hard dick in the room."

With great effort, Simon struggled to his feet and moved closer to the two men. He paused, then walked behind the black man. "That's some scar you have there," he remarked. "How'd you get it? One of them police dogs in Selma get a little too close?"

The black man, his right hand touching the scar on his cheek, glared hard at Simon. "Car crash, when I was a kid."

"You know, you're the first black person—I mean, Afro-American—who's ever been on this vessel," Simon said. "Except, of course, for the servants."

"I'm honored," the big black man said.

Simon circled the two men again, slowly, finally stopping in front of the Indian. "You must be Seneca. I've heard a lot about you. Why, there are those of my acquaintance who speak of you in almost reverential tones.

They say you're the best, that no one comes close. That true, or is it only a lot of talk from your fork-tongued redskin brothers?"

"He's the best, make no mistake about that," the black man said, turning toward Simon.

"I don't recollect asking for your opinion, spade. I asked the man himself. Well, how about it, Cochise? You as good as they say?"

The Indian flashed a quick grin. "Better," he replied, his voice barely above a whisper. Just as quickly, the smile vanished and his right hand shot out and grabbed Simon's testicles. "And the name isn't Cochise, fatman. It's Seneca. Got it?"

He increased the pressure. "Got it?"

"Yeah, yeah, I got it, I got it," Simon belched. "Take your fuckin' mitts off my balls."

More pressure.

"What's the name, fatman?"

"Seneca, goddammit . . . fuckin' Seneca."

"That's better."

The Indian released his grip and pushed Simon back against the bar. Simon's face was bathed in fear. He grabbed a napkin and wiped sweat from his forehead.

"I didn't come here to listen to your redneck bullshit," the Indian added. "I'm here to find out where Karl wants to meet. Tell me that, and I'm gone."

Before Simon could answer, Hannah walked into

the cabin, looked around at the three men, and smiled. "Sounds like you boys are getting a little rowdy down here."

Simon coughed. "Get enough sun, Kitten?"

"Don't I look tan and lovely?" she answered, turning toward the Indian. "Simon, why don't you introduce me to your friends?"

"The one in front . . ."

"Seneca," the Indian said, cocking his head in the direction of the black man. "That's Deke."

"Pleased to meet you, ma'am," Deke said, relieved to see her fully clothed.

Simon coughed again, louder this time. "Honey, I have important business to discuss with these gentlemen. Why don't you take a shower? Freshen up a bit before dinner."

"She can stay if she wants," Seneca said.

"It goes against my beliefs to talk business in front of a woman."

"Maybe you need some new beliefs." The Indian looked at Hannah. "Have a seat."

"I don't think that's such a good idea," Simon grunted.

"Simon is right," Hannah said. "I do need a shower, but thank you for offering to let me stay. A lady always likes to feel wanted."

The three men were quiet until she left. Simon followed, locked the cabin door behind her, then turned back toward his visitors. "Dumbest broad on God's green earth. But you can't argue with a body like that.

Makes up for a lot of those missing IQ points."

"You ought to treat her better," the Indian said. "If you don't, she might not be around much longer."

"She'll be with me when they're kickin' dirt on my coffin," Simon growled. "She's not that dumb. She's read my will."

Simon opened a drawer and pulled out a bottle of Tennessee whiskey. "I understand everything went well in Arlington." He took a drink straight from the bottle. "That true?"

The Indian slid past Deke and sat on the couch. "Karl. When do we meet him?"

"You don't. Not yet, anyway."

"Why?"

"He has another assignment for you. Another run-through to make sure everything is hunky-dory."

The Indian stood. "Doesn't work that way, fatman. I don't audition for anyone, including Karl. Tell him that. And while you're at it, tell him I said he can fuck off."

"You're making a big mistake, my Indian friend. Karl won't take kindly to attitude."

The Indian walked to the door and unlocked it. "Tough shit. Tell Karl the next time he wants me, he'll have to come looking."

Simon laughed. "What makes you think there'll be a next time?"

Seneca reached up and grabbed Simon by the throat.

"Because what he wants done is big. Big enough that he knows I'm the only one who can do it."

He released his grip and pinched Simon's sweating cheek. "See, when you're the best at something, fatman, there's always a next time. But being the best isn't something you'd know much about, is it?"

CHAPTER THIRTEEN

Lucas had been right. There was nothing in the file on Seneca that Collins didn't already know. Nothing he couldn't recite from memory. He leaned back on the couch and tossed the folder onto the table. An 8x10 black and white photo slipped out and fell to the floor. He bent down, picked it up, and held it in front of him.

Dwight David Rainwater. Full-blooded Cherokee Indian, born on a reservation in Oklahoma, son of a chief, descendent of warriors.

Code name: Seneca.

Profession: hired assassin.

Weapon of choice: knife.

Those were the only bits of information that counted. The rest of the data was insignificant.

Collins leaned the picture against the crystal decanter. Even now, even in a photo, Seneca's dark eyes radiated hatred. Hate and power.

It has often been said that the eyes are the windows
to the soul. There was no doubting that Seneca's eyes
surely revealed the truth about the man within. They
always had. No mysteries there, nothing hidden. But
in this case, the philosophers and poets were only half
right. Seneca's eyes were windows not only to the soul;
they were also a portal to some dark, forbidden place. To
look into his eyes was to glimpse hell.

No one understood this better than Collins. Seneca
was a killer, pure and simple. And in his twisted mind,
killing had nothing to do with duty or survival or right
and wrong. He killed because he loved the act itself, the
slaughter, the bloodletting. For him, politics never figured into the equation. For him, there was nothing more
satisfying than the taking of a human life. There were
no conventional enemies, only a world filled with potential victims waiting to be eliminated, swiftly, brutally.

For Seneca, there was an unquenchable thirst that
could never be fully satisfied, no matter how much blood
was shed.

And that made him the most dangerous opponent
possible.

Collins dug deeper into the folder. He couldn't remember the year Seneca came to him at the Shop—he
thought maybe it was summer 1968, but he suddenly
wanted to know for certain. He found the record sheet
and ran his forefinger down the page until he found

what he was looking for. Close. Seneca came to him in February 1968. Valentine's Day, to be exact.

The notation jogged Collins's memory. How could he have forgotten? A snowstorm had shut down all transportation, delaying the arrival of new recruits for at least twenty-four hours. Bored, he'd gone to the officers' lounge and shot some pool before retiring to the barracks. On his way back, he heard footsteps crunching the snow behind him. Instinctively, without thought or hesitation, he turned, moved his body slightly to the left, and reacted to the arm he saw stretching toward him. Grabbing it at the elbow, he lifted it skyward, moved his right leg behind the man's right hip, and using the leverage he'd created, sent the man sprawling into the powdery snow. Standing above his attacker, his breath coming out in dying clouds, killing hands drawn back with fingers extended, he stared down at the stunned man lying on the ground.

"Wait, Major, I'm one of your recruits," the man said, breathless but strangely unaffected by what had just happened. "My name is Rainwater. Sergeant David Rainwater. From Fort Campbell, Kentucky."

Collins helped the man to his feet. "How did you get here? I was told all transportation was down."

"Hitchhiked," the man said without adding the required *sir*.

The man brushed the snow off. When he looked

up, his face was illuminated by a light coming from a barracks window. It was the first time Collins looked into the face of Dwight David Rainwater.

Into those dark and penetrating eyes.

The same dark and penetrating eyes now staring back at him from an old 8x10 black and white photograph sitting on the table.

He reached out, picked up the photo and brought it close to his face. He could almost smell the stench of death, hear the laughter, that ancient and primal sound of a predator announcing another kill.

And now this predator was on the prowl again. Doing what he did best.

Killing.

Collins dropped the photo onto the table, leaned back, and rubbed his eyes.

Yes, Lucas, Seneca will be a problem.

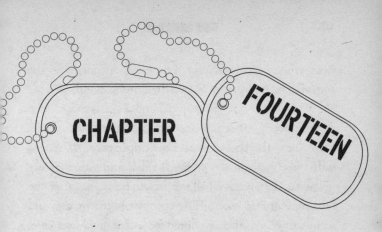

CHAPTER FOURTEEN

Moss shut off the Pontiac's engine, took a final drag on his cigarette, then ground the butt into the ashtray. He rested both arms on top of the steering wheel and stared straight ahead. Only after a few seconds did he finally turn to look at Bungalow nine. Taylor's bungalow. He wasn't anxious to get started, but he could no longer put it off. The remainder of Taylor's belongings had to be shipped to a cousin in St. Louis. Moss should have taken care of this task two weeks ago, but it was one of those dreaded chores that only get done when there is absolutely no more time for procrastination.

Some of Taylor's belongings were shipped three days after the incident occurred; the rest had been boxed. All that remained was for Moss to make a couple, maybe three trips to the post office. He should have borrowed the Pinewood Estates van and taken care of the matter in a single trip. But he hadn't and it was no big deal. These days, when many residents were back up north for the summer, he had plenty of free time on his hands.

A white BMW drove past Taylor's driveway. The driver offered a friendly wave and an ear-to-ear smile. Moss liked the young man, Brad McGregor. What he didn't like was the idea of Brad and Kelli living together outside of marriage. Of all the broken traditions, that one bothered him the most. If two people love each other and want to live together, it should be as husband and wife. Whatever happened to the term "living in sin" anyway?

Moss sighed. What the hell difference did it make in the long run? The world's going to hell in a hand basket. Terrorism, hunger, pollution, drugs, kids killing kids in schools all across the country, disrespect, politicians banging young interns . . . Let us count the ways. Look what happened to a nice guy like Taylor. Living alone, minding his own business, harming no one, then— murdered. Further proof that the world is heading down the toilet. With so many real troubles, what could possibly be wrong with a couple of fairly decent kids living together? Nothing. Yet, for whatever reason, however old-fashioned or outdated, Moss was bothered by it.

He opened the door, put on his L.A. Lakers baseball cap, got out of the car, and walked down the brick path leading to bungalow nine.

The bungalow was dark and smelled of musk, so Moss opened the curtains in the living room, then went into the kitchen and opened the blinds covering the window that looked out over the inlet. After getting a drink of water, he went into the living room and counted the boxes stacked in the corner. Six, plus two small ones still upstairs. Definitely three trips, he figured. The old Pontiac might be roomy—Taylor once called it an ark—but it wasn't nearly roomy enough to get the job done in two trips.

Moss decided to get the two boxes in the upstairs bedroom first. When he reached the top of the stairs, he waited a few seconds to catch his breath, adjusted his Lakers cap, then took one last look in the hall closet. Satisfied none of Taylor's belongings had been overlooked, he went into the bedroom.

And froze.

He wasn't alone. A man was standing by the large window that opened to the balcony.

Moss surveyed the intruder. Tall, lean, handsome; dressed in Levis, a T-shirt, and white Nikes. Brown hair on the longish side, bluish-gray eyes.

And perfectly calm. He smiled, nodded as though he anticipated Moss's arrival, and continued what he was doing.

Moss didn't react so nonchalantly. He took a step back, looked to his right, spied a brass candleholder on the dresser, picked it up, and clutched it tightly in both hands.

"Who are you?" he stammered. "And how the hell did you get in here?"

"Relax, Moss. I'm—"

"How'd you know my name?" Moss interrupted.

"It's my business to know things." Striding across the room, the man put out his hand. "I'm Mickey Collins. And you can put down that weapon. You won't need it."

Moss looked at the man's large hands, still unsure of what exactly was happening and even less sure of how he should deal with it. *Cautious* was the first word that came to mind. *Danger* was the second. After all, one man had already been murdered in this bungalow. He had no intention of becoming victim number two. Not if he had anything to say about it.

He took another step backward. "Okay, so your name is Mickey Collins. You still ain't told me why you're up here and how you got in."

"I'm here to look around. As for getting in, I picked the back door lock."

"That's known as breaking and entering. People go to the hoosegow for doing that." Moss stared at Collins's hands. "Just what is it you're lookin' for, anyway? And why?"

"Cardinal was a friend of mine."

"Who was a friend of yours?" Moss asked.

"Cardinal." Collins saw the confused look on Moss's face. "Taylor. Taylor was a friend of mine."

"Then how come I've never seen you here before?"

"Because I've never been here. I haven't seen Cardinal for many years."

"Why do you keep calling him Cardinal?"

"Cardinal was Taylor's code name."

"Code name? What was he, some kind of James Bond spy?"

"No."

"What about you? You got a code name?"

"Cain."

"Cain? Like in the Bible?"

"Yes."

"He murdered his brother, didn't he?"

"So the story goes."

"Well, how can I be sure you ain't a murderer?"

"Because I'm not."

Moss thought about it for a few seconds, then said, "Listen, mister, I'm not sayin' you're lyin' to me or anything like that, but I'm in charge of security around here. So I gotta check you out."

"No need to bother. I'm kosher."

"Look, man, even if I did believe you, I'd still need some proof. I could lose my job if you don't check out A-OK. This job don't pay much, but it's all I got."

"You won't lose your job, Moss. Promise."

Moss cut his eyes downward. "From the look of those hands of yours, maybe I ought to be worried about more than losin' my job."

Collins reached for his wallet, hesitated. "You're gonna have to trust me, Moss. Just like I trusted you."

"Trusted me?" Moss said, his interest suddenly piqued. "How'd you trust me?"

"By telling you Taylor's code name. And mine. There aren't ten people in the world who possess that information."

"Well—"

"I've heard you're a good man, Moss. I also heard you were pretty close to Cardinal. I'm banking on all that being true."

"Why?" Moss asked, leaning slightly forward.

"I may need your help somewhere along the way."

Making an outsider think he's being brought into some secret inner circle is the greatest of all baits. Collins knew from the look in Moss's eager eyes that the bait had been snapped up and swallowed. But offering the bait was only half of the proposition. Now came the closer— a dash of fear.

Always throw in fear.

"In my business, trust isn't something one can assume. I have to be very careful who I give it to. When I do extend that trust, and if it's broken, well, let's just say bad things happen."

Collins paused briefly, then said, "really bad things," in a stern whisper.

Moss leaned forward like a deaf man straining to hear. When he was sure nothing more was coming, he took the bait a second time. "What kind of bad things?"

"Like what happened to Cardinal."

Moss glanced down at Collins's hands. "You didn't kill Taylor, did you?"

"No. But I've got to find the man who did. And fast."

"You a cop?"

"I'm no cop."

"Private investigator?"

"It's not important who or what I am, Moss. What is important is finding Cardinal's killer."

Moss put the candleholder back on the dresser. His face was set in that frown that accompanies deep thought. Finally, he looked up at Collins. "This may be the dumbest thing I've ever done, but I'm goin' along with you on this. It'll probably end up bein' my ass." He paused, looked around the room. "What the hell? Anyway, you stand a better chance of catchin' Taylor's killer than those peckerhead cops downtown."

"Those peckerhead cops are not to know anything at all about me. That clear?"

"Right, perfectly clear."

Collins went into the bathroom and opened the medicine cabinet. Except for two loose Tylenol capsules on the bottom shelf, it was empty. He bent over the tub and ran his forefinger around the inside of the nozzle. He unscrewed the showerhead, raised himself up on his tiptoes, and inspected it.

"If you'll tell me what it is you're lookin' for, maybe I can help you out. Save you some time," Moss said.

"I don't know what it is I'm looking for."

"Then how will you know when you find it?"

Collins laughed. "Good question."

"Want me to unpack the boxes downstairs?" Moss asked.

"No need."

"How do you know?" Moss said, adding, "unless you've already checked them."

Collins smiled.

"You fox," Moss said. "You know, I had you figured for bein' a sharp cookie the very second I laid eyes on you. What else have you done?"

"Let me ask the questions, Moss."

"Fine by me. Only one thing, though."

"What's that?"

"Did you know three boxes of Taylor's stuff have already been shipped? To a relative in St. Louis."

"They've been checked."

"I should have guessed." Moss sat on the bed. "Okay, fire away with your questions."

"For starters, I need the name of every person who came to see Cardinal during the last six weeks or so leading up to the time he was killed. Everyone. Visitors, delivery people, maintenance, anyone you can think of."

"Wow, that's a tall order. I don't know if—"

"Don't you keep records at the guard shack? A log of some sort?"

"Only after six at night. But I can plainly remember

the ones who came to see him after dark."

"Who?"

"Well, naturally, there was that dippy trio who found the body. They came here two or three times. I can't remember exactly, but I'll look it up for you when I get back to the shack."

"Forget them, they're clean. Anyone else? Think hard; it's important."

"Let's see. Yeah, I remember a couple of times when Taylor ordered pizza from the Pizza Hut down on the strip. Both times it was the Hendley kid who delivered them. He's in and out of here all the time. Early last month, Taylor's air conditioning shut down and old Elvis Chandler had to come and work on it. Other than that, I can't recall anyone else comin' to see Taylor after dark. He pretty much stayed to himself. Day and night."

"Did he ever have a visitor who was an Indian?"

"An Indian? You mean like Ghandi?" Moss asked.

"No. A Native American Indian."

"Nah. Nobody like that came to see Taylor."

"Who's the one person living here who knows the most about what goes on around the island? The island gossip, so to speak."

"That would have to be . . ." Moss's eyes widened. "Hey, wait a minute. I do remember one other person coming to see Taylor at night. He came twice, in fact. How could I have forgotten him?"

"Who was he?"

"I don't know his name, but Taylor must have known him. He called the guard shack to let me know the man was on his way and for me to let him in."

"When was this?"

"First time . . . about three weeks ago. Second time . . . maybe four or five days later."

"Can you remember anything about him? What he looked like? How he dressed? Anything at all?"

Moss laughed. "Sure can. He was a black dude."

Collins's eyes darted. "A black guy?"

"Yep. Big as a mountain, too."

"Did you log in his name?"

"Nah. When Taylor okayed him, I didn't bother getting a name. Sorry."

"Anything else, Moss? Think hard."

"Well—"

"Did he have an L-shaped scar on his left cheek?"

"Sure did. Hey, how'd you know that?"

Collins headed out of the bedroom and down the stairs. Moss followed close behind.

"Did I do something right?" Moss asked as Collins opened the front door.

"You did good, Moss. Very good. Cardinal would be proud of you."

Moss was still beaming when Collins drove away.

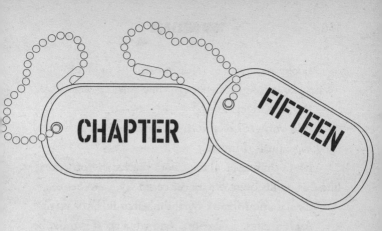

CHAPTER FIFTEEN

"So, my boy, it looks as though you knew what you were talking about," Lucas White said. "As usual, of course."

Collins pressed the phone against his left ear and covered his right ear with his free hand. "Speak up, Lucas. I can barely hear you."

"You and your damn penchant for pay phones," Lucas said, chuckling. "The rest of the world long ago entered into the era of the cell phone. You should consider joining us."

"Old habits are like old friends. Besides, I feel safer doing it this way."

"You need not worry. This line is static free. You can take my word on it." Lucas tapped the bowl of his pipe into the ashtray. "You're convinced it was Deke?"

"Yes."

"But Deke and Cardinal were close, weren't they?"

"At one time, yes. But I'd say they had a falling out of sorts, wouldn't you?"

"Looks that way." Lucas paused to light his pipe. "Where do you figure Seneca fits into this little scenario?"

"Primary executioner."

"And you are convinced he's involved?" Lucas said, exhaling a puff of smoke.

"More than ever. Deke would never do something like this on his own. He never could say no to Seneca."

"That damn Indian. What the hell could he be up to?"

"A hit, Lucas, a takeout. And whoever it is must be big. Very big. Seneca and Deke are involved, and obviously they were trying to recruit Cardinal. But Cardinal would never hitch on with those two. So he said no. When he did, his fate was sealed. They had no choice but to eliminate him."

"I am truly sorry about Cardinal. I know you were especially fond of the man."

That was true. Collins had always cared deeply for Cardinal. Perhaps it was because Cardinal was the oldest and most out-of-place member of that first (and best) group of recruits. Out of place because he, unlike the others, detested killing, hated it to the very fibers of his soul. Seneca thrived on the kill. Deke did it blindly, obediently. It was simply part of the job for him. The same with Snake and Moon and Rafe, the only one to die in combat. Not so with Cardinal. The taking of a human life was abhorrent to him, even in a combat situation. He did it, reluctantly, and he did it for those long-forgotten reasons of duty, honor, and patriotism. Even with that to fall back on, he seldom succeeded in convincing himself the killing was justified. Cardinal was the odd duck in that first group, the one who probably shouldn't have been there. He was too decent, too humane. Yet, when you got right down to it, he was the one whose reasons for being there were the soundest. If, indeed, there is ever a sound reason for killing.

"You there, my boy?" Lucas finally asked.

"Yes."

"Where do you go from here? There seems to be precious little to go on."

"I have Taylor's last words. 'Fallen angels.' You do remember that, don't you?"

"I remember. What was the term you once used to describe it?"

"Magnificent maybe."

"Yes, that's it. How did you put it? Let's see, I think you said something very poetic, like 'Operation Fallen Angels will always go down as a great magnificent maybe.' That may not be precisely verbatim, but it's close."

"Operation Fallen Angels, had it been given the green light, and had it been successful, which it would have been, would have ended the Vietnam mess three years earlier. Ended it favorably, I might add. You know

I'm right, too."

"My boy, we've debated this a million times. Another debate is useless. I have always said the payoff would have been great, but the risks were too high. I was never able to convince myself that it could have been done successfully. Maybe I was right, maybe not. It was a judgment call."

"Lucas, we could have been in and out of Hanoi before anyone had a whisper of what was happening. You know that. Old man Ho and his bunch would have been history. We could have taken them out. Without them, there would have been total chaos in North Vietnam for months. No way they could have recovered."

Lucas sighed out loud. "Perhaps. But we'll never know."

"No, I don't guess we ever will."

Lucas sensed the old fire was gone from Collins's argument. For that he was thankful. It was a debate that had gone on long enough, a debate that had no final resolution.

"How do you go about finding Seneca?" he asked.

"By finding Deke."

"Where do you start?"

"Chicago. Where else? Go to enough blues joints and you'll eventually run into Deke. He can't stay away from them."

"Keep me posted. If you find out anything concrete, let me know about it. The same applies here. If we learn anything, I'll get it to you pronto."

Collins laughed.

"Why the jocularity?" Lucas asked.

"You work in military intelligence, Lucas. You guys never get anything first."

CHAPTER SIXTEEN

Collins stood at his office window and looked out. The threat of rain hung over the campus like a dark blanket. Thunder rattled in the distance. Lightning creased the sky with streaks of gold.

"Pepsi, Diet Coke, orange juice, or Gatorade. What's your choice?" He turned and opened the small refrigerator on the floor next to his desk.

"Doesn't matter," Kate said. "Whatever you give me will be fine."

"You don't get off that easily. Life is filled with tough choices. What'll it be?"

"Diet Coke." She took the soft drink from him. "When are you leaving?"

"Tomorrow."

"So soon?"

Collins shrugged.

"When were you planning on sharing this little

tidbit with me?" Kate asked, a hint of sarcasm attached to every word. "Or were you just going to sneak out in the night and not say anything?"

"I'm telling you now."

"You're working for that Army guy, aren't you? The one I didn't care for?"

"Men like him work for me."

Kate set her Diet Coke on his desk. "Could I ask you a question?"

"More questions? You should be a reporter."

"Am I being nosy?"

"Yeah. But ask anyway."

"That bucket of gravel behind your desk. What's that for?"

"It's for an exercise that strengthens my hands."

"Exercise? What kind of exercise?"

"You asking for a demonstration?"

"Yeah. Sure."

Collins swiveled in his chair, grabbed the bucket, picked it up, and put it on his desk. He stood, looked down at the gravel, took several long, deep breaths, drew his right arm back, straightened the fingers on his hand, then violently thrust his arm forward. When the tips of his fingers made contact the gravel parted like water.

Kate watched, fascinated and frightened, as he repeated the action, alternating hands in rapid succession. She looked up into his eyes, and for a split second she could have sworn they were gray.

He continued, his hands ripping the gravel with increasing intensity. After more than a minute, he stopped. "That's how it's done," he said, wiping his hands on a towel. "No big deal, really."

"Don't the rocks cut your hands?"

"No." He bent down, picked up an old fruit jar, and opened it. Almost instantly, a pungent smell filled his office.

"What's that?" Kate asked.

"It's called *dida-jou*," Collins answered. He poured some of the dark liquid onto his hands. "This hardens my hands."

"What's it made of?"

"I'm not sure. Alcohol and a variety of herbs, I think. Or so I've been told."

"Where do you get it?"

"China. I get mine from Chin, the guy I told you and Pete about."

"I never realized until now just how large your hands are," Kate said.

"All the better to explore every inch of that marvelous body of yours."

She reached out and took both of his hands in hers. "I'm afraid to ask what these hands have explored in the past," she whispered.

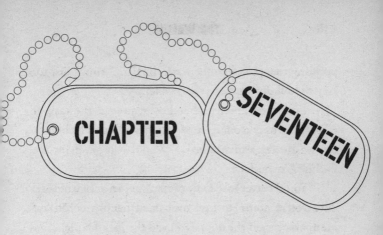

CHAPTER SEVENTEEN

The heat was oppressive, heavy. Simon Buckman removed his coat, tossed it onto the back of a chair, and walked straight to the bar. He scooped up a handful of ice cubes and mashed them against his face. Water dripped from his chin to the floor.

"Hannah, get in here," he growled.

Hannah Buckman descended the steps from the deck into the cabin. Her hair was pulled back and tied in a ponytail, and a blue bandana was tied around her head. She wore a white bikini that contrasted vividly with her sun-baked skin.

"For God's sake, Simon, what do you want this time?"

Simon held up an empty bottle of Jack Daniels. "How many times have I told you? Never let me run out of whiskey. The only damn thing you have to do around here, and you can't even do that."

"There's plenty in that cabinet," Hannah said,

pointing to a glass door beneath the bar. "You're just too lazy to look for it; that's the problem."

Simon attempted to bend over, judged the task an impossible one to complete, straightened up. His breathing was heavy and strained. "Would you get it for me, darlin'?" he said.

"You'd better lose some of that weight or one of these days you're going to keel over dead from a coronary." Hannah opened the door, removed the Jack Daniels, and ceremoniously handed it to Simon. "You'll croak like an old water buffalo."

"No doubt that would cause you a great deal of grief."

"Yes, it would."

Simon grumbled something under his breath, poured a drink, and gulped it down. He refilled his glass two more times and drained the whiskey in a matter of seconds.

Hannah opened the cabin door and started up the stairs. "And another thing," she remarked, looking over her shoulder. "You'd better cut down on your drinking. You're going to become an alcoholic if you're not careful."

"Hell, I already am an alcoholic," Simon shouted, refilling his glass again. "Charter member of AA and damn proud of it, too. But don't you worry your pretty little self about it for one minute. It don't affect you in the least."

Hannah left without answering, went to the deck, found her favorite recliner, and spent the next five minutes adjusting the back to a comfortable upright position.

She sat down and was about to unbutton her bikini top when she saw the man coming toward the boat. Her heart fluttered with excitement. It was the Indian with the dark, movie star good looks.

She thought about giving the Indian a good show—let him see her breasts again—but quickly decided that wasn't such a wise idea. Simon was down below drinking like a fish, and when he got drunk he could become violent and dangerous. The last thing she wanted was to cause trouble for her or the Indian.

She tapped on the cabin window.

"What do you want now?" Simon said gruffly.

"Someone is coming."

"Who?"

"That man who was here before."

"You mean that crazy goddamn Indian?"

"Yeah."

"Is that damn big black shadow with him?"

"No, he's alone."

"Wonder what the hell he wants."

"How would I know?" Hannah said, picking up a paperback. "He's here to see you, not me."

"Send him down here."

Simon drained the last drops of whiskey from his glass. He opened a drawer, pulled out a Beretta, checked to make sure it was loaded, then tucked it into his back pocket. He wanted to be ready. Any trouble, even the slightest hint, and he'd blow that crazy bastard Indian's ass back to the happy hunting ground where it belonged. No sense taking any shit from him again. Simon put his right hand in his pocket and let his fingers touch the cold steel of the gun.

"Just watch your step this time, Indian," Simon said aloud. His right foot tapped nervously against the bar rail.

Hannah watched the Indian jump from the dock to the boat. He moved with the ease and grace of a ballet dancer. And, damn, what a looker. This was a man who was delicious enough to eat.

"Hello again," she said, smiling.

He nodded.

"Seneca, right?"

"Ah, beautiful, bright, and with a good memory." He moved next to the recliner and put his hand on Hannah's shoulder. "A trifecta."

"Thanks for the compliments," Hannah said. "They're few and far between around here."

"I can believe that."

"Guess you're here to see Simon."

The Indian nodded.

"Too bad," Hannah teased. "I'd be much more fun."

"I can believe that, too."

"Maybe later, then?"

"You never know."

"He's waiting for you in the cabin."   Hannah

touched his hand. "Until later."

Simon was standing at the end of the bar. His foot tapped the brass rail with increased tempo as he watched the Indian descend the stairs.

"Well, well, the mighty brave returns." Simon's voice barely held, despite his firm grip on the Beretta.

The Indian was silent, his expression unchanged. Those dark eyes bore into Simon.

Simon giggled nervously. "Looks to me like that business about letting Karl find you was just a lot of talk. So much hot air. Leads me to believe your reputation's been padded somewhat."

The Indian bent down, picked up a silk nightgown, looked at Simon, and smiled. "Bet the wife looks nice in this. Must drive you crazy to have a fox like that and not be able to do anything about it."

"Never give it a second thought; that's how much it bothers me," Simon grunted. "Know what does bother me, though? You bein' here. See, I don't like Indians any better than I like niggers."

"Where's Karl?" Seneca demanded, tossing the gown onto the couch.

"You're shit outta luck, squaw lover. I don't know where he is, and if I did, I wouldn't tell you."

"Oh, you know where he is, fatman. And you'll tell me."

"Think so?"

"I'm positive."

"You're pretty sure of yourself, aren't you, redskin?"

"Karl? Where is he? I want an answer now."

"Check the smoke signals. Maybe they'll tell you where to find him."

The Indian moved forward. When he did, Simon took a step back and pulled out the Beretta.

"One more step, Cochise, and you won't need to know where Karl is." Simon's voice was steady, controlled. The gun in hand gave new life to his nerves.

"It's Seneca, remember?"

"It's 'Dead' if you take another step."

"I don't think so, fatman. You see, if you're going to use that thing, you really ought to take the safety off."

"The safety is off," Simon said. His words came fast and strong, but lacked much conviction.

"You trying to convince me or yourself?"

"I don't need to be convinced of anything—I know I'm right."

The Indian took two more steps forward, his dark eyes focused on Simon with blazing intensity. "But you're not real sure, are you?"

Great droplets of sweat fell from Simon's face. The hand holding the gun began to tremble. "I can take care of that problem," he said. "It's as simple as flicking this switch."

The instant Simon turned the safety upward, the Indian made his move. Stepping forward, he grabbed the gun with his left hand, straightened Simon's arm and lifted it upward, then hooked his right arm behind the big man's elbow. It only took a minimum of pressure before Simon let the revolver fall to the floor. The Indian moved behind Simon, taking the big man's arm with him. He bent the arm at the elbow and applied upward pressure. The hammerlock elicited a loud pig-like squeal from Simon. The Indian took his left hand and covered Simon's face, plunging his forefinger and middle finger into the groaning man's eyes. "You fool, who do you think you're dealing with? Some rag-ass redneck clown?"

"Please, Seneca, don't kill me," Simon begged. "I wasn't going to shoot you. I was scared . . . just protecting myself. I swear."

"Where's Karl?"

"I don't know."

"Not good enough," the Indian said, driving his fingers deeper into Simon's eyes.

"I swear, I swear I don't know where he is. But I can find out. Give me two days."

The Indian exerted more pressure on Simon's arm. "Tell me where Karl is or I'll tear your arm off. Then I'll rip out your eyeballs and feed them to the fish. Think about the pain, fatman; think about the agony I can cause you."

"Please, Seneca, I'm not lying. I don't know where he is. I've never even met him. Only talked to him on the phone."

The Indian released his grip and pushed Simon hard against the bar. Simon hit the bar, reeled to his left, and tumbled onto the couch. One of the couch's legs gave way, causing him to roll onto the floor. He quickly righted himself and began rubbing his eyes.

"Twenty-four hours, fatman; that's all you've got. You don't find out by then, that pretty little thing upstairs will be a widow this time tomorrow."

Simon reached for the silk nightgown, brought it to his face, and gently pressed it against his eyes.

"Got it?" The Indian stooped down and picked up the revolver. "Got it?"

"Yeah, yeah, I got it. What do you think—I'm fuckin' deaf or something?"

"No, I think you're an idiot." The Indian pointed the gun at Simon. "The safety was off. You let me talk you into putting it on."

He ejected the magazine clip, emptied the bullets into his hand, cleared the chamber, and tossed the gun onto the floor. It landed with a loud *clunk*.

"Twenty-four hours, fatman. No more."

Nearly ten minutes passed before Simon was able to clear the blurriness from his vision and another ten minutes before he was able to stand. On unsteady legs, he went to the bar, picked up the phone, and began dialing. Things had to be done. Without further delay. That damn Indian had to be eliminated. He was too fuckin' crazy to deal with.

Simon continued to rub his eyes, listened to the phone ring, and waited. After half a dozen rings, he heard the cell phone click on.

"Hello."

"Karl?"

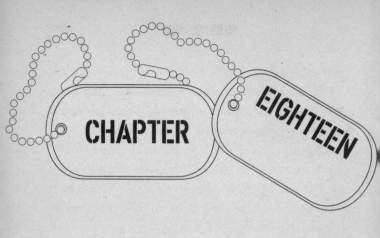

CHAPTER EIGHTEEN

"Jesus God, did you see that?"

"Yeah, I saw."

"The look, did you see the look in his eyes?"

"I saw, I saw. The little dink bastard never knew what was happening."

"No, not him, not the dink. The captain. Did you see his eyes while he was wasting the little motherfucker?"

"No, I wasn't watching his eyes."

"They were cold, like a cobra. Like a wild animal. Scary, man. I'm tellin' you, it was spooky."

"Forget his eyes, man, did you see that dink's head tumble into the river? It hit the water so hard it bounced."

"Look at the captain now."

"Yeah, he's out there, man, out there in that killer's zone."

"First kill, sir?"

"Forget it, man, he's too far out there to hear you. I saw one other guy with that look, and he sometimes didn't come *back for hours. He'd stand there, like the captain is now, lookin' down at the victim's body, studying it, you know, like he was sizing it up, analyzing it. It's almost like he was lookin' for ways to kill more swiftly, more efficiently."*

"You can't kill more swiftly or efficiently than he just did."

"No, you're wrong. Guys like him make killing a game, something personal. They're always lookin' to find ways to streamline it, to execute it perfectly. A 'masterpiece kill'—that's what they call it."

"First kill, sir?"

"I'm tellin' you to forget it. He's not hearing you."

"Sir, sir."

"Sir, sir."

Collins's eyes snapped open.

"Sir, would you please fasten your seat belt? We'll be landing in Evansville in ten minutes."

Collins smiled at the flight attendant, yanked his seat to the upright position, and clasped the seat belt buckle together. His head ached; his mouth was as dry as a sand dune. He stared out the window, hypnotized by the setting sun and dreamy from his own fatigue. Closing his eyes, he listened as the plane's engines groaned their familiar, monotonous tune.

Seconds later he found himself once again poised on the banks of that muddy river in Nam, kneeling next to a headless corpse, hearing from a distance the whispered voice calling out to him, hearing again—how many times, now?— that singular question, "First kill, sir?" as it pierced the darkness and hung suspended, waiting for an answer.

But he hadn't answered, not then, not ever. He didn't need to. The answer was in the question.

Every kill is a first kill.

The plane's rough landing jarred him awake, mercifully retrieving him from the river's edge, from a past littered with the bones of countless dead, drenched in a sea of blood. This return, he knew, would be brief, a stopover. The past summoned him, and before this journey was finished, he would have to find that river of blood once again. Find it and embrace it.

Assassins are only given a one-way ticket.

The killing never ends, does it, my boy? It just goes on and on.

An hour later, Collins stood in a small strip mall parking lot, staring at the front of a red brick building with a large tinted front window. On the window, written in gold letters trimmed in black, was the name of the man he'd come to see.

SNAKE'S POOL HALL
&
GRILL

The interior was exactly what Collins expected: heavy with atmosphere, smoke filled, dark, and dingy. A dining area to the left, consisting of a grill, counter, and five stools. Two booths, both empty, next to the big window. Like a hundred pool rooms he'd been in over the years. Standing there, he half-expected Willie Mosconi or Minnesota Fats to tap his shoulder and challenge him to a game of straight pool.

A tall, thin, fortyish-year-old woman sat in a chair behind the counter, talking to a balding man wearing an Evansville Aces baseball cap. She smiled at Collins. "What can I do for you, stranger?" Her voice was deep, rusty. "We've got the best homemade bean soup in the tri-state area. I know because I made it. Like some?"

"Nothing, thank you," answered Collins.

The smoky playing area was spacious enough to accommodate five Brunswick tables, one snooker table, two old-fashioned pinball machines and a jukebox, out of which The Righteous Brothers belted "You've Lost That Lovin' Feeling."

Two twenty-somethings were at the front table playing nine ball for fifty bucks a game. Collins watched the taller of the two miss an easy shot on the seven, leaving his opponent with a simple run out.

"Shit, how could I miss a shot like that?" the man asked, looking at Collins. "That was a gimme."

Because you're a lousy pool player; That's why. Collins

shrugged, moved past the front table, easing his way toward a group of four men sitting in a circle a few feet past the jukebox. Two of the men, both wearing solemn expressions, were lost in a game of chess. One of the players, the one whose chair leaned against the wall, was the man Collins had come to see.

Grady Wilson.

The Snake.

Without realizing it, Collins wiped his watering eyes with the back of his hands. He wasn't sure if the tears were caused by the heavy smoke or by his old friend's appearance. What he did know was that he suddenly felt very sad, depressed.

He also felt betrayed by his memory.

In Collins's mental scrapbook, Snake was tall and wiry, with the sinewy, defined muscles of a well-conditioned athlete in his prime. Snake had been considered the best pure athlete in that first class. He lacked Seneca's brute strength and great agility, or Deke's quickness, or Cardinal's brains, but in the overall analysis, taking everything into consideration, Snake was judged the best all-around athlete.

Not anymore.

In no way did this man resemble that once-great athlete. Snake had changed—drastically. And in ways not measured strictly by years, by the passing of time. It was something else. He was a stranger now, someone

Collins had never seen before and likely wouldn't have recognized under other circumstances.

Snake was only a shell of what he once was, a skeletal outline covered by a layer of skin stretched so tight it looked ready to snap. His bony shoulders, once wide as goal posts, sagged forward, pitiful victims of gravity's relentless forces. His gray-speckled hair, pulled tight into a ponytail, fell to the middle of his back. His eyes, once wild and filled with life, were deep and dark-circled. His face was mostly hidden by a thick, bushy beard. But most striking of all was his weight, which couldn't have been much in excess of a hundred pounds.

He looked like a biblical prophet or a concentration camp survivor.

"I believe that's what is known as checkmate," Snake declared to the man sitting across from him.

His opponent studied the board carefully for several seconds, removed his cap, scratched his head, then said, "Yeah, kinda looks that way."

"That's another sawski you owe me."

The man dug into his pocket, pulled out a ten, and slapped it into Snake's palm.

"Nice doing business with you," Snake said. He took a long pull from a bottle of Smithwick's. "Come back anytime. I'm always here."

As the group began to disperse, Snake stuffed the bill into his shirt pocket, peered up, saw Collins, looked back down, then quickly glanced up again. It took another look before recognition hit. Smiling, he stood and walked slowly toward Collins. It was, Collins thought, a very sad smile.

"Goddamn, I can't believe it. Cain. What brings you to this crummy part of the world?"

"You."

"Well, damn, that's great . . . terrific. Hell, I never expected to see you again."

"Here I am."

"No shit. Here you are . . . a ghost from the past."

The two men hugged, stepped back, and stared awkwardly at each other for nearly a minute. Collins finally broke the silence. "You have a place where we can talk? In private?"

Snake's expression turned serious. "Sure, sure, right this way. My office in the back. Ain't much, but it'll do."

Snake's assessment of the office as "ain't much" was more than modest. In fact, the office was large, cool, and surprisingly clean. And judging from the casino-like furnishings that filled the room, this was probably where the big profits were raked in. A card table surrounded by six chairs sat in the center of the room. To the left stood a craps table. In the right corner were two slot machines.

Collins sat in one of the chairs, picked up a deck of cards, cut the deck with one hand, and turned over the top card. It was the ace of hearts.

"Looks like this is where the real action takes place," he said.

"It's the money room."

"You run a high-stakes game here?" Collins asked.

"Too big for me; that's for sure. I just let 'em play, then take my cut off the top. Straight ten percent. They're pretty big high rollers, so I do okay."

"I don't see a license, so this has to be illegal."

"Yep, a definite criminal enterprise."

"How do you avoid the law?"

"The D.A. has a serious love affair with the dice."

Collins laid the cards on the table. "You look like shit, Snake. What's going on?"

Snake sighed and looked away. His eyes were hollow, distant. "Can't you guess? Smart guy like you ought to know."

"I'm not that smart. Tell me."

"Junk, man."

"What kind of junk?"

"What kind? Coke, heroin, meth, pills. You name it, I've done it."

"How long?"

"Man, I've been fighting the monkey man for years. Hell, practically ever since we got home. He's tough, man. Always there, waiting. Some days I wake up and say, 'Okay, Snake, today's the day. You're gonna whip that bastard. You can do it.' And I will whip him for a while. Then something happens, or I'll have a dream, or flash on some memory, something like that, and here comes the monkey again. The laughin' motherfuckin' monkey. Believe me, Cain, he's one heavy, persistent bastard."

"Have you tried to get help?"

"Help? Man, there's not enough help in the world to rid me of my nightmares. You're bound to have them, too. There's no way you can't. I mean, look at all the shit we did. We were savages, beasts, mercenaries fighting our own private war, keeping our own personal body count. Hell, what we did had nothing to do with Vietnam, or our country, or any of that American flag shit they talked about. You know that. Keepin' our country free? Free from what? Those scrawny dinks in pajamas? What the hell were they gonna do to us? Come over here and rape our mothers? Fightin' the tidal wave of Communism? Man, we wouldn't know a commie if we were introduced to one. What we did wasn't about patriotism or Communism; it was about killing. That's it, pure and simple. Killing. And, man, we were wild, crazy, and ruthless, and there's no other fuckin' way to describe it.

"Then . . . *boom!* We come home one day and it's over. Finished, just like that. The fun and games are called off, the body-count scorecards torn up and thrown away. What are you left with after that? Besides the nightmares? And the bloodstains on your hands? Nothing; that's what. What comes after the killing? How do you match the high you get when you chop off a man's head? Or cut off his ears to keep as souvenirs? Where do you find that kind of rush again? You don't. It's not possible. So you turn to something else. For me, that something was dope." Snake leaned forward, his elbows on the table. Tears streamed down his sunken cheeks.

He continued, "Remember how you used to talk about 'the look'? About how a successful assassin had to have it or else he couldn't make the grade? Eyes of the predator, isn't that what you called it? Well, one day you wake up, look into the mirror, and realize the person looking back at you doesn't have it anymore. It's gone, history, just like the war. Then it hits you that you're really nothing more than a cold-blooded murderer, that killing is what you've been trained to do, and that those skills, your body count, mean nothing in the real world. That's when you understand it was all just a game run by politicians and businessmen, and that we were the fools who played the game for them.

"Crazy, man, it's all so fuckin' absurd. And look what it did to the players. None of us ever married. We have no family, no real friends, no close attachments of any depth. We're adrift, man, adrift on a sea of blood and bodies and bad memories. It's no fun, man. No fun at all." Snake paused, held out his right arm, opened and closed his fist. He stared at it absently for nearly a minute before he spoke again.

"You're the only one who came out of the shit okay. Know why? Because you were a natural, a born killer, just like your namesake. Whoever christened you Cain knew exactly what he was doing. The perfect name for the perfect assassin. The ability to kill was God's gift to you. Some irony, huh? Did you know I used to say a prayer before every mission? I did. And it wasn't a prayer for safe deliverance, or even for forgiveness. I prayed I could kill like you did. You know why I prayed for that? Because your kills were humane. So swift, so sudden, without pain. You were the best, Cain, the absolute top-of-the-line assassin. Compared to you, the rest of us were rank amateurs. Only Seneca could even dare to dream the dream of Cain. You were something, man, really something." Snake fell silent, his haunted eyes glassy, tired, wet with tears.

Collins put a hand on his friend's shoulder. There were a thousand things he wanted to say—should say—to help ease Snake's suffering. To try one last time to bring Snake back from those jungles. But— "Listen, Snake, have you heard from Seneca recently?"

"Not since we left Nam. Why?"

"I need to find him."

"The last I heard he was in Africa, or Russia, someplace like that."

"What about Deke?"

"He was around here a month or so ago. Just popped up one morning, like you did today. Surprised the hell out of me."

"What did he want?"

"Nothing, really. We talked for a couple of hours, then he left."

"What did you talk about?"

"Mostly, we talked about the past, about the guys. Some of the things we did over there. Nothing serious."

"Did he ask for your help?"

"Help? No. Why? Is somethin' going down?"

"Yeah, but I don't know what," Collins said. "That's why I need to find Deke ASAP."

"Chicago, man. That's where he lives. He's a bouncer at one of those blues clubs he loves so much. He shouldn't be hard to find."

Collins looked straight into Snake's eyes. "Did you hear about Taylor?"

"Taylor? No. What about him?"

"He's dead."

"The Cardinal? Dead? No, I hadn't heard. When? How?"

"Murdered. A couple of weeks ago."

"You know who did it?"

Collins shrugged.

"Cardinal was a good guy. He . . ." Snake looked down. "It's all bullshit, man, bullshit by the bucket loads."

Collins went to the craps table, picked up the dice, and tossed them. Boxcars. "What can I do to help?" he asked.

"Erase the past; make the dreams go away."

"Sorry. That's beyond me."

"And I thought the great Cain could do anything."

"Is the monkey close?"

Snake snickered. "He's always close, man. Always ready to climb right up my ass and gnaw at my heart."

"If you need anything—anything—call me at this number." Collins handed Snake a card. "Anytime."

Snake opened the office door, and they walked into the pool hall, now empty except for the woman behind the counter.

"How's the Grey Fox doin' these days?" Snake asked.

"You know Lucas. Same tough old bird as always."

Collins stepped outside into the darkness, turned, and looked back at Snake. "If you happen to hear from Deke again, let me know. And don't wise him to the fact that I was around here asking questions. Okay?"

"Okay."

Collins climbed into his car and drove away, leaving Snake standing framed in the darkened doorway. Seldom had he felt such overwhelming sadness. Sadness for Snake's pain and anguish, for his personal horde of demons, for the nightmares that wouldn't fade, for the torment that would never end.

For his inability to conquer the most devastating enemy of all.

The enemy within.

CHAPTER NINETEEN

On certain nights the District of Columbia is a spectacular sight, magnificent and majestic, a spit of land more worthy of Olympus and the Greek gods than the very human politicians who run America. To see it on one of those special nights, to walk within that beauty, is to be awed. There is no way to remain unmoved; the delicate blending of light, shadow, moon, and marble is enough to humble even the most indifferent observer.

Simon Buckman was the exception. Never one to see beauty in inanimate objects, he gave no thought to the glorious mixture of time and place, of history and legend, as he pulled himself from his car and shuffled apprehensively toward the Tidal Basin in Potomac Park. To his left, across Independence Avenue, was the Lincoln Memorial. To his right, safely tucked behind the south corner of the Basin, was the Jefferson Memorial. Those sculpted monuments to two towering figures in American

139

history were of no concern to Simon now. Not at night. Not at 2:30 in the morning.

For Simon, night meant shadows and sound . . . especially sound. Night sounds had always terrified him. Trees jostled by a soft breeze, leaves brushing against objects hidden by the darkness, grass whispering—sounds he associated with nightmares, with some inner fear that left him gasping for breath. Simon Buckman preferred the safety of daylight.

On his way through the park, he had to step aside to avoid collisions with midnight joggers. Not once, but twice. "Stupid idiots," he mumbled. *What kind of fool would jog at this hour, in this city, with its outrageously high homicide rate?* Without realizing it, he reached inside his coat pocket and felt the small-caliber pistol. Small-caliber, maybe, but big enough to do considerable damage. He felt reassured.

Simon pushed his way to the edge of the Basin. Another jogger, a young man running hard to keep up with a Great Dane, sped past. Simon scooped up a handful of water from the Basin and splashed it onto his face. Relief from the stifling heat was instant.

A sudden gust of wind whipped through the park, stirring the cherry trees. And his imagination. Those nightmare sounds surrounded him, engulfed him. Half-turning, hand on pistol, he met the darkness.

"Goddammit, man, would you please hurry up?" he

whispered. "I'm not fuckin' stayin' here all night."

Standing alone in the Washington night, plagued by his worst fears, he couldn't help but question the wisdom of this trip. Maybe he should have waited, let things pass, maintained the status quo. That would have been the prudent thing to do: to leave well enough alone. Most certainly, standing here alone in the middle of the night was anything but sane. It was crazy, ridiculous. Only an idiot would have made this trip.

Not true, he quickly told himself. This meeting was essential.

Simon had flown to D.C. to meet with Karl. There were grievances that needed to be addressed, issues resolved. Simon hadn't been anxious to make this trip— he detested flying, a fear even greater than his fear of night—but these were important matters. Urgent matters. This trip also served a second purpose: he would finally meet Karl. At last, he would match a face with the voice he'd heard countless times.

He had tried to paint a mental picture of Karl. The portrait he invariably came up with was that of a short, thin, perhaps effeminate, middle-aged man. It was the voice that triggered the image: high-pitched, reedy, supremely confident. Karl's speech was different, too: clipped, distinctive, English-sounding, always spoutin' those big fuckin' fifty-cent words. Simon saw Karl as an actor, a slight figure alone on the stage, Gielgud-like, a fuckin' fairy reciting Shakespeare to a theatre full of fairy watchers.

Standing alone in the darkness, Simon heard with surprising clarity that familiar voice calling out his name—once, twice. *Jeezus, that fuckin' voice sounds close,* Simon thought, *like it's real, like it's . . . oh, fuck, it's coming from behind me.*

Startled, Simon whirled, his hand clutching the pistol. "Karl? Is that you?" Simon tilted his head, straining to see into the darkness. Nothing. He took a small, tentative step forward, his fingers now squeezing the pistol. "Is that you, Karl?"

"Don't come any closer." That voice, distinctive, confident. Gielgud at the top of his game. "What you have to say can be said from there."

"I prefer to see who I'm talking to."

"What you like or don't like is of no consequence to me," Karl snapped. "Just do as you're told. Understand?"

"Sure. You bet," Simon said.

"You buffoon. This—"

"But, Karl, I—"

"Never interrupt me, do you understand? Never."

"I, I—"

"This meeting is unnecessary," Karl said, his tone still nasty. "I'm growing weary of your alarmist attitude. Your . . . weakness."

Simon slumped against the side of the Basin, stunned

by Karl's words. He felt tired, beaten, as if everything—the flight, the shadows, Seneca, Karl's anger—were suffocating him. He gulped the hot night air.

"I don't mean to sound alarmist," Simon said. "It's just that we have a problem that needs to be taken care of immediately."

"It's not your job to worry about problems. You're to follow orders and nothing more."

Simon took out a handkerchief and wiped his face. "Yes, yes, I'm aware of that. But there's this problem."

"What problem?"

"That crazy Indian."

"Seneca?"

"Yes, he's—"

"You called this meeting to tell me you think Seneca is a problem?"

"I did," Simon admitted, meekly. His hands were shaking, and beads of sweat had begun to collect on his upper lip.

"You fool. I should have you shot for such an imbecilic move." Karl's voice was deeper now, more hard-edged, with a hint of controlled fury. Gielgud had given way to De Niro.

"I just thought—"

"Shut up. In the first place, you don't think; I doubt you even possess that particular capacity. Second, I'm the one who decides what's a problem and what isn't.

And third, I'm the only one who takes care of problems. Right now you're the only problem I see."

"Look, I don't mean to make waves or anything, but I'm the one who has to deal with that crazy bastard. It was my balls he nearly pulled off. I know what I'm talkin' about. He's crazy out of control. He needs to be taken care of."

"You're overreacting, as usual," Karl said. "Seneca will follow orders. If he doesn't—"

"If? You mean 'when.'"

"*If* he doesn't, he'll be dealt with accordingly. Same as you, if you interrupt me again."

"Well, you'd better be prepared, because he's a renegade who has no loyalty or respect."

Karl said, "*Loyalty? Respect?* Those are rather nebulous terms, don't you think? Especially in our line of work. Myself, I prefer more concrete words, like *efficient, cunning, resourceful*. Words that accurately define that *crazy* Indian, as you like to call him."

"I don't know from nebulous, or whatever the fuck that word means. I'm just tellin' you how it is." Simon was relaxed now, his fears having been somewhat assuaged by Karl's less-menacing tone. "Out of curiosity, what is our line of work?"

"You're to act as intermediary between Seneca and me. Right now that's all you need to know."

"Have it your way. But don't forget I warned you."

"I always have it my way," Karl said. "Never forget that."

"By the way, the Indian said he needs to know when and where you want to meet. Said he needed to know yesterday."

"Seneca has many wonderful attributes, but I'm afraid patience isn't among them. Tell him I'll be in touch within the next two weeks. Tell him I'll know by then the precise time and location of his next task."

"He said no more dress rehearsals."

"That sounds like Seneca," Karl said. "You inform my Cherokee friend that this is no dress rehearsal. Make it clear to him that this is the real thing. That he'll be more than pleased."

Simon Buckman stood at his hotel window and watched the sun rise out of the eastern sky, a bright orange avenger come to drive away the demons of night. Simon's eyelids drooped as he stared at the expanding orb. He had never felt more exhausted, yet sleep wouldn't come. His body, indeed his entire being, was spent, worn. He needed to crash, to sleep for hours, but it wasn't going to happen. There were too many thoughts crisscrossing in his head, too many ideas, too many words. No way sleep could break through that mental wall.

He was especially troubled by Karl's words.

What you like or don't like is of no consequence to me.

Simon sneered, paced, still smoldering from what Karl had said four hours earlier in the frightening D.C. night.

You're to follow orders and nothing more.

Simon's blood boiled inside him. He didn't have to take that kind of shit from anybody, and that included Karl. Who was this Karl, anyway? Some kind of a god? Hell, no. And even if he was some big hotshot, that didn't give him the right to treat people in such a shabby, disrespectful manner.

Right now, you're the only problem I see.

That one particularly galled Simon. How dare anyone challenge him, or admonish him, like he was some amateur? Hadn't he performed countless tasks over the years, often with little or no monetary remuneration? Dirty, thankless tasks, some of which were plenty hazardous? Had he ever complained? Never. Had he once asked for special favors? No. He had always been a good soldier, had always done as he was told. He deserved respect.

Buffoon.

Fuck Karl.

Simon went into the bathroom, filled a glass with cold water, gulped it down. The liquid cooled his throat but not the fire that burned within, or the stinging resentment he felt for Karl. Nothing could quench that.

Karl. What rock did he slither out from under? What hole? It bothered Simon that he knew so little about the man. In all the years, through all the jobs he had performed, Simon had never so much as heard Karl's name mentioned, not even in passing, until three months ago. Until then, for all Simon knew, the man didn't exist. Then, like some fiery meteor, Karl appeared, a king barking orders and treating a loyal warrior like some second-class citizen.

It wasn't right. It had to stop.

Simon fell back onto the bed and closed his eyes. The weariness he felt was overwhelming, almost painful, yet any thought of sleep was out of the question.

Karl's words kept getting in the way.

After tossing and turning for another two hours, Simon swung around and sat on the edge of the bed. He looked at his watch: 8:30. Three hours until his flight departed. He looked out the window. The sun, now clear of the horizon, made its steady climb upward. The day held great promise.

At that moment, Simon made his own promise. He would see that Karl paid dearly for his disrespect, for saying those hateful words that refused to go away.

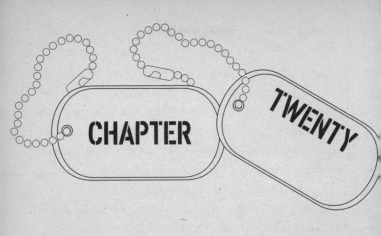

CHAPTER TWENTY

The morning dawned much differently in Sarasota, Florida, than it did in the nation's capitol. A midnight storm, the last remnants of a major hurricane south of Cuba, had drenched the area and sent the temperatures tumbling nearly twenty degrees. By mid-morning, little had changed. A steady drizzle fell, and thick, gray clouds kept the chill in the air. Florida weather forecasters were promising a less-than-beautiful weekend.

Hannah Buckman awoke to the sound of waves slapping against the sides of the yacht. She lay on her back, eyes closed, and listened as the rain assaulted the deck with increasing intensity. It was a sound she loved: the rain. So romantic. She also loved the rocking of the yacht, the peaceful swaying back and forth. It was so soothing, like being in a hammock gently caressed by the breeze. But those weren't her feelings this morning. Today, she felt anything but peaceful. She had consumed too much alcohol last night at the Old Salty Dog on Siesta Key, and now she was paying the price. Her stomach was angrier than a live volcano, her eyes sandy as the desert. Probably, she was going to throw up, no matter how hard she fought it. For the moment, until the inevitable occurred, she decided remaining perfectly still was the best course of action to take.

It wasn't until she dozed off and awakened again nearly an hour later that the volcano erupted. She dashed for the bathroom, making it just in time. Throwing up was bad enough; the dry heaves were worse.

After splashing cold water on her face, Hannah lifted her head and looked in the mirror. And flinched. The face staring back was virtually unrecognizable. A horror movie queen in full makeup. A trickle of dried blood curled from the corner of her mouth to the bottom of her chin, a narrow thread giving her mouth a slanted, lopsided look. Both lips were noticeably swollen; there was puffiness under her left eye and a series of bite marks beneath her right ear. Even more prominent were the bite marks on her neck and breasts. Several were ringed with dried blood; all had left deep bruises. She closed the bathroom door, removed her robe and examined her body in the full-length mirror. What she saw repulsed her, caused her to shake with fear. Her flesh, from shoulder to ankle, front and back, was a mass of purple bruises, bites, and welts. Nearly every inch of her skin had been battered mercilessly.

Hannah struggled to remember. Had there been an accident? Had she slipped and fallen? Had she . . . ? She couldn't remember. She shook her head, blinked her eyes, as if that would somehow lift the alcohol haze and allow her to remember. But it didn't help. Last night was a million years ago, distant, unreachable.

Jesus, what happened to me?

She waded into that haze again, pushing hard to break through. It lifted, briefly, revealing fleeting impressions, grainy, flickering newsreel scenes that lingered teasingly, then faded. One image—the Indian, dark eyes burning like hot cinders, his skin hard, smooth. A second image came, then disappeared as quickly—hands around her throat, contracting, suffocating.

Finally, the dam broke, releasing a wave of images, faster, each one clearer, longer. His mouth covering her breasts, teeth biting into her nipples. Her hands and legs tied to the bedposts, spread-eagle, helpless. The long knife blade, glistening as it trailed across her body. The numbing fear she felt when the Indian guided the blade from her sternum to the top of her pubic area. Through the rapidly disappearing haze, she heard the grunting sound he made when he entered her. She felt his savage thrusts, the strange, yet exquisite pleasure she experienced as he drove deeper inside her. Pleasure mixed with pain and fear. She felt his climax, heard his deep, guttural groan, the most primitive sound she'd ever heard. She remembered being untied, flipped onto her stomach. She could see him take the long strap of soft leather, feel him flog her, softly at first, then with frenzied enthusiasm. She tried to scream, but he silenced her by covering her mouth with a scarf. And always the knife in plain view promising pain, maybe even death. He entered her again, stayed inside for what seemed like an eternity, climaxed, his breath coming fast. Then he slept, his body covering hers, a deep, peaceful sleep. An animal fully sated. Sometime during the night, her pain and fear dulled by the alcohol, she too found sleep.

Hannah leaned over the sink, retching. For ten minutes, her body tried to purge the alcohol and the memory and the terror of last night. When there was nothing left inside her, she covered herself with the robe and returned to bed.

She closed her eyes, softly whispered the Indian's name, then drifted off to a troubled sleep.

CHAPTER TWENTY ONE

Sitting at a booth in an Indiana truck stop, a half-empty cup of cold coffee in front of him, Collins stared absently at the television set perched high above the counter. His brooding eyes saw the pictures, his ears heard the words, but nothing registered. He was tired, drained. The television images and sounds flew by like a hurried dream.

The History Channel—what else at this hour?—was replaying a special on the current war in Iraq. Collins listened with growing interest as various personalities, some military, some civilian, all with proper credentials and speaking with absolute authority, dissected the reasons for our second incursion into that faraway country in a little more than a decade. And there was no shortage of reasons. Eliminate Saddam, regime change, locate and destroy weapons of mass destruction, spread democracy and democratic ideals in that region of the world. Take your pick.

There is, Collins knew, never a shortage of reasons for going to war. Some real, some imagined, some manufactured. In this particular case, the one that mattered most was seldom mentioned—oil. No matter what the so-called experts said, if Iraq had no oil, the United States would have no interest.

But Iraq did have oil, so young Americans were once again put in harm's way for questionable reasons. *No,* Collins reminded himself, *that doesn't even rank as a questionable reason.* Blood for oil is a devil's bargain in every respect.

"Victory in Baghdad" was the cheesy B movie title they'd tagged it with. An entire war condensed into a neat, one-hour package. With plenty of commercials, of course. Leave it to the media to trivialize something as deadly and ugly and horrific as war, presenting it as though it were nothing more than a glorified video game. War must never be taken lightly, and no one knew this better than Collins. *Shock and awe* may have a nice ring to it, but it translates to death and destruction. Soldiers on both sides fight and die. The dead come home in flag-draped coffins. Families are shattered, cities and villages torn apart. Blood is spilled. That's the reality.

War is the ultimate truth, and to portray it in such a clean and antiseptic manner is a lie. The dead and wounded deserve better. The country deserves better.

Collins was convinced that if politicians worldwide

were forced to spend fifteen minutes in actual combat, war would become a thing of the past. That was an observation he once shared with Lucas many years ago.

"That's a wonderful sentiment, my boy," Lucas responded. "Wonderful, but inaccurate. Money is the engine that drives warfare. Politicians are only puppets on a string. So long as billions of dollars can be made, wars will continue to flourish. Never allow yourself to think otherwise."

Staring up at the TV screen, Collins wondered how long it would take before the History Channel aired the sequel to this ongoing military entanglement, which would include Iraq, part two, and the war in Afghanistan. No doubt it was already in the works.

"We have kicked the Vietnam Syndrome," commentators and politicians proclaimed after the first Gulf War. "America can feel good about itself once again."

Hearing that, Collins could only wonder how many future war syndromes lay in store for the country.

That haunting question only added to Collins's already heavy mood. What did it mean, anyway, kicking a war syndrome, be it Vietnam or Iraq? Nothing. They were only words spoken by a cheerleader with short-term memory and a long eye on popularity. Taken seriously, the statement was yet another slam at the veterans and the job they performed in shit-hole countries thousands of miles away. Men and women sent into combat with hands too often tied behind their backs, with shabby equipment, and for the most tenuous reasons. Soldiers fighting despite an appalling lack of support from the folks back home. It pissed him off to hear shit about how we "lost" in Vietnam. We didn't lose in Vietnam. No way did we fuckin' lose. And we won't lose in Iraq. What will eventually happen is there will be a replay of what happened in Nam: our leaders, "the best and the brightest," will one day simply decide to take the ball and go home. We won't lose; we'll quit.

Then we'll be left to wonder why. To ask ourselves what it was all about and whether or not the results were worth the price we paid. All the while, as we seek answers to those questions, our next generation of the "best and brightest" will be looking around for the next war.

"We sure kicked ass big-time, didn't we, Sally?"

Collins initially thought the question came from one of the History Channel commentators. It was only when he looked up that he realized the speaker was a man sitting alone at the counter. Tall—maybe six-five—and thin, he wore tight jeans, a tank top, leather cowboy boots, and a black Peterbilt cap. There was a tattoo on his left shoulder: a cross, under which was written, "Glory to Jesus."

"I'd say you're right," Sally agreed, placing a cup of coffee in front of him.

The man wheeled on his stool, coffee cup in hand.

"We kicked old Saddam's ass, didn't we, partner?" he said to Collins.

Collins smiled, indifferent to the man and the question.

"Well, you do agree with me, don't you, partner?" the man insisted, sipping coffee.

"Wrong enemy, wrong war," Collins replied. "Bin Laden is the guy we want."

"Yeah, whatever. But you gotta agree; taking out old Saddam was easy as takin' candy from a baby."

"Kicking ass is never easy," Collins said.

"I don't buy that," the man said. "And I don't imagine Saddam did either, especially when he was standing on the gallows with a rope around his neck."

"You ever been in a war?"

"Nah, but I'd dearly love to have been in that first one. Or the one we're in now. I'd like nothing better than to hunt down that coward bin Laden."

"It's an all-volunteer army."

"Believe me, I gave plenty of thought to joining. Talked to the recruiter about it a couple of times. But I doubt they'd have me. See, my blood pressure tends to run a little high." The man paused to stir his coffee. "But, hell, they don't need me. Those boys did just fine. Women, too, although I have to admit I'm not all that keen on sending females into a war zone. But, shit, old Saddam didn't know who he was messin' with. Neither will Osama. We'll blast him out of those caves. Wait and see. Before all is said and done, that Muslim lunatic will regret the day he decided to go against us."

The man took a sip of coffee. Judging it too hot to drink, he added more cream.

"These Gulf wars—they ain't like Nam," he said quickly. "Over there, we let those little bastards push us around pretty good. Not this time. This time we went in there and showed 'em who was boss. We flexed our muscles, you know? Showed the world we're still the baddest ass-kicker on the block."

Collins felt a strange mix of feelings toward this man-child. There was a certain appreciation for his simplicity, for that concise black and white outlook toward complex issues. Collins had long ago come to realize his own world would be easier if there were fewer gray areas. Conversely, he detested the man's kick-ass mentality, the tough-guy posturing. Of all the misconceptions, that was the biggest. Tough guys don't posture or bluff. They don't feel the need. Tough guys merely do the job and let the job do the talking. Joe Louis didn't brag. Lou Gehrig didn't brag. They beat your brains in every day. Tough guys don't stand on a ship and tell you, "Mission accomplished." Of course, Collins understood the man was caught up in the fervor of an ongoing military campaign and the residual anger of 9/11. He was riding on a new wave of patriotism that had swept through the country like napalm on a hillside. In Collins's view it was Super Bowl pizza party patriotism, more fashionable than heartfelt. But maybe that was okay. Maybe that was what the country needed. It wasn't his style, or to his liking, or something he could relate to, but that didn't really matter. How could it? He was from another time, another era.

Another war.

The killing never ends, does it, my boy? It just goes on and on.

Collins signaled for another cup of coffee. The waitress brought it, answered his frown with a cheery smile, then sashayed away. He gazed deep into the dark liquid, his thoughts swinging like a pendulum, forward to Deke, backward to Snake.

At some point the machinery broke, causing the pendulum to become stuck in the past.

On Snake.

There was no mystery why Collins felt so down. Meeting Snake again, listening to his old friend's troubled words, looking into those cadaver eyes—how could he not be down?

Snake had been to the abyss, peered into the darkness, and seen absolute evil. They all had seen the same darkness, the same evil. Been to the same abyss. They had negotiated its unique confines, performed their duties, then withdrawn to the light and its safety. All except Snake. The darkness followed him, pursued him relentlessly, trapped him, and ultimately swallowed him.

Snake was being held hostage by countless ghosts from his past. By the secrets left behind in those steaming jungles of death. His soul was on fire, and the flames were unquenchable.

"I hope you find peace." Those were the last words Collins said to Snake.

Snake, his head lowered like a monk in prayer, didn't answer for almost a minute. Finally, he lifted his head, directed those sad, hollow eyes at Collins, and said, "Not in this world, my friend. Not in this lifetime."

Snake nailed it. There would never be peace, not for him. There would only be more pain and suffering. The Angel of Death offered the only means of escape, the only end to all his agony. Collins could envision it—Snake with a gun in his hand, his head in a halo of blood, or a rope around his neck, or a dirty needle in his arm . . . some shabby way to lay the monkey to rest, to finally set himself free. To leave the ghosts behind. One more casualty of the Vietnam War. How many more would there be before that war's long arm of death ceased to harvest victims?

The killing never ends, does it, my boy? It just goes on and on.

Those dark thoughts followed Collins all the way

to Chicago. So did the image of Snake's tortured eyes. Even as Collins lay sprawled on the huge bed in his motel room, he heard Snake's words rumble through his head like a locomotive. Words that pleaded for redemption and peace. Words Collins couldn't allow himself to hear. They had to be erased, like the enemy.

Sympathy, pity, concern—the inevitable signs of weakness. And weakness led to defeat. There was no place for sympathy or pity, now or ever, not even for a wounded comrade-in-arms. He had to forget Snake; the man was lost. He had to be cold, indifferent, distant. There was no other way. Somewhere out there, Seneca was waiting. And Seneca pitied no one.

Neither could Collins.

Because it's time for Cain to be born again.

Pity was foreign to the great Cain. That's why Lucas called for his resurrection. Pity, sympathy—they simply didn't exist within him. Neither could they exist within Mickey Collins. In truth, Mickey Collins could no longer exist. He had to be discarded like an old suit of clothes, laid away until this drama was finished.

This was Cain's time.

That meant journeying back to the riverbank, to the abyss, and looking once again into the darkness. For there, on the edge, he would rediscover the assassin's heart.

Collins eased closer to sleep, his curtain of conscious-ness rising and falling delicately. Noises from outside the motel mingled with scattered, broken voices heard during a firefight. Automobile horns were in harmony with helicopter rotors. Dogs barked, water buffaloes bellowed. The chill air from the air conditioner was a cool answer to the hot breeze of the jungle. Two maids exchanged pleasantries in the hallway; two shadowy figures on a riverbank whispered in the early morning mist.

Because it's time for Cain to be born again.

As the abyss neared, a question arose: was he closing in on it, or was it closing in on him? He hoped for the former, would accept the latter. Either way was fine because, ultimately, it wouldn't matter.

Cain was there . . . waiting.

First kill, sir?

CHAPTER TWENTY TWO

In combat, life and death are always at the mercy of chance. Nothing else figures in. Odds against living or dying can't be computed; therefore, any contemplation is a waste of time. The randomness of death is such that all calculations are useless. A mortar shell explodes fifteen yards to your right: you walk away unscratched; a soldier to your immediate left becomes hamburger meat.

How do you begin to account for such absurdity?

You don't. You move on, hopeful that chance is on your side when the next shell explodes.

Collins seldom dwelled on such matters. He instinctively understood war, thus eliminating questions concerning matters beyond his comprehension. Understanding erased the mystery. Anyway, questions seldom led to answers, only to more questions. Questions also led to doubt, to undue caution: deadly traps for any soldier.

What he did know was this: he was still alive. Four

months in Vietnam, countless firefights, and he was still breathing, still in one piece. In the end, it was all that mattered. Being alive, healthy, still functioning. He had been in country, in confrontations with the enemy, face to face with death enough times to understand war is a very elemental enterprise. War isn't about nations or philosophies. It's not about right or wrong. War is about surviving, about staying alive. It's about killing the other guy before he kills you.

Pleiku was scalding on that March afternoon in 1967. The monsoons had ended two weeks earlier, replaced now by unrelenting heat. It was as if the whole world had become hell and the jungles of Vietnam were at the center. Lucifer himself would have trouble breathing in this furnace.

Collins guided his company through the steaming jungles surrounding a small village several kilometers east of Pleiku. The village, inhabited by fewer than two hundred people, was a suspected Viet Cong stronghold. Collins, only nineteen and already a captain in the First Air Cav, had been ordered to infiltrate, look for signs of Viet Cong activity or sympathizers, kill the sympathizers, and torch the village if positive evidence was found.

They entered the village at fourteen hundred thirty hours. An emaciated old man came out of his hut, approached rapidly on spindly legs, and in broken English told Collins that no Viet Cong sympathizers lived there.

He cursed Ho Chi Minh, praised the United States, railed against the war's toll, saying in a voice choked with emotion that he had lost two sons, a daughter, and a grandson.

Before the old man could finish his tearful litany one of Collins's men emerged from a small building, holding a large burlap sack in each hand.

"It's the mother lode, Captain," the man said. "Weapons, Army rations, more than five grand in cash, clothes. Don't listen to what he says, Captain. These dink pricks ain't pure."

Collins aimed his M16 at the old man's head.

"Viet Cong?" Collins asked.

The old man backed away. "No Viet Cong," he said, shaking his head frantically. "G.I. boo koo number one. United States boo koo number one."

"He's boo koo full of shit, Captain," the soldier said, holding up the sack.

"Viet Cong?" Collins repeated, pushing the old man to the ground.

"No, no, no Viet Cong," the old man screamed.

Then came the shots, *pop, pop, pop*, from behind and to the left. Automatic rifle, probably a single shooter. Collins dropped to one knee, let the old man go, then motioned for his men to fan out in all directions. More shots rang out—five to be precise, one smashing into Willie Dickinson's chest. The young corporal fell backward, dead before he hit the ground.

Pandemonium was unleashed. Villagers ran scream-ing for shelter, women yanked crying babies out of harm's way, soldiers struggled to find cover.

Pop, pop, pop.

Collins heard—felt—a bullet whiz past his head. He fell to a prone position and began crawling toward a water trough. To his left, maybe fifteen feet away, an-other soldier took a hit in the lower abdomen. He fell to the ground, screaming. Someone called for the medics, but a second bullet, this one to the fallen soldier's temple, arrived first.

"How many you figure, Captain?" someone asked.

"One," Collins replied.

"You're fuckin' nuts," the soldier mumbled.

The next few seconds seemed to happen in slow motion, and Collins would always remember it that way. Im-ages moved in a halting, almost poetic way, voices and noises sounded as though they might be coming from a phonograph record played at the wrong speed. His own movements, slow and precise, were more dreamlike than real.

Straight ahead, directly in his line of vision, Collins saw the sniper darting between huts, running low, rifle in hand. Collins scrambled to his feet, raced to his right, intent on intercepting the sniper before he could disap-pear into the jungle or the network of tunnels running underground. Collins knew if that happened, the shooter, and any chance of killing him, would be lost.

When Collins came around the last hut, he saw the man running toward him, not more than thirty feet away, struggling to insert a banana-shaped clip into his AK-47.

The sniper stopped dead in his tracks. Collins raised his M16, sighted, squeezed off a single round. The sniper's head exploded, coming apart like a watermelon dropped from a skyscraper. The bullet entered directly below the man's nose, blowing out the back of his head, opening a hole the size of a grapefruit. Most of his teeth were splintered by the bullet's impact, and his left eye, blown free from its socket, dangled on his cheek. Although he died instantly, his right leg continued to twitch for several seconds after he hit the ground.

"Goddamn, what a mess," one of Collins's men said.

"Served the little gook motherfucker right," said another.

Collins looked down at what seconds before had been a human face, but was now a grotesque mixture of dark red blood, flesh, brain matter, and bone fragments. He pushed his foot against what remained of the dead man's head. It rolled to the side like the broken head on a child's doll. Several teeth worked their way through a glob of thickening blood and dropped to the ground.

It was his first confirmed kill, although he suspected there had been others. In combat you didn't always know for certain. Combat is chaotic, given to sudden bursts of high energy and uncontrolled madness. Bullets fly, bodies fall. Which bullet kills what enemy is not always clear. Accurate scorecards are impossible to keep. More often than not, the killer is as random as the victim. Seldom is the equation clean and simple. But with this kill there could be no question, no doubt. He had squeezed the trigger, seen the bullet do its damage, and watched the target fall.

Collins felt total exhilaration. He also felt a strange calm inside, a sense of detachment, like he was standing outside the scene looking in. There was no voice inside his head pleading for compassion, for empathy. Those were signs of weakness, and in this moment, in the searing heat and dust of some shitty gook village, he understood with clear certainty that weakness did not reside within him.

He possessed the stone-cold heart of a killer.

"First kill, sir?"

The voice coming from behind him sounded as if it were coming from another planet.

"First kill, sir?" the voice repeated.

Collins didn't answer; there was no need. Numbers didn't matter. Something inside him had been set free, some force that had no need for numbers. At that moment he knew what he was going to do, what he was condemned to do: create new and terrible numbers.

The mathematics of death.

Cain had been born at that moment, although neither Collins nor Lucas would know it for many months. That first tour of duty in Nam only fertilized the egg; birth wouldn't occur until well into his second tour. It was then that his unparalleled ability to kill manifested itself in ways no one could have anticipated; it was during his second tour that Cain grew to manhood. Somewhere in those Vietnam jungles, Captain Michael James Collins shed his own persona like a snake shedding its skin.

Cain was born.

And quickly became a legend, a myth, more feared than any predator in those jungles. U.S. soldiers spoke of him with hushed reverence, invoking his name as if he were a deity. To them, he was godlike. A man above all rules, immune to the stings of conscience, a killer without remorse. Stories of his kills wove their way from the DMZ to the Delta. Much of his legend was fueled by the "midnight missions," those solitary excursions into the jungle darkness, where, using only his bare hands, he sometimes killed a dozen or more of the enemy before returning to base camp at sunrise.

Among the Viet Cong, Cain's legend took on a powerful, even sinister force. They saw him as a demon spirit, indestructible, immune to death. He was the shadow that awaited them in the night. He was their nightmare come to life.

Lucas was the first to recognize the change, later noting that he saw it more in Collins's eyes rather than his actions. At certain moments, Lucas said, those blue eyes turned gray, revealing something dark, hidden, empty. They were, Lucas sensed, the eyes of a jungle predator: cold and keen, brutal, cunning, and savage.

In late 1967 Lucas needed those predator eyes, those killing skills. He had been ordered back to Washington, where he was put into place to oversee a new operation, one that would eventually replace the infamous Phoenix Project. This new project would be highly covert and even more secretive than its predecessor.

The Phoenix Project, also known as Operation Phoenix, was born deep within the belly of the CIA in the mid-1960s. It was designed to identify and "neutralize"—capture, induce to surrender, kill, or otherwise disrupt—anyone supporting the Viet Cong or pro-Communist sympathizers. The operation was introduced as the Intelligence Coordination and Exploitation program (ICEX). Among those running the program was legendary CIA spook Ted Shackley, the CIA Saigon station chief, and Shackley's long-time friend, General Lucas White.

From its inception, Operation Phoenix was nothing less than an assassination program. Its mission was to cripple the Viet Cong by killing influential local village and hamlet leaders, such as mayors, teachers, and doctors. Guerrillas from the North, or any leader suspected of aiding the South's parallel government, were also deemed legitimate targets for assassination.

Operation Phoenix was a natural successor to an earlier CIA black op—Project Pale Horse. Named for a passage from the Book of Revelation, Project Pale Horse ran for six years, operating primarily in the northeastern provinces of Laos, where it proved to be so effective against Soviet KGB and Red Chinese military advisors that a $50,000 bounty was placed on the head of the Pale Horse commander.

Pale Horse eventually ran its course, giving way to Operation Phoenix, which proved to be both efficient and highly controversial. Before Operation Phoenix was turned over to the South Vietnamese and spiraled out of control, the estimated death toll exceeded 40,000.

Operation Phoenix was, in the eye of one critic, "the most indiscriminate and massive program of political murder since the Nazi death camps in World War Two."

"Maybe so," Lucas commented to Shackley and Westmoreland upon reading that assessment. "But no one can say we weren't effective."

With Phoenix flaming out, the need for a new operation became a high priority matter for the generals running the war. Big wars always contain smaller, secret wars, and Vietnam was no different. Thus, the plan for a new assassination operation went into effect. It was to be known as Project Armageddon. Lucas, because of his close association with both Pale Horse and Phoenix, was the natural choice to head the operation.

Lucas wholeheartedly believed in the project and was only too willing to oversee it. In Collins, he had the perfect instructor. Who better to teach the art of killing than a man with a doctorate in death?

"You don't need me, Lucas," Collins had argued at the time. "I'm needed here, in-country. This is where I can do the most good."

"You'll return, my boy. I promise." Lucas countered. "And when you do, you won't be alone. You'll bring your heirs with you."

"I don't know."

"Come with me, my boy. Let us make full use of your special talent."

Collins went with Lucas, reluctantly leaving Vietnam for the first time in two years. The real world held no interest for him anymore; his home was the jungle. That's where he wanted to be—needed to be. That's where Cain had come of age. Where he had carved out his legend.

He declined a lengthy leave, arguing in favor of immediate reassignment. Lucas was more than happy to oblige. The school, or "Shop," as it was called, officially began operations in February 1968.

Lucas and Collins spent many weeks carefully

screening potential candidates. More than one hundred were given initial consideration. Of that number, after further screening, fewer than half were called in for an interview. None were told the true purpose of the interview, or the nature of the project. That would happen only after acceptance.

That first class, which convened in the snows at Aberdeen Proving Grounds in Maryland, consisted of thirteen men, ranging in rank from captain to private first class. All had served at least one hitch in Vietnam. Nine were Army, three Marines, one Navy. There were six Caucasians, four blacks, two Puerto Ricans, and one Native American Indian.

Of that original group, only six survived the cut.

Collins could remember every face, every code name. He had taught them, christened them, unleashed them. Now, four decades later, he could see them clearly, as if they were standing in front of him. Cardinal, Snake, Deke, Rafe and Moon.

The heirs of Cain.

But it was the Indian, standing slightly apart—always—from the others, arms folded, black eyes burning, that he saw most clearly. Dwight David Rainwater.

Seneca.

From the beginning, Seneca had been a different animal in every way. He never sought comradeship, never forged alliances, never relied on a fellow soldier. He was a lone wolf trapped in a pack. There were other differences, as well. He had instincts the others could never acquire. Natural instincts. While they were learning various killing techniques, he was honing skills that somehow seemed innate. Skills that accompanied him from the womb. But the biggest difference was his thirst for blood. While the others wondered, *In the end, will I be able to do this?* Seneca never doubted himself or his ability to kill. He knew.

Collins saw a madness in Seneca that went beyond what was needed. Assassins kill, but they don't have to be crazy. Collins argued strongly for Seneca's dismissal from the Shop, but Lucas adamantly refused the request. After all, Lucas reasoned, Seneca was precisely what was needed: the perfect killing machine. No guilt, no hesitation, no conscience. What more could you want in an assassin?

Seneca would stay.

"Okay, Lucas, have it your way," Collins said. "But someday you'll regret it."

"That's a risk I'm willing to take," Lucas responded.

"It's not a risk, Lucas. It's a certainty."

Now, after all these years, that day had arrived.

CHAPTER TWENTY THREE

As the afternoon shadows began to sweep through the room, Collins stood in front of the mirror and studied his naked body. It had held up well. The muscle tone, the definition, the strength—he looked good. Better than most men half his age. Except for the two scars—one on his left shoulder, one on his right side—he looked no worse for wear than he had twenty-five years ago.

He still had the predator's body.

The predator's mentality.

He stared at his face in the mirror, beyond his own cold blue-gray eyes, into the deepest recesses of his own being. Into the darkness of his heart.

He smiled.

Blood time was about to begin.

His time.

174

Vietnam, November 1967

The jungle heat attached itself to the skin like a blanket of fire. Mosquitoes and other insects swarmed with impunity. Silence screamed.

Cain leaned against a large tree, waiting until the sun moved beyond the jungle canopy, waiting until darkness fell.

Waiting for blood time to begin.

His time.

This was the first of what would become legendary midnight missions. On this night, the ultimate assassin made his debut. The night predator was unleashed. In the deep jungle darkness was the genesis of Cain's legend.

He knew, even at this moment, that he was entering into a different realm. That from this night onward, his life would be changed forever. That once he began the killing, there was no turning back.

Cain would be more assassin than soldier. A ghost. A shadow among shadows.

Lucas had approached him with the idea, arguing that certain types of "nocturnal killings" were more valuable and would carry more weight. They would, he contended, make a "more emphatic" statement, play on the "enemy's psyche" like a nightmare come true.

"I will find you targets," Lucas said. "Get you locations.

You, with those marvelous skills of yours, will do the rest."

"Your confidence is reassuring, Lucas."

"My boy, the level of confidence I have in you does not come close to matching your talent," Lucas answered. "As I have said on many occasions, what you have is a very unique gift indeed."

"Has this been cleared?"

Lucas chuckled. "My boy, this is Vietnam. Nothing needs to be cleared. If we want to do it, we simply proceed."

Cain's first two targets were a North Vietnamese captain and the mayor of Da Lat, a small village west of Cam Ranh. The mayor, a distant cousin of Vietnam's flamboyant vice president Nguyen Cao Key, was a CIA asset who had been supplying the North with valuable U.S. military intelligence plans for almost a year. The two men had a 3:00 a.m. meeting scheduled in the back room of a small bar right off the main street.

Cain left Cam Ranh Bay by chopper and was dropped off in a clearing three kilometers from Da Lat. He worked his way through the jungle, eventually reaching the edge of the village an hour before sunset. There, back against the big tree, he waited until darkness fell. Until he was merely one more shadow in the night.

His two targets weren't alone. A third man, armed with a machine gun, stood watch outside the back entrance. Cain was not surprised at seeing an extra body at the site; his faith in the accuracy of Army intel had long ago given way to doubt and skepticism. That led to Cain's first Golden Rule: never put your fate in the hands of others.

The sentry leaned his weapon against the building, took out a pack of cigarettes, extracted one, and put it in his mouth. As he reached into his shirt pocket to take out a box of matches, Cain closed in quickly from behind. He delivered a sharp blow to the man's throat, then a second blow to the neck. The man grunted, stumbled, and dropped to one knee. He was dead by the time his second knee touched the ground, his neck broken by a savage snap of the head.

Cain rolled the man's body behind a large barrel, laid the machine gun in a flower bed, then slowly opened a screen door. As he moved down the narrow hallway, he could hear the sound of laughter coming from a small room to his left. He eased forward until he could see the two men. They were sitting at a table, each with a large paper cup in hand. An almost-empty bottle of Jim Beam rested on the table between them.

Perhaps it was the shock of seeing a black-face intruder coming at them like a crazed panther, or maybe it was the alcohol fog that denied movement, but neither man rose from his chair when Cain entered the room. The man dressed in military clothing fumbled his cup while reaching for his pistol. Cain went for him first, hitting him across the bridge of his nose with a judo chop. Blood spurted from the damaged nose, spraying the table and the Jim Beam. Cain moved behind the captain and snapped his head violently to the right, instantly ending his life.

The mayor sat frozen, immobilized by fear, eyes wide. He seemed incapable of moving, even as Cain reached out and grabbed him by the throat. His mouth moved, but no sounds came out.

Cain's large right hand increased the pressure on the mayor's throat, cutting off his air passage. Next, Cain pinched the mayor's nostrils, eliminated the breathing process entirely. The panicked mayor began to violently thrash his lower body, kicking the table and knocking over the bottle of Jim Beam.

Cain looked the mayor squarely in the eyes and smiled. As the man continued his futile struggle to free himself, Cain tightened his grip. After several seconds, he removed his fingers from the mayor's nose.

"I have one question for you," Cain whispered. "Answer it and I'll let you live. Answer by nodding or shaking your head. Got it?"

The mayor, gasping for air, his eyes wide and filled with tears, quickly nodded.

"Someone has been giving you top secret intelligence. Is that someone CIA?"

The mayor shook his head.

"Army?"

A quick nod.

"Out of Saigon?"

Another nod.

"Dooley?"

Shake.

"Maddox?"

A nod.

"You're an honest man for a politician. I like that," Cain said as he snapped the man's neck. "But I'm not."

Two days later, Cain met with Lucas and Westmoreland in Saigon. Neither man was surprised when Cain told them what he had learned.

"We have suspected it for some time now," General Westmoreland said. "This simply confirms those suspicions."

"Colonel Maddox has always valued money over duty," Lucas added. "He's not the first, and he won't be the last."

"This war is unlike any we've engaged in before," Westmoreland said. "It's certainly far different from the ones I have fought in—World War Two and Korea. The enemy here is strange and complex, but that's only part of it. I have been here four years now, yet I have no concrete answer. And certainly no concrete solution."

"The opportunity for corruption is the biggest difference I see," Lucas said. "Hell, there are more two-legged snakes walking around in this country than there are snakes crawling on the ground. On both sides. I doubt God could tell the saints from the sinners in this country. Colonel Maddox is one bandit among many, and a small one at that."

Westmoreland sighed. "I'm afraid you're right, Lucas. This war, this country—it's a breeding ground for criminal behavior."

After Westmoreland departed, Lucas filled a glass with Chivas Regal and took a long drink. He moved to the window, stood there silently for several seconds, then turned back toward Cain.

"I know what you are thinking, and the answer to your question is no," he said. "Maddox will be handled properly, in a military manner. I say that with some reluctance because my instinct is to let you have him. He's committed treason, been a traitor, and for that he should pay the ultimate price. But . . . in this instance, that would not be the prudent action to take."

Lucas set his glass down and moved next to Cain. "Are you okay with your new role? Are you at peace with it?"

"I'm a soldier, Lucas. Killing goes with the territory."

"Yes . . . but—"

"Relax, Lucas. It's blood time, and blood time is my time."

CHAPTER TWENTY FOUR

Collins needed but two stops before finding a link to Deke's whereabouts—a place called The Blues Cave on Chicago's Southside. The owner, a rotund white man with large saucer eyes and a hideous hairpiece, was the chatty type, only too willing to provide information.

"Listen. Ask anybody about Big Lonnie. They'll tell you I don't want trouble with no one. But the big son of a bitch is just plain bad news. Has been ever since I've known him, and that's been more years than I care to remember. I tried to get along with him, keep the peace, but not anymore. Now I don't give a shit about him, so long as he stays out of my way."

Collins ordered a ginger ale.

"Stayin' away from the hard stuff?" Big Lonnie asked.

"Starting today," Collins answered.

"Know what you mean. I gave it up years ago. Right before it got the best of me."

Collins took a drink and looked the place over. Only two other customers were at the bar: a man sitting three stools to his left and a woman at the far end. The jukebox was on, Miles Davis playing soft and sweet and true.

"When was the last time you ran into Jefferson?" Collins said.

Big Lonnie scratched his head, careful not to disturb the hairpiece. "Couple of months ago, I guess. Let me think. Yeah, around the first of March. He was in here lookin' for Trish."

"Who's Trish?"

"His old lady."

"Wife?"

"I don't know about that. Who gets married these days? All I know is they've been together off and on for about fifteen years. That's who you need to talk to. She can tell you where he is."

"How do I find her?"

"Place around the corner, up two blocks. Mariah's. She'll be there. Tell her Big Lonnie sent you. Me and her, we're real close."

Collins emptied his glass and placed two dollars on the bar. "Thanks."

"Hey, man, you go easy on Trish. She's one fine lady."

Mariah's Tavern was a small, intimate bar badly misplaced in what was otherwise a gaudy, blues-oriented district. It had an almost genteel '50s feel, more

Tony Bennett's kind of place than John Lee Hooker's. The slightly elevated stage, which was bare except for a Baldwin piano, might have been awaiting the arrival of Frankie Laine or the young Ray Charles. Nostalgia was thicker than the cigarette smoke hugging the ceiling.

Collins walked to the end of the bar, where he was greeted by a tall, elderly woman with white hair, a still-beautiful face, and an aristocratic manner. Like the place she owned, Mariah also seemed to belong to another era.

"Hello," the woman said, smiling broadly. She offered Collins her hand. "Name's Mariah."

"Pleased to meet you," Collins said, accepting the hand.

"What'll you have?"

"Actually, I'm looking for someone and I was told she might be here."

"Oh, yeah? Who told you that?"

"Big Lonnie."

"Big Lonnie tends to talk too much."

"He's definitely not the shy type."

"So . . . who's the mystery lady you're trying to find?"

"Trish."

Her smile gave way to a look of concern. "You the law?"

"No."

She scrutinized his face with narrow, intense eyes. "What business do you have with Trish?"

"I need her help; that's all. I'm not here to hassle her. A couple of questions and I'm gone."

Her face relaxed. "That's her at the table in the corner. Make it brief. Her next set begins in five minutes."

The woman sitting alone in the dark was a petite brunette, mid-forties, dressed in blue slacks and a white blouse. A blue silk scarf was tied neatly around her neck, and a large diamond-shaped earring dangled from each ear. The passing years had not been particularly kind to her, yet they hadn't been so unkind as to erase completely the evidence of a face that had once been truly beautiful.

Looking at her, Collins was struck by two things: the deep sadness etched on her face, and the color of her skin. Trish Underwood was white. He had never known Derek Jefferson to be particularly interested in white women.

She looked up, sensing his approach. Her brown eyes, swimming in sorrow, met his.

"Trish?"

She nodded but didn't speak.

"My name is Mickey Collins. I need your help. Mind if I sit?"

She pointed to a chair across from her. He sat, then leaned forward, elbows on the table.

"What kind of help?" she asked.

"I need to locate Derek Jefferson. Big Lonnie said you might be able to help me."

"How do you know Derek?" she inquired. Her voice was deep and strong.

"The Army. I was his commanding officer."

"He told me about the Army. About Vietnam and the things that went on over there." She breathed deeply. "Truth is, I suspect that's the cause of most of his problems."

She unfolded her hands and placed them palm down on the table. They were young-looking hands with unusually long fingers. Her fingernails were painted a deep red.

"Collins," she said. "I don't recall Derek ever mentioning anyone by that name."

"What we did was highly confidential. We were trained to keep secrets."

She stared straight at Collins. Once again he was struck by the deep sadness written on her face. This was a woman who had been through a lot in life, most of which hadn't been pleasant.

"You know, some people are beyond help, no matter how hard you try," she said. "Derek is one of those people. I tried to help him. Believe me, I tried. But he couldn't—or wouldn't—change."

Tears welled in her eyes.

"Do you know where he is?" Collins asked.

"Around. He's always around."

"When was the last time you saw him?"

"About a week ago. He came by to let me know he was back from Florida."

"Did he say why he went down there?"

"No."

"Did he mention the names of anyone he knew in Florida?"

"Not that I remember."

"Think hard, Trish. It's important."

"He didn't say much at all about Florida. About anything, really."

"What about South Carolina? Did you ever hear him talking about a man named Anthony Taylor?"

"No."

"Cardinal. That mean anything to you?"

"No. Listen, we don't see each other like in the old days. Things have changed."

"You aren't together anymore?"

That sad smile again. "Not for several years now. I wanted to make a go of it, make it work, and God knows I tried. But . . . how much is someone supposed to take? The race thing—we overcame that pretty good. But the violence, the beatings. I couldn't take it anymore. So I left him."

She looked at her watch. "I only have a minute or two." She tilted her head toward the piano. "Gotta sing for my supper."

"Do you have any idea where I might find him?"

"Butterfield's most likely. He sometimes works there as a bouncer."

"Thanks," Collins said, standing. "If you happen to see him, don't mention I was here."

"Still keeping secrets?"

Collins nodded.

"Don't worry," Trish said. "Keeping secrets is something I've been doing most of my life. I'm very good at it."

He turned to leave.

"Derek isn't a bad guy. He just . . ." Her words faded into silence.

She rose from the table, climbed onto the stage, and settled in behind the piano. Her sad eyes found his.

"He's a violent man," she said, her voice softer than a whisper. "And he'll die a violent death. I only pray that . . ."

As he walked away, the sweet melody of "Stardust" began to fill the room.

Two men stepped out into the Chicago night, walked several paces, then disappeared into an alley. The smaller man led the way, walking briskly and purposefully, as though he were late for an important engagement. The larger man trailed behind by a few feet, his eyes darting from side to side. Together, they were a peculiar-looking duo. The smaller man, thin and wiry, resembled a bird. A very nervous bird. He constantly shifted on the balls of his feet, giving the appearance that he was engaged in some type of exercise. The bigger man was black, and moved slowly, cautiously, with a grace belying his enormous size.

Upon reaching the end of the alley, the two men stood several feet apart. Neither spoke. A light from above shone down on them, casting their silhouettes against the side of a building. The smaller man lit a cigarette, took a deep drag, then tossed the match onto the concrete.

"Look, Derek, I'll have the money for you by Friday. You have my word on it." He blew a cloud of smoke into the night. "You have to give me until Friday."

"I don't have to do anything," the black man said. "The man wants his money now. I aim to see he gets it."

"He'll get it. He always has, hasn't he? It's just that I'm a little thin at the moment."

"You're always a little thin."

The little man fidgeted with the cigarette, flicking ashes with his thumb. "Look, I know you've got a job to do. I understand that. But you've got to give me a break. Square it with the man for me. You can do that. Tell him I'll have the money by Friday. At noon. No later. The full ten grand. You have my word."

Deke turned slightly, lifted his eyes, and stared into the light. The look on his face was calm, serene, like that of an overgrown black child praying in an Alabama church. He looked blissful, as though God were speaking directly to him. But it wasn't God's voice he was hearing; it was the other voice, the one preaching anger and violence.

In less than a flash he wheeled, slamming his huge fist

deep into the little man's stomach. The force of the punch doubled the little man over, sending him reeling hard against the building. He groaned, coughed, spit up blood.

"Friday, by noon," the black man said, looming over his stricken companion like a dark cloud. "If you don't have it—all of it—you're dead meat. You get my drift?"

The little man struggled desperately to refill his lungs with oxygen. "You'll have it," he moaned. "The full ten large. I swear."

"Good. Then that's settled."

Just as suddenly, the calm, serene look returned to the black man's face. With the gentle fingers of a loving father he smoothed the little man's tie, straightened his collar, then asked, "Now, what was it you wanted to tell me?"

The little man's trembling hands lit another cigarette. He took a quick puff, exhaled. "Some guy was looking for you earlier tonight. Over at the Cave."

"You sure he was looking for me?"

"I'm positive. A friend of mine heard him ask Big Lonnie about you."

"Did your friend happen to catch a name?"

"No. But Big Lonnie sent the guy to Trish. Maybe she can tell you."

"Trish, huh? And that's all you can tell me?"

"That's all I know."

"Guess I'll see Trish, then."

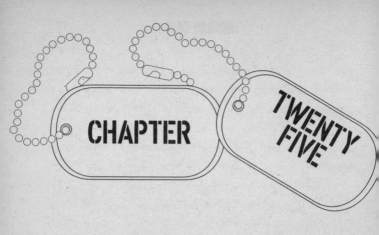

CHAPTER TWENTY FIVE

Butterfield's rated as the number one blues joint in Chicago, perhaps in all of North America. The best professional singers and musicians—individuals and groups—counted this as one of the must venues on their regular schedule. So did any young artist who harbored aspirations of making it to the big time. A gig at Butterfield's, like an appearance with Leno or Letterman, could provide that desperately needed shot in the arm for up-and-comers.

Collins sat at a table directly across from the front door. Three hours of waiting had left him numbed by the noise and convinced Jefferson wasn't going to show. The bartender had said Jefferson left on an errand and should have been back by eleven. It was now a quarter till one. Collins debated calling it a night, decided to give it another hour, then leaned back in his chair just as the band finished its set.

The bartender, carrying a tray filled with shot glasses, worked his way in Collins's direction.

"Have one. It's on the house," he said.

"What is it?"

"I call it The Blues Bomber. A little concoction of my own."

"What's in it?"

"That's top-secret information."

"I'd better pass. It's too late for surprises."

"You don't know what you're missing." The bartender looked around. "Derek hasn't showed yet?"

"Haven't seen him if he has."

"Hell, you can't miss that big galoot." The bartender shrugged his shoulders. "He should've been back by now. It's not like him to stay away this long."

"Must've gotten tied up."

"Shouldn't have. All he had to do was talk to a guy for me. That shouldn't have taken more than a few minutes."

"Could he be at another place?"

"Nah. This is Derek's joint. I can't imagine what's keeping him."

A pretty woman, late twenties, walked past, smiling at him. Collins kept his eyes on her until she disappeared from his view.

"That's Jamie," the bartender said. "She's a regular. Want an introduction? She'd be better company than Jefferson; that I can guarantee you."

"Better pass," Collins said, grinning. "Like I said, it's too late for surprises." He stood, feeling the blood flow again in his legs. "Maybe I'll catch up with Jefferson tomorrow."

"Oh, yeah, he'll be here. Saturday nights he helps me out. Keeps the rowdies in line."

Collins walked outside, thankful to leave the noise and smoke behind. His ears were ringing, his eyes burned, his throat felt like parched bark. He took several slow, deep breaths. The cool, clear Chicago air felt good.

He pondered Jefferson's failure to show. That was troubling. Unexplained absence usually meant something was wrong. Most likely, Jefferson got wind that someone was asking about him. Perhaps Trish wasn't so good at keeping secrets. Or maybe Jefferson forced the information out of her.

But the violence . . .

Walking toward the parking lot, past a crowd heading into Butterfield's, Collins was dogged by an uneasiness clutching at his insides like a steel claw. He felt observed, the watcher being watched. Eyes trailed his every step. He could feel it, like some special sixth sense working in overdrive. Someone was watching him at this very instant.

His survival instincts, especially his hearing, went to Code Red.

That had always been the case, even back in Nam.

When danger threatened, when warning signals flashed, he could detect even the smallest, most insignificant sounds from two hundred yards away. Not only detect them, but identify them instantly as either threatening or non-threatening, then react accordingly.

The sound that saved his life came from fifty feet away—a click barely audible to the average person but louder than a cannon blast to him. It came from behind his left shoulder and was immediately classified as menacing.

He dove to the ground a split-second before the bullet shattered the windshield of a BMW. As he scrambled to the other side of the car, a second bullet blew out the left front tire. A third bullet hit the pavement and ricocheted beneath the car.

Collins worked his way down a row of cars until he was in a direct line with his would-be assailant. He felt safe enough to stand; the assassin had had his chance and failed. There wouldn't be a second opportunity, now or ever. Collins's eyes, now gray, continued to study the darkness, searching for the shooter. Off to his right, he saw a silhouette moving between buildings and then vanishing into the night. For an instant he thought of giving chase, but quickly decided against it. There was no need to rush. He would have his revenge.

On his terms.

By this time, several bystanders had begun shouting for someone to call the police. Patrons from at least four nearby clubs, drawn to the excitement like passers-by to a bloody accident, flooded out onto the street, oblivious to the potential danger. One man screamed, "Firecracker!" Another said it was gunfire.

Within five minutes two police cars, a Cook County Sheriff's car and an emergency medical unit, arrived, lights flashing, horns screaming, giving the scene a carnival-like atmosphere. Several men pointed in the direction of the gunfire, while others pointed toward the parking lot. As spotlights scanned both directions, policemen, weapons drawn, began to fan out over the area. Several gawkers tried to follow but were quickly—and forcefully—herded back into the bar.

Collins was far enough away to avoid being hit by the lights. Remaining in the shadows, he worked his way back toward the crowd, quietly slipping in among the curious. No one noticed—or seemed to care—about his sudden appearance. That was fine with him. The last thing he wanted was to be questioned by the police.

"You're positive it was Jefferson?" Lucas asked, concern registering in his voice.

"Had to be. I'm in Chicago, and this is his turf."

"You're very lucky, my boy."

Collins looked out his hotel window. "Not really.

Deke has become careless. His choice of location was terrible. So was that loud-ass weapon he used. I taught him better than that."

"I'm thankful he was careless. Otherwise, you might be on a slab right now." Lucas waited several beats before continuing. "What precautions have you taken to ensure this doesn't happen again? Have you changed hotel rooms?"

"That's not necessary."

"You needn't take any chances. Next time he might not be so sloppy."

"There won't be a next time, Lucas."

"I understand. Do you think Seneca knows about you yet?"

"Hard to say. Deke will undoubtedly make contact with Seneca as soon as possible. So if Seneca doesn't know about me, it's only a matter of time until he does."

"Which only adds a sense of urgency to locating him."

"And eliminating him."

"Who would have thought it would come to this—brother against brother?"

"Ever read the first chapter of Genesis, Lucas?"

"I'm familiar with that story. I'm also familiar with the outcome. Cain survives, if I'm correct."

Lucas waited another beat. "Be wary, my boy. Study the shadows closely."

"The shadows, Lucas? They're my sanctuary."

CHAPTER TWENTY SIX

Kate Marshall entered Collins's office, slung her shoulder bag onto his desk, opened it, removed two books, and returned them to the bookshelf. Now came the difficult part: finding an old, tattered paperback copy of *The Brothers Karamazov* buried somewhere amid all the clutter. She searched through a multitude of books, on the floor and the shelves, only to come up empty. Next, she plowed through the desk drawers. Still, the famous Russian brothers remained hidden. It wasn't until she brushed a package off the top of the refrigerator that Dostoyevsky's classic tale of family trials and tribulations presented itself.

Kate slammed the book into her bag, silently cursing Ivan and his brood for causing her such consternation. Were a bunch of dysfunctional Russians worth all this trouble, anyway? Probably not, although she damn sure couldn't tell that to her lit class.

Without thinking, she opened the white package that had fallen onto the desk. Inside was a brown folder containing several pieces of correspondence. There were letters, photos, memos, all held together by a single paper clip. Frowning, she studied the bundle and wondered what in the world it could be. None of it looked related in any way to an English or literature class. Or to the college, for that matter. It was some strange-looking stuff, whatever it was.

She removed the first letter, laid the rest of the papers on the desk, and began reading.

THE WHITE HOUSE
Washington, D.C.
March 3, 1968
Dear Mickey,

Lucas White recently informed me that you have agreed to join us in our new project. I'm delighted. I don't think he could have made a better choice. Your skills, your dedication to the cause of this great nation of ours, and your good work in the past are well-documented and appreciated. I am excited about the task we are undertaking. It is my firm belief that in today's world there exists a need for what we are doing. These perilous times demand extraordinary action. The project you and Lucas are overseeing will help us maintain the strength to continue as a beacon of freedom and hope in the world.

I have made a firm commitment to the task at hand, and have full confidence that it will be successful.

Congratulations on your recent promotion to the rank of major. It is well-deserved.

LBJ

Kate read the letter again, slowly this time, finally letting her eyes come to rest on the scribbled initials near the bottom of the page. LBJ. *Lyndon Baines Johnson*, for christsakes. Only then did she make the connection—a long-gone president and Professor Michael Collins.

But what was the connection? When? At what point in time could the paths of these two men have possibly crossed? In what way? For what reasons? Her curiosity now in high gear, she dove deeper into the folder, holding her breath like a scholar who had directly stumbled onto a rare and ancient manuscript.

On top were twelve color photographs, two close-up face shots for each of six men. She thumbed through them quickly, looking for a picture of Collins. There weren't any. Beneath the photos were more letters and other official-looking forms. She removed the clip holding them together, took the first letter, and began reading.

May 1, 1968

Mick:

I was happy to hear that the laborious task of interviewing potential candidates is nearly completed. As I told you in our Tuesday phone conversation, Rear Admiral Cunningham is sending three Seals he thinks can be of help. I trust you will judge their merits before making your final decision.

Plans here in Washington are being finalized. We will set up shop at Aberdeen Proving Grounds. Several alternate sites were proposed, but APG seems the most logical. Have you decided how many candidates will be needed? My feeling is no more than twenty. Of course, in that matter I will yield to your wishes. I should be finished here NLT Sunday, which means I'll be available to help in the selection process should I be needed.

Please keep me apprised of the situation. I look forward to rejoining you soon.

Lucas

June 24, 1968

Mick:

Your list of thirteen looks good to me. I was particularly pleased to see that you included one of Cunningham's men. That should make him happy, and keep him off my back. Whether we like to admit it or not, politics are always present, even in a project such as this.

Teach them well.

Lucas

July 2, 1968

Mick:

Orders are being cut at this moment for your return to Vietnam. You should have them by Friday. Sorry we had to rush things, but recent events have put a sense of urgency on everything. People are running around the War Room with blood in their eyes.

I'm sure you will be more than happy to return to those God-forsaken jungles. As for me, I have mixed emotions. When I think I fought alongside your father and will now be fighting alongside you, well, you can imagine how old that makes me feel. I'm not sure war is for old men. But duty calls, so you'll be seeing my smiling face more than you care to.

One other matter. Some are wondering if six men are enough. Are you positive that's all you'll need? Remember, even our Savior needed twelve. Give this matter some consideration. If you are comfortable with six, we'll proceed as planned. Please advise.

Lucas

January 25, 1969

Mick:

Just finished briefing Nixon's people. They appear to be even more enthusiastic about the project than their predecessors were. I have a feeling the kind of work we're doing is right up their alley. They seem to have a thirst for blood that many in LBJ's crowd lacked. RN, the "Dark Prince," is a man I've known for almost two decades, since he was a congressman. I've never much cared for the man, and I wouldn't trust him under any set of circumstances. Having said that, I can't argue with the enthusiasm he and his fellow henchmen showed when informed of this project. It almost rivaled that of the Kennedy brothers, and God knows JFK and Bobby certainly had an affinity for wet ops. As I have learned after many years in this business, you dance with certain devils in order to kill other devils.

I'll see you in about a month.

Lucas

August 10, 1970

Mick:

Everyone here is raving about the success of Operation Clean Sweep. One CIA big shot called it state of the art. Jolly good show. The green light has been given for Operation Silent Night. It is my understanding that you plan to proceed within the next three weeks.

Keep me advised, and let me know if there is

anything you or your men need.

Lucas

P.S. As for that other matter, it is still under consideration.

March 3, 1971

Mick:

I have passed along your blueprint for Operation Fallen Angels. It is being met with near-unanimous approval. I must add, however, that I have some reservations, which I shall discuss with you in detail at a later date.

I ran into your father yesterday. He is doing well and sends his love.

Lucas

January 13, 1972

Mick:

It is my understanding that Ted Shackley has informed you that Operation Fallen Angels is off. I'm sure he also informed you that I had the deciding vote and that I cast mine against proceeding. No doubt you are steaming—I know you well enough to know that.

My vote was cast not so much against the

mission, but rather in consideration of your safety. I cannot convince myself that it's anything less than a suicide mission. I simply don't see how you and your men can get into Hanoi, do what needs to be done, then get out safely. And the logistics trouble me. How would you get to Hanoi in the first place? Up from the South, down from the North, from the West?

I can't envision a route that eases my fears. Another stumbling block is accuracy of the targets' whereabouts. Our people in intelligence tell us the North Vietnamese leaders have several command centers. Which one would you attack? Then we get to the matter of getting out once the task has been completed. For me, that's the greatest cause for concern. I could hope for nothing more than the success of this mission, but not if it means sacrificing you and your men, which is precisely what I foresee as the ultimate end.

To be sure, the plan has much merit.

As you have suggested, the extermination of Giap, Dung, and the rest of the top echelon would most certainly cause great chaos among the North Vietnamese. However, my boy, I fear we are facing an enemy that relies less on upper-echelon leadership and more on an inner resolve that appears to be unbreakable. I offer as evidence the recent death of Ho. If anything, his loss has only served to further galvanize the will of the North Vietnamese people. It is a many-headed monster we face. To cut off one, two, even three heads will not diminish their strength. You disagree, of course, and you can take comfort in the knowledge that yours is not the lone voice of protest. Many here in the Pentagon are in agreement with your assessment that a successful mission to Hanoi would bring a quick end to the conflict. You are a warrior; it is only natural for you to see resolution in military terms. I've become somewhat more cynical over the years. Military machinery is easier to defeat than a nation's collective will. It has become clear to me that we have stumbled blindly into a pit of quicksand and that we must begin to extricate ourselves before we are completely swallowed up. Our nation is tearing itself apart because of the futility of what is happening over there. We cannot allow this situation to drag on much longer.

I'm sure my words are like poison to you. As one who also considers himself a warrior, I feel a certain contempt for my reluctance to OK the mission. I yearn for the old days, when things weren't so complicated, when matters such as these were viewed in black and white. I wish I could tell you to go for it, but the truth is, we are in a no-win situation in Southeast Asia. We can eliminate Giap, we can eliminate his successor and his successor's successor, but nothing would change. We would still be left to face a nation's resolve. The French couldn't defeat it, and neither can we.

Therefore, given my personal feelings for you and your men, given my gut-level feeling that even a successful mission would be for naught, Operation Fallen Angels is off. It is my judgment that the mission would ultimately prove to be futile. Just the way the Vietnam War is destined to be futile. This conflict will be decided not on the battlefield but in dark rooms by diplomats wearing expensive three-piece suits. That's the reality.

Take care.

Lucas

Hands shaking, heart racing with excitement, Kate finished reading the last letter, put it down, and looked out the office window. Darkness had descended. Her plans for the night were shot. She didn't care. What she had planned seemed terribly insignificant now. But this . . . this was intriguing, interesting.

She had stumbled into the past, a past involving the man she probably loved, and she wasn't going to leave until she found out all she could.

Kate looked at the twelve photos, hoping she'd overlooked one of Collins. She desperately wanted to find one, to match the Collins who knew presidents with the

Collins who taught Melville and Eliot and Conrad with such passion and force. A photo of him as a young man would help unlock the many secrets he kept hidden from everyone, including her. She needed something—anything—that would give her the key to his past.

But there was no picture, and that only added to the intrigue. So did the last letter, written by someone named Cain, which had a list of strange names. How did it fit into this fragment of history? And why was it marked *EYES ONLY*? She laid the pictures down, picked up the undated letter, and began reading.

Lucas:

As per your request, here are the names, code names, and hometowns of the six men I have chosen for our operation:

CAPT. Anthony Leon Taylor (Cardinal)—St. Louis

SSG. Dwight David Rainwater (Seneca)—Tulsa

SFC. Charles Grady Wilson (Snake)—Terre Haute

SFC. Raphael Diego Martinez (Rafe)—The Bronx

SFC. Derek Louis Jefferson (Deke)—Chicago

ENS. Douglas Martin Walker (Moon)—Oakland

There will be a seventh member, a young second lieutenant who possesses a remarkable talent for procuring and scrounging. His name is Andrew Tyler

Waltz (code name: Houdini), from New York City.

I leave in your capable hands the task of pulling records and cutting orders. Hopefully, it can be done expeditiously. We need to get on our merry way. The jungle cries out for us.

Cain

Kate studied the faces of the six men in the photographs, trying to match them to the names in the letter. The Hispanic, the one with the dark hair and low forehead—surely that was Martinez. And the one with jet black hair and midnight eyes—he had the look of a Native American. That had to be Seneca. But the three Caucasians and the one black man—she couldn't begin to make an accurate pairing of face to name. What about Cain? Who was he? Where did Collins fit into all this? What role did he play?

Kate leaned back and sighed. History as mystery. She hated it.

CHAPTER TWENTY SEVEN

Derek Jefferson entered Butterfield's through the back door, stopped briefly to say a few words to one of the singers waiting to perform, then climbed the stairs leading to a private room overlooking the bar area and dance floor. Leaning against the glass, he scanned the crowd, studying each face with deadly seriousness. Back and forth, his eyes moved slowly for a full five minutes, straining, searching for that one particular face.

His face.

The face of death.

As his eyes zeroed in on each male patron, his right hand came up and caressed the scar on his cheek. It was an involuntary action, perhaps even an unconscious one, something he did when he felt scared or threatened.

The scar. He was three years old when his drunken father plowed the car into an oncoming truck on the icy Dan Ryan Expressway. The old man died instantly, crushed behind the steering wheel. Jefferson's older brother, Rudy, suffered massive head injuries resulting in permanent brain damage. Jefferson, alone in the back seat, was thrown through the windshield, a jagged piece of glass tearing a chunk of flesh from his cheek. The wound required seventy-six stitches and left him with a deep L-shaped scar.

"Has anyone been askin' for me?" he asked one of the waitresses.

"No one's interested in your sorry black ass," she said, smiling.

"I'm serious. Has a white guy been in here askin' about me?"

"You need to clean those big ears of yours, honey. Like I said, no one's been inquiring about you—white, black, or pink."

"You're positive no one named Cain has been look-ing for me?"

"Not Cain, not Abel, not Moses, not sweet Jesus himself. No one has been asking about you."

Jefferson began reviewing his options. To start with, he needed to keep a low profile, stay out of sight, go into hiding. That was imperative.

Okay, so maybe he was overreacting, making too much of nothing. After all, it had been dark; maybe it wasn't him. Could as easily have been any one of a dozen guys with grudges.

But . . . if it was, or even if the slightest chance existed that it might have been him, there was only one prudent course to follow—get lost. He could stay with Trish; she was always good in times of trouble. But there was a down side to that. It was too obvious. That would be the first place anyone would think to check out. His best bet was to hide out in The Projects, maybe hang out with Ramon or Louis. He'd be safe there. No one would come looking for him in The Projects, least of all a white dude.

But this wasn't just any white dude. This was . . .

He refused to think it, refused to let the name roll off his tongue. If he didn't pronounce it, didn't give it life, then maybe the man didn't exist. Maybe silence would keep the man from being real. Maybe the man would disappear.

His hand pressed hard against the scar.

He had to piss.

The bathroom door in the private office was locked; that damn Giselle. She stayed in there forever, snortin' that white powder up her nose, gettin' high, gettin' crazy. That's one black bitch who had to go. Trouble all the way.

He walked down the stairs and into the hallway. Before opening the restroom door, he glanced over his shoulder, saw no one following him, then went inside.

There were four men in the restroom: two standing at urinals, one washing his hands, another sitting in one of the stalls. Although the need to relieve himself had reached the painful stage, he stayed by the door until the three men he could see walked out.

Only the man in the stall remained.

Jefferson couldn't hold off any longer. The pain was becoming too great. He had to take care of business. To hell with the man in the stall.

He rushed to the urinal, unzipped, and with eyes closed, began relieving himself.

It was his first mistake of the night.

When he heard the restroom door open behind him, heard that first sound of movement, he should have reacted instinctively. He should have sensed trouble, felt the danger closing in, been ready.

Most of all, though, he should never have put himself in such a defenseless and vulnerable position. Any amateur knew better.

Almost instantly he felt the heavy weight of a man's body pressing hard against his, felt the man's forearm against the back of his neck, pushing forward with relentless force. Jefferson's face smashed against the white porcelain wall, his body arched inward, bent freakishly at the lower back, his penis touching the wet, cold tile. He could feel his attacker's right hand inside his jacket, feel the fingers extracting his .45 with the skill and expertise of a pickpocket.

In his panic, Jefferson sprayed urine everywhere.

"Zip it up, Deke, and come with me. Quietly. Don't make me end it here. There's no dignity in dying with your dick hanging out."

The voice was frighteningly familiar.

"You've got it all wrong," Jefferson stuttered. "You've got to listen to me."

Jefferson, his pants soaked, overwhelmed by sheer terror, zipped his pants. The warm urine cooled as it ran down his legs. He worried about how he would smell once it dried.

By any set of standards, this had not been a pleasant piss.

"I'll come with you, man," he said. "I don't want no trouble." His voice was urgent, tight, panicky.

When the pressure against his body eased, he thought of bolting for the door. But that would be a foolish tactic. Running meant signing his own death certificate. He mentally calculated his odds and quickly realized his best chance—his only chance—would be to wait, pray for an oversight or a mistake, anything that might shift the balance of power in his favor. Then he would make his move.

But—

This was Cain, the legend, and he never blundered. Ever.

Jefferson did hold one card: a small can of Mace hidden in his right sock had miraculously gone undetected. That would be his salvation.

"We're going out the front door, then to the right," Cain whispered. "Don't be foolish. It's not worth it."

Jefferson felt the gun press into his back. "Listen, Cain, you've got it all wrong. Let me explain."

"Outside."

They left Butterfield's, made a right, walked a few yards, and turned down an alley. Jefferson felt his old confidence returning; this was, after all, his home turf. He'd smacked around dozens of guys here. One poor *putz* called it "Derek's Alley." If there was any place where he might have the upper hand, this was it.

But it was also an alley of shadows, and Cain thrived in shadows.

Without realizing it, Jefferson's right forefinger traced the L-shaped scar.

At the end of the alley, he turned and saw Cain for the first time in more than twenty-five years. Seeing his former commander did little to lift his spirits. Or his hope of surviving. Cain was wiry, hard, strong, as fit as he had been in the jungle. He looked untouched by the passing years.

And, of course, those eyes. Gray, steely, cold. One look at them and Jefferson knew his situation was extremely delicate. He knew blood time when he saw it.

He was going to die.

Unless—

He could maneuver close enough to hit Cain's eyes with a shot of Mace. It was risky, dangerous. It was also his only option. Distance between the two men was critical. And tricky. He had to get close enough to administer a blinding dose without getting so near that Cain's lethal hands would become a factor.

No one, regardless of the circumstances, wanted any part of Cain's hands.

The gun? It would never come into play. The great Cain was too arrogant to ever use any weapon other than those hands.

"You've become sloppy, Deke," Cain said. "I taught you better than that."

Jefferson inched his feet closer. "Look, Cain, you don't have any reason to treat me like this."

"Way I see it, I have three reasons."

"Give me one."

"You tried to kill me," Cain said.

"You're wrong. I never tried to kill you. We're family, remember? It's what you always said—that we were family and we had to stick together."

"What about Cardinal? He was family."

"I heard about him. That was a bad break."

More movement.

"Why'd you waste him?"

"Me? I didn't kill Cardinal. It must have been Seneca."

More movement.

"It was you, Deke. You killed Cardinal, and you tried to kill me. Seneca wouldn't have botched things like you did."

"I swear, man, you got it all wrong." Jefferson eased

forward another six inches. He was almost there, almost where he needed to be. Only a few more inches and he would be within striking distance.

"You have ten seconds to tell me what's going on," Cain said. "The clock's ticking."

"I don't know what you're talking about."

"Tick, tick, tick."

"I swear, Cain. I don't know nothin'."

"What's Seneca got planned?"

"Look, Cain, I don't know anything worth telling. I swear on my mother's grave. All I know is Seneca called me, told me to go see Cardinal and Snake, and see if they'd be interested in doing something like Fallen Angels. Just like Nam, remember? He told me to waste them if they refused. Snake was too far gone—the junk done got the best of him—so I let him slide. With Cardinal, I—"

"Killed him."

"Man, I had to. I didn't want to deal with Seneca. He's crazy; you know that."

"Where is Seneca?"

"I don't know. New York City, maybe. I think he's stayin' there these days."

"When was the last time you saw him?"

"Couple of weeks ago. We went to Florida to meet some guy." Jefferson moved forward another three inches.

"What guy?"

"I don't know his . . . wait. Simon something. A real

fat ass. Lives on a boat with a good-looking young ho."

"Why, Deke? Why turn against family?"

"Like I said, Cain, I didn't want to deal with that crazy Indian."

"But now you have to deal with me."

"You ain't gonna kill me."

"Oh, yeah."

"Why?"

"Sinners must pay."

"Come on, Cain. Please. I'll help you find Seneca."

"I'll find him, or he'll find me."

"You have to believe me, Cain. I didn't want to kill Cardinal. Or you. I was afraid; that's all. It was nothin' personal."

"And there'll be nothing personal when I kill you."

Jefferson caved in to his fear. Although he was still three inches too far from Cain to initiate a strategically sound move, he let his hand reach for the canister of Mace.

It was his second blunder of the night.

The last one he would make.

Cain anticipated the move long before it occurred. Not only anticipated it, but visualized it, broke it down into microscopic detail, and played it out in his mind. He'd even orchestrated it by purposefully leaving the Mace untouched, fully aware Deke would see it as his means of escape.

By his calculations, it would all be over in five seconds.

Jefferson went for the Mace too quickly, fumbling the canister—another blunder that, in the final analysis, wouldn't have made any difference to the ultimate outcome, because in his haste he also lunged forward, becoming easy prey for Cain's hands.

Cain had seldom been quicker or more precise. The result: few kills were this easy. It was a simple matter of shifting his body slightly to the left to avoid unnecessary contact with the bull-like Jefferson, then executing two clean karate chops, one to the temple, the second to the bridge of the nose. The first blow may have been fatal, but in all likelihood, it was the second blow, the one driving bone into brain, that ended Jefferson's life.

Jefferson fell like a wounded elephant, dead before he hit the ground.

There was no need to check for a pulse, but Cain did so anyway. Never leave an opponent breathing. How many times had he told that to his students? Never give an opponent a second chance. It was one of Cain's sacred commandments. If Jefferson had listened, if he had made sure Cardinal was dead, he might still be alive.

There can be no mistakes during blood time.

Kneeling next to Jefferson, feeling for a pulse he knew wasn't there, Cain heard Lucas's words echo in his head—"brother against brother"—and felt a strange sense of anger and disappointment. He felt something else as well: arrogance. His men were good, among the finest killers this country ever produced. He had taught them well, made sure they were exceptional. Yet he, Cain, was the best. Jefferson, good as he was, never had a chance. He was simply overmatched.

The great Leonardo once said that the student who does not surpass his master fails his master.

Leonardo would have been displeased with Deke.

Deke allowed his skills to atrophy. Even more crucial, he failed to keep a wary eye on old friends.

That was the one secret Cain elevated above all others, the one edge he refused to share. Study your comrades as closely—perhaps even more closely—than you study your enemy. Friends don't always remain friends, and no one is more dangerous than a comrade who becomes the enemy.

CHAPTER TWENTY EIGHT

The phone rang twice before Lucas picked up.

"Deke is history," Cain said.

There was a momentary pause. "How appalling. I hoped it would never come to this."

"What did you think would happen, Lucas? That Deke and I would sit down, hoist a few beers, and discuss old times?"

"No. But I do remember how hurt you were when Rafe bought it in Nam."

"That was different. Rafe died in combat, doing his job."

After a lengthy pause, Lucas said, "How many of the six are dead?"

"Cardinal, Rafe, Moon, and now Deke," Cain answered.

"Two because of this business with Seneca. Even Moon. We suspect he was working for Seneca when he died in Afghanistan. What a messy world this has become."

"It's always been messy, Lucas."

"Ah, yes, my boy, I'm afraid you're right." Another pause. "Did you learn anything regarding Seneca's whereabouts?"

"Deke went with Seneca to see a guy in Florida. His name is Simon. You might want to check him out."

"Simon Buckman."

"You're familiar with him?"

Lucas chuckled. "My boy, you've been away too long. Everyone knows Simon."

"Fill me in."

"What do you want to know?"

"For starters, who he works for and what he does. Minor information like that."

"Simon has done many things for many people, including us. He was never a major player, always the middle man. All it takes to secure his services is a healthy stack of bills. His loyalty, such as it is, belongs to whoever is waving the most cash at any given moment."

"Sounds like a real jewel."

"My boy, you don't know the half of it. Simon is a rare gem, indeed."

"He doesn't sound like someone Seneca would hook up with. How do you figure their connection?"

"I can't even begin to speculate," Lucas said. "Simon has been known to act as a broker for arms shipments around the world. If there's a war or revolution or *coup d'état*, Simon usually makes a few bucks. Perhaps he's working with Seneca on an arms shipping deal."

"This isn't about arms shipments, Lucas. And it's not about revolutions. This is about a planned assassination. A take out. Who the target is: that's what we've got to find out. And fast. I have a feeling we're running out of time."

"What's next for you?" Lucas asked.

"Florida. See this Simon Buckman."

"Do you have any idea where Seneca might be?"

"Maybe New York City. At least, that's what Deke said."

"Why don't you go to New York? See if you can locate Seneca? I'll send some of my people to Florida. We like to make periodic visits to our friend Simon. This is the perfect time to find out what he's been up to lately."

"I'll catch an early flight to New York."

"Be very careful, my boy. Seneca isn't like the others."

There was a long silence. Finally Lucas said, "I'm truly sorry you had to eliminate Deke. It couldn't have been an easy thing to do."

"It's always easy to kill a traitor, Lucas."

Cain hung up the phone, undressed, showered, and lay down on the bed. Within seconds he was back on that riverbank, watching a gook's head bobbing in the dirty water.

Silence, then whispered voices, past and present, ran through his head.

"First kill, sir?"

"Every kill is a first kill."

"Couldn't have been easy."

"No, you're wrong, Lucas. Killing Deke was easier than snuffing the dinks in the jungle."

"Shadow Ghost. Isn't that what the dinks called him?"

"Goddamn right. Deke made too many mistakes, became too sloppy, allowed himself to get swept into the shadows."

Cain's Law: the shadows are mine.

Trespassers will be punished with extreme prejudice.

No exceptions.

Seneca, I am coming for you.

CHAPTER TWENTY NINE

Lucas White sat alone, empty glass of Scotch in hand, eyes fixed straight ahead into the darkness. The weight of depression rested heavily on his shoulders. He needed to refill his glass, many times, enough to buoy the weight and strip it away, but he couldn't bring himself to move. He couldn't sleep, and he couldn't move. He was a man frozen.

Finally, with great effort he pulled himself up, went to the liquor cabinet, picked up a bottle of Chivas Regal, and carried it back to his chair. He refilled the glass, drank the Scotch straight, felt it burn.

He leaned his head back and closed his eyes. Sleep had never been a friend, even during the best of times. By all accounts, these were far from the best of times. These were nightmare times—confusing times. He yearned for the old days, when black and white squared off against each other, when there were no gray areas . . .

Poppycock. Such talk was pure poppycock. There

had always been gray areas. Indeed, he had operated in those hidden areas, much like Cain had operated in his own world of shadows. Nothing was ever clear-cut.

Except death.

Death was always clear-cut, final.

Lucas didn't mind death. He had seen many men die, ordered thousands of good men into combat, written the letters home to grieving loved ones. While death was never a welcomed guest, it wasn't an unexpected one. Not for a professional military man. He had learned to accept it—and handle it. A good soldier had no other choice.

And Lucas was a good soldier.

Then why this gloomy mood? What was causing this heavy weight bearing down on him? Was it Deke's death? He thought about that for a moment. Yes, the death troubled him, but . . . the circumstances ate at his insides. The in-house killing, the brother-against-brother aspect. It was unnatural. Military men do not kill their own. They simply do not. It is their duty to kill the enemy. That's the nature of their occupation. This . . . this fratricide violated sacred laws.

Alone in the darkness, his brain sluggish from too much Scotch, Lucas thought of different times. He retraced the footsteps of his life, a journey that had taken him from Iowa to West Point to Korea and beyond. It had been a good life, eventful, full, and productive. What he had done counted. It added up. In his own small way, he had made a difference. There had been honor, praise, glory. More important, there had been respect from both his peers and his enemies. They had seen him as a good soldier, a true warrior. They still did, and the evidence proved it. Hadn't they come to him? Hadn't they pleaded with the old lion to come out of retirement one last time and handle yet another crisis?

Yes.

General Lucas K. White. A soldier's soldier. *Goddamn fucking-A-right.*

At moments like these, when sleep was elusive and introspection reared its ugly head, Lucas's thoughts invariably returned to Vietnam. To the one matter haunting him like a recurring bad dream.

Operation Fallen Angels.

Had he made the right decision? Was he wrong to say no? Should he have given the green light? If he had, and if the mission had been executed successfully, would the end result have been a quicker and more favorable conclusion to that damned war? Had those voices opposing his been correct?

He would never know. Perhaps that's what haunted him the most.

Lucas sipped at his Scotch.

And remembered.

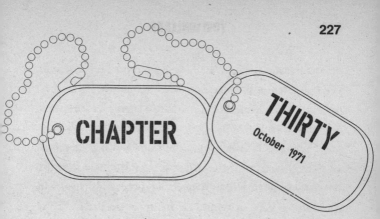

CHAPTER THIRTY

October 1971

Operation Nightcrawlers was Cain's idea from the beginning. He conceived it, drew up the plan, and orchestrated every movement. From the moment intelligence had first learned of the meeting and given it to Lucas, it had been Cain's show.

What intelligence learned was that nine high-level ARVN leaders were meeting with two Russian generals at Hoa Binh, a medium-sized village located less than an hour from Hanoi. The purpose of the meeting was unknown; however, most U.S. military experts guessed that plans for another Tet-like offensive were being finalized.

Another full-fledged invasion of South Vietnamese cities could be devastating to morale, both on the field of battle and in the riot-torn streets of America. The Nixon White House, already under siege on the home front, couldn't tolerate another battlefield setback ten thousand miles away.

The situation couldn't have been more hotly debated. For Cain, it was perfect.

"An impossible mission," one general had intoned, "better left to B-52s."

"Suicide," another said. "No way it could succeed."

Cain welcomed the mission, seeing it as a forerunner to Operation Fallen Angels. If successful—and why shouldn't it be?—it would be his most persuasive argument yet in favor of Fallen Angels: five assassins, within miles of Hanoi, eliminate eleven key high-ranking enemy personnel and get back safely.

Lucas would have to listen.

Cain and his men helicoptered from DaNang to Xam Hua on the western border of Laos. From there they crossed over into North Vietnam, moved through the jungle to Moc Chau on the edge of the Black River, picked up a small gunboat from a CIA operative, and began the short trip to Soui Rut, where they met—and killed— Lucky. The final leg of their journey, four tough miles through jungle, they covered on foot.

They arrived at Hoa Binh an hour before sunrise. According to intelligence, the meeting was to take place in an ancient brick building situated on the northern tip of the village. Strategically, the location was perfect, allowing for quick access to the jungle once the mission was completed. That is, if intel was right. If intel got it wrong, always a possibility, neither the jungle nor anything else would matter. There would be no exit, safe or otherwise.

The building, two-storied and surprisingly well kept, dominated the village. To Cain's great surprise, the building was unguarded. He dispatched Snake to the side entrance, and within two minutes Snake had picked the lock and was waving the rest of the group forward.

Cardinal was the first to enter, followed by Deke, Seneca, Snake, then Cain. Next came a bit of educated guesswork—finding the room where the meeting would take place. That task turned out to be a simple one: the building had but one room large enough to accommodate such a gathering. It was located on the ground floor, next to the kitchen area. At the center of the room was a long rectangular table surrounded by a dozen chairs. Several large maps of South Vietnam covered the wall behind the table. Each map was divided into sectors, with the larger towns and villages marked in red ink with Xs.

Cain positioned his men for the wait. Less than an hour until blood time.

Outside, a rooster crowed. Daylight broke.

The first to arrive, an ARVN colonel, had the misfortune to open the door, turn and face Seneca. The man's mouth dropped open, but he never had time to utter a sound. Seneca's knife was swifter and more accurate than a rattlesnake's strike. Four fierce thrusts were all it took to turn the colonel's heart into a pin cushion.

Seconds later, three more arrived for the last sunrise

meeting of their lives, two ARVN colonels and a Russian general. Deke and Cardinal took out the colonels—Deke with his knife, Cardinal with a piece of piano wire he picked up outside—while Cain easily killed the Russian by administering a judo chop to the Adam's apple, then driving his fingers deep into the man's throat.

A harrowing two minutes followed. Five men, all ARVN officers, entered the room single file. Two of the five carried AK-47 rifles. The weapons, of course, posed no threat of death, only noise. The men would be dead before ever having the opportunity to fire a killing shot. However, one of them could accidentally get off a round, and the noise from that blast would be as deadly as a bullet.

Single file was what made the dynamics somewhat problematic for Cain and his men. It was essential that the fifth and final man entered the room before the killing began. That meant for a fraction of a second the men would see their assassins, the surprise element lost. That reduced any margin for mistakes. For the mission to succeed, everything had to click perfectly.

If it didn't, they were dead.

But this was their finest hour. This was the moment they would settle all debate about future operations. This would transform them into legends.

This was blood time in its most perfect form.

They weren't about to fail.

By the time the fifth man was even with the door,

the killing was under way. One step into the room, and two men were dead, the first taken out by Cardinal, the second by Snake. One step farther, and men three and four were falling. Seneca's knife eliminated the third man; Deke's machete lopped off the fourth man's head and sent it rolling across the floor. The fifth man was not even three full steps into the room when he came eyeball to eyeball with Cain. For a brief moment, the man seemed torn between going for his rifle and screaming for help. He did neither. Cain drove his fist deep into the man's solar plexus, effectively rendering him breathless and incapable of making a sound. Next, Cain grabbed the man's head on both sides and gave a savage twist, quickly breaking his neck.

Snake and Cardinal disposed of the final two victims—an ARVN captain and the second Russian general—with no problems. Their weapon of choice was the machete. Both men had been impressed by what Deke accomplished with his.

Cain surveyed the scene. Eleven dead, not a sound made, no more than five minutes elapsed time.

It couldn't have been done more efficiently.

Cain walked to the corner of the room, picked up a decapitated head, and set it at the center of the table. He then reached in his pocket, took out a playing card, the ace of spades, and propped it up in front of the dead man's face.

Mission accomplished.

Lucas lay on the couch, the glass of Scotch resting on his chest, rising and falling with each breath. How much Scotch had he consumed? Too much. No, that wasn't correct. Enough to kill the pain; not enough to erase the doubts.

There was never enough Scotch to erase the doubts. No matter how hard he tried to drown them in liquor and self-reproach, those doubts forever remained with him. If Operation Nightcrawlers failed to erase them, nothing could. Not Scotch, not time.

The first glimpse of sunlight cast a slim reed of light across Lucas's desk. He let his weary eyes follow the light from the narrow opening in the curtains to the old desk, where the light hit directly on a framed picture of him standing with his arm on Cain's shoulder. He had a smile on his face; Cain, as always, displayed no emotion.

Qui Nhon. Summer 1972. Behind them the blue South China Sea glistened like glass. The picture had been taken only weeks before Cain left Vietnam for the last time.

There was something about that photo. Something Lucas couldn't remember. Something that made it special. But what? Cain, maybe? Something in those cold, unflinching eyes? That faraway look?

No, that wasn't it. What, then? Lucas thought hard but couldn't pin it down.

The ringing phone pierced the silence. Lucas rose on wobbly legs, walked to the desk, picked up the receiver.

"Yes," he said.

Then listened.

"Not to worry, General Nichols," Lucas said. "I wasn't asleep."

He sipped the Scotch and listened for several more seconds.

"Noon, your office, sounds fine. I'll be there."

He sat in the leather chair behind the desk, his head cupped in his hands. *Tired. Goddamn, I'm so tired, so fucking tired of it all. When does it end? When do the wars and battles end?*

The killing never ends, my boy. It just goes on and on.

Lucas picked up the photo, brought it to his lips, and kissed Cain. After staring at it for several more seconds, he set the photo down, angling it so the incoming sunlight also kissed Cain.

Suddenly, as if the light of God had provided the answer, Lucas realized what it was about the picture that had been troubling him.

It had been taken by Seneca.

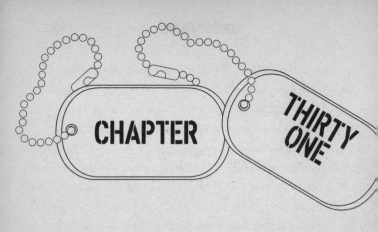

CHAPTER THIRTY ONE

Cain was the last member of the group to leave Vietnam, finally departing those bloody jungles forever in late 1972. Seneca, Deke, Snake, and Moon all rotated back to the states three months earlier, while Cardinal, the only one who would make the military his career, left two weeks after they did. The first to leave was Houdini, who, true to his gift for salesmanship, had somehow managed to finagle the last seat on a C-141 transport plane bound for Fort Lewis, Washington.

Cain remained behind at Lucas's request to take care of a particularly delicate situation that had arisen within the South Vietnamese government. "A bit of in-house tidying up" was how Lucas phrased it.

Killing was what he meant.

"Who are the targets?" Cain asked.

"Hoang and Trung."

"Consider it done."

Lucas chuckled. "My boy, I never cease to marvel at your complete lack of curiosity."

"Meaning?"

"Not once during any assignment I've given have you ever asked why. Aren't you the least bit interested in the reason why a pair of fellow Homo sapiens must perish?"

"No."

"Never?"

"Never."

"A rare quality, I must say."

"I don't want to know why, Lucas. *Why* is irrelevant. *Why* is unnecessary information. *Why* is for someone else."

"On this occasion I shall tell you why, if for no other reason than to annoy you. And despite your well-earned reputation for not tolerating foolish behavior, as your superior officer I retain the right to be annoying."

"Annoy at your own risk, Lucas."

Lucas chuckled, louder this time. "The aforementioned Hoang and Trung have been playing both ends against the middle for quite some time now. They drink from our river of money while at the same time drinking like camels from the monetary waters of our enemy. As you surely know, such double-dipping is frowned upon. Of course, we have been aware of these nefarious activities for more than two years and have used that knowledge to our full advantage. Fortunately for us, they are far more ambitious than skillful. 'Eager incompetents' is how I would classify this pair of numbskulls, who have been christened 'Laurel and Hardy,' and for good reason. As a result, they have passed along enough *bad* information, *mis*information, and downright *inaccurate* information to confuse even the brainiest military strategist. However, with this war beginning to wind down, they are no longer useful. Furthermore, they need to be held accountable for past sins."

"So they must die?"

"Like a bad vaudeville act."

"That's all I needed to know, Lucas."

Lucas nodded. "Your indifference to *why* is perhaps even more frightening than your ability to kill."

Two days later, Hoang and Trung were dead. Cain put an end to their double-dipping, taking out both men in Saigon: Trung in a hotel room, where he was expecting to meet a Japanese prostitute, then Hoang in an alley behind a CIA-fronted bar.

They were his last two victims in that country, his "final acts of madness," Lucas said.

At some level, Cain knew, Lucas was right. What he and his men had done during their time in the jungle bordered on madness. How could it be otherwise? In the eyes of most civilized people, killing indiscriminately, for whatever reason or cause, was the one unforgivable sin. Throughout history, nothing was deemed more sacred or valuable than human life. To rob another of his own existence was the ultimate theft, stealing from that person his present and his future.

But for Cain, the killing was justified. Always. This was war, and in war the object was to kill the enemy. To put him down before he took away your existence. To steal his present and future. There was nothing complex about it.

Also, nothing personal. This one element separated Cain from his men. Each of them, at various levels, felt something when they took another person's life. With the exception of Seneca, who killed with glee and for the joy of tasting blood, that something might be sadness, relief, repulsion, or profound guilt. Not so for Cain. He was blessed with the capacity for indifference. To him the victims were faceless men, obstacles to overcome, roadblocks to success. If they had the misfortune to find themselves standing between him and his goal, they had to be removed. No questions asked, no second-guessing.

Lucas once asked Cain why he thought Seneca had such an unnatural thirst for blood. What part of Seneca had gone so haywire that it enabled him to actually enjoy the act of taking another person's life? Was a part of his soul missing?

Of course Cain knew he, not Seneca, was the real subject of Lucas's questions. Lucas had no interest in analyzing a man like Seneca, who was, in all likelihood, beyond understanding or comprehension. But Lucas was now—and always had been—intrigued by Cain's ability to execute those "acts of madness" and yet be untouched by guilt or remorse.

What part of Cain is missing? Lucas silently wondered.

"The wall you have constructed for psychic protection must reach to the heavens," Lucas once commented. "I have yet to decide if I envy you or if I'm appalled."

"What would you have me do, Lucas? Brood deeply on each kill? Feel sympathy for the fallen?"

"My boy, I would be relieved to know you felt *something.*"

"Oh, I feel something, Lucas. Alive."

"You are on the side of the angels," Lucas said. "I can only hope that is your shield."

"I am on the side of the living," Cain answered.

"'And there went out another horse that was red: and power was given to him that sat thereon to take peace from the earth, and that they should kill one another: and there was given unto him a great sword.'"

"You're quoting Scripture now, Lucas?"

"The book of Revelation seems appropriate."

"What do you want to hear from me, Lucas?"

"A heartbeat."

Cain understood Lucas really sought a confession, a trace of remorse, perhaps a bit of sympathy for the dead. Repentance for past crimes committed. Anything that would make the great assassin more humane. But that wouldn't happen. *Couldn't* happen. What Lucas failed to comprehend was that the executioner must always remain neutral, numb to his actions, beyond feelings, humane or otherwise. The executioner must, ultimately, be more dead than his victims.

CHAPTER THIRTY TWO

General David Nichols pushed back his chair, stood, and slowly walked to the coffee pot. He filled two Styrofoam cups with steaming coffee, started back to his desk, hesitated. "Do you want cream and sugar?" he asked.

Lucas White shook his head. "Black's fine."

Nichols handed the cup to Lucas. "You look like you haven't slept for days."

Lucas laughed softly. "These are busy times, uneasy times. Sleep is a casualty, I'm afraid."

"Most of us were surprised when we heard you had come out of retirement. We figured it was ocean air, Chivas Regal, and ladies in distress for you. Easy living, easy women."

"Ah, that does have a nice ring to it," Lucas said. "Except for the easy women part. I've always found that gender to be anything but easy. Maybe when this business is concluded, I can live the scenario you've painted.

But for now, I'm afraid the good life is on hold."

Nichols picked up a pencil and began doodling. He drew a cross with the figure of a man hanging from it. Beneath the cross he wrote "Cain."

Lucas looked at the rendering. "Not bad. You have some talent."

Nichols drew a huge X over the drawing, wadded the paper into a ball, tossed it in the wastebasket.

"Why the fascination with Cain?" Lucas inquired.

"It's impossible not to be fascinated with a man who has done the remarkable things he's done."

"That's a very generous assessment."

"What do you mean?"

"Most civilized people would be repulsed by what he's done."

Nichols nodded. "How many men do think he's killed?"

"I wouldn't presume to guess. Probably he doesn't even know." Lucas let out a soft sigh. "Too many, I would say. Far too many."

Nichols resumed doodling, this time drawing a coffin with a man inside. When he drew the man's eyes, he made a straight line, giving the dead man an Asian look. Under the coffin, he wrote "Charlie."

Nichols looked at Lucas and smiled. "I met Snake once. At Fort Lewis, right after I rotated back to the states. He was working in a local pool hall at the time. He'd tell these wonderful stories. How Cain could take out three, four, even five men before they could react. How they never stood a chance. He said when it was happening Cain's eyes were . . . Snake called them 'Lucifer's diamonds.' He said only the devil could have eyes like that."

"Snake always had a tendency toward hyperbole."

"Do you discount the stories about Cain?"

Lucas smiled. "Not for an instant. In fact, he likely did much more than Snake was aware of. Rest easy, General. Cain's legend is well-deserved."

Nichols seemed relieved. He picked up his coffee cup and sipped. "I never killed a man. Two stints in Nam and I never even fired a shot. How's that for helping the cause?"

"You did your duty," Lucas said. "That's all anyone can ask of a soldier."

"When I think of what Cain did, what his men did, then compare that with what I did—what I didn't do—I can't help but feel like a fraud."

"Pitting yourself against Cain is a sucker's proposition. What he did was abnormal, an aberration. Even under combat circumstances."

"What he did was . . ." Nichols struggled for the right words.

"Go insane," Lucas interjected. "Five years in those jungles, taking God only knows how many lives—how could he not have gone mad? It's a miracle he came back with any degree of sanity at all."

"That's it; that's what makes him so damn intriguing. How can a man kill that often, that personally, and come back at all?"

"I can't answer that. Maybe he was ordained to kill, just as Christ was ordained to die on the cross."

"Ordained? By whom?"

Lucas shrugged. "All I can tell you is that Cain was born with a predator's instincts. Predators kill. Today, tomorrow, forever. It's what they do because that's the hand nature dealt them."

Nichols leaned back and propped his feet on the desk. He swirled the coffee cup in his hand. "Why did the Shop go out of business? I can't help but believe that men with Cain's experience and skills would have been useful to us in many ways."

Lucas handed his cup to Nichols and watched the younger general refill it. He had no interest in rehashing that bit of ancient history. His blood sizzled every time he did. But he could tell by Nichols's interest that he wasn't about to let the question go unanswered.

"Changing times, mainly," Lucas said, taking the cup from Nichols. "After Nixon got the boot, there was a housecleaning mentality around Washington. Ford, Carter . . . they had no taste for what we did. Vietnam and Watergate had soured everything. So it was only a matter of time until they shut us down. A grave error, in my judgment. I told them so at the time, but nobody listened.

To them I was only some old-line Cold War hawk looking to shed more blood. Well, given world events in the past quarter-century, it turns out I was right. Some of these terrorist leaders wouldn't sleep so soundly at night if we were still in operation. That includes bin Laden. Believe me, General, they are novices compared to Cain."

"Must have been disappointing for you when orders came to close the doors."

"It was disappointing for all of us. Especially so for Cain. A man like that needs the action."

"Are you telling me Cain just came home and that was it? He simply stopped? Seems to me an asset like that could still be useful."

"I said the Shop was shut down. I didn't say Cain stopped."

"So, you did utilize him."

Lucas leaned back in his chair. "There were occasions in the seventies and eighties when he applied his unique skills and talents to our benefit. Not many, but a few here and there. Special situations that required handling in a somewhat delicate manner. Certain obstacles best removed."

"Wet ops," Nichols said.

Lucas smiled. "I'm not at liberty to discuss such matters in detail, which I'm sure you can appreciate, General."

"Of course."

"This current situation is, to the best of my knowledge,

the first time Cain has been called into play since my retirement." Lucas sipped at his coffee. "Like old times, except . . ."

"What, General?"

"Old friends have become the new enemy."

"What's Seneca like?" Nichols asked.

"Brutal, efficient. But lacking any restraint. Cain killed. Cold, methodical, like the jungle predator. Seneca relished the act of killing. The brutality. Inflicting pain. A kill meant nothing to Seneca unless the victim suffered."

"What if Cain finds Seneca? How will—?"

A knock at the door interrupted the one question Lucas knew was inevitable. It always popped up, anytime men asked about Cain and Seneca. A black lieutenant colonel entered and handed Nichols a memo. Nichols waited until the man retreated before reading it. When he finished, he handed it to Lucas.

"Peace in the Middle East?" Nichols said. "Never gonna happen. Not in our lifetime, anyway. Three thousand years they've been at each other's throats. That's never gonna change."

"July 30, Camp David, the president, Israeli prime minister, Palestinian president, and a representative from Hamas," Lucas summarized. "And you're to oversee security. Four parts nitro. A volatile mixture. I don't envy you, General."

Lucas reread the memo, paying particular attention to the time and place of the meeting. *Saturday, July 30,*

Camp David. He handed the memo back to Nichols.

"Do you have a problem with me informing Cain?" he asked.

"No, not at all. Who better to have on your side than the perfect predator?"

Lucas stood and shook Nichols's hand. "Let me know if there is anything I can do. Anything at all."

Lucas left the general's office in the Pentagon, hurried to his car, got in, and quickly scribbled the memo information onto an envelope. His thoughts were racing at blinding speed. One thought stood out: time was growing short. July 30 was less than two weeks away. There was still much to be done.

His first priority was a phone call.

It had to be made.

Now.

CHAPTER THIRTY THREE

Houdini.

Andy Waltz.

Cain smiled as he mentally clicked through Waltz's bio *Readers' Digest* style: smart, hip, Jewish, streetwise son of a wealthy New York senator and his socialite wife; ex-CIA/military intelligence; married and divorced twice; now a columnist for *The New York Times*.

Also: One of the initial candidates at the Shop; solid soldier in every respect, yet lacking the "intangibles" necessary to become a successful assassin; a smooth-talking con man of the highest order. He possessed a different set of talents that could be beneficial to the group, namely the ability to "scrounge," and had the hustler's knack for always being one step ahead of the posse. Perhaps most importantly of all, he was one of the few men Cain trusted without reservation.

For almost five years Houdini's greatest gift, and his

major benefit to Cain, was an uncanny ability to make seemingly non-existent supplies magically materialize. Houdini would steal Westmoreland's balls if they were deemed necessary to the success of a mission. His motto: if it's real, it's mine to steal.

Waltz was sitting alone in his glassed-in office, feet propped up on the desk, reading *Newsweek*. Cain knocked, then opened the door. Waltz peeked over his glasses, narrowed his birdlike eyes, and smiled a familiar, crooked grin.

"No proselytizing, so get your ugly Jehovah's Witness ass out of here." He slammed his feet down, jumped from his chair, and gave Cain a hug. "I cannot believe what I'm seeing. You ugly *schmuck*, how you been doing?"

"Boot Hill is filled with men who called me ugly," Cain retorted, grinning. "Better be careful."

"Okay, so you're just a *schmuck*."

"That's better."

Waltz went into a martial arts stance. "I can take you, Cain. We both know it." He straightened up, put a hand on Cain's shoulder, and said, "No shit, man. It's great to see you. I miss those days. All the guys."

Cain closed the door. "We need to talk."

"This sounds like business, not pleasure." Waltz pointed to an empty chair. "What's up?"

"Cardinal is dead." Cain said.

"I heard. Any idea who did it?"

"Deke."

"What? Deke killed Cardinal? Killed one of his own?" Waltz pulled out a cigarette, lit it, inhaled deeply, let out a cloud of white smoke. "Goddammit, why would he kill Cardinal? Cardinal, of all people?"

He crushed the cigarette into the ashtray and looked straight at Cain. His fingertips drummed the desktop. "This has to be dealt with."

"It's been done."

"Good. I hope you made that big spade suffer."

Waltz lit another cigarette, took one long drag, then smashed it into the ashtray. "Fuckin' Cardinal. He was one of the good guys."

"You heard from Seneca lately?" Cain asked.

The question surprised Waltz. "Seneca? No. Why?"

"Deke was working for him."

"That figures. Hell, those two always were joined at the hip."

"It's time to scrounge again, Houdini."

Waltz's face lit up. "Tell me what you need."

"Information."

"My specialty. Name it."

"Seneca might be living here in the City. I need an address."

"No problem. What else?"

"Cardinal managed to say something before he died. 'Fallen angels.' That can only mean—"

"A hit."

"Yeah. And my hunch is, it's a big one. So keep your ears open. Snoop around. If you get wind of a visit, a meeting, anything that might interest Seneca, I need to know about it."

"I'm on it."

Cain took a pen from the desk, wrote two phone numbers on a memo pad, and handed it to Waltz. "The top one is mine."

"And the other one?"

"Lucas."

Waltz whistled through clenched teeth. "You and Lucas. Damn, this must be bigger than big."

"I have a feeling it'll happen soon."

Waltz smiled. "Leave it to Houdini. I've never failed you before, and I won't this time."

CHAPTER THIRTY FOUR

Simon had just dozed off when the phone rang. He shook himself out of his sleepy stupor, cursed loudly, and picked up the receiver.

"What?" he yelled. He suddenly snapped to an upright position when he recognized the voice on the other end of the line. Reaching up with his left hand, he rubbed both eyes, yawned, listened. "A pen? Got one right here. Shoot."

Simon squeezed the phone between his ear and shoulder while scratching the caller's words onto a notepad. When he finished writing, his beefy hand dropped the pen and he stood up.

"Yeah, got it, right. Okay, no sweat. I'll give it to him." Simon listened for several seconds, anger rising within him. "Why do you want me to read the damn message to you? Hell, you just gave it to me."

Simon cursed silently, then read the message back to

the caller. He expected the worst, but was pleased when the caller praised him for pronouncing the words correctly. Simon hung up the phone and fell back onto the bed. *That asshole Karl,* he said to himself, *what does he think I am—an idiot?* He sat up, grabbed the bottle of Jack Daniels, and took a drink.

"Fuckin' bastard," he mumbled.

He held the piece of paper up to the light and reread the message. What was the big deal, anyway? It seemed simple enough—a time, date, and location.

Simple enough, except for that last line, which Karl made him repeat three times.

Tuez le messager.

Simon Buckman was a great believer in dreams, reasoning that if all those old Bible big shots put so much faith in them, why shouldn't he? Maybe there was something to them. Maybe sleep's images were worth paying attention to. What if the future could be found in that nocturnal landscape? What if dreams were where the answers to important questions could be found? It was something to think about.

Last night Simon dreamed that he killed the Indian. Sliced him up with a sword and fed his body to alligators. Simon didn't own a sword, or alligators, and had no clue why they would find a place in a dream of his. Dreams, especially those that lingered long after he awoke, rarely made much sense. But that was a minor detail. All in all he thought it was an awfully good dream, one he was more than willing to turn into reality.

He paced the deck of his yacht, stopping only on those occasions when his empty glass needed a hit of Jack Daniels. The dream had him wired, thinking angles, scenarios. In the dream he shot the Indian in the back of the head, cut off his penis, stuffed it into his mouth, took the sword, sliced and diced the body, then made the alligators happy. It was an exhilarating dream. Simon awoke that morning with his first full erection in nearly three years.

But the dream failed to address one important issue: how to explain the Indian's death to Karl. Simon knew that would be a problem. His explanation would have to be precise and believable. Even so, Karl wasn't likely to be pleased. He would no doubt view such a bold and daring move as open rebellion.

"Fuck Karl," Simon muttered. He fortified his growing courage by belting down another shot of Jack Daniels. "Fuck 'em all. None of 'em mean a goddamn thing to me."

Simon jumped when a gull flew overhead and squawked loudly. His hand moved inside his coat pocket and touched the Beretta. The cold steel further braced his courage. So did yet another blast of whiskey.

Though his nerves were jangled and his energy could jump-start a dead battery, Simon felt a great surge of joy coursing through his veins. He was about to do something big, something many others, perhaps dozens of others, hadn't been able—or courageous enough—to do.

He was going to kill Seneca.

His step quickened as he paced the deck. This was dangerous, he knew, but it was also something more. Much more. The prospect of actually killing the Indian, with that arrogant smile and invincible attitude, was thrilling.

Simon could barely keep from shouting his plan to the heavens.

But the specter of Karl curtailed his joy. How best to handle him was a question that couldn't be dismissed lightly. As Simon played the scene out in his head, he kept coming back to a single answer: use the Indian's reputation as the reason for the kill. Everyone knew the Indian was a renegade, a bully, with an infamous temper. His rep was legendary. Karl surely knew that. So he would tell Karl the Indian caused trouble and the troublemaker had to be done away with.

It was logical. It made perfect sense. Karl would understand. But what if Karl didn't buy the story? What if he challenged Simon? What if—?

Simon drained the whiskey from his glass. *No problem,* he thought. *If that happens, there are people I know who would be more than happy to rid the world of Karl.*

For enough money, anyone, even a top-echelon man like Karl, can be taken out. In this business, money always trumps sacred cows.

Simon looked at his watch: 9:28. He breathed deeply. Only thirty-two minutes until his meeting with the Indian.

Or so he thought.

"Hello, fatman."

Simon spun around so quickly he became dizzy. Fearing he would topple over, he dropped the glass into the Gulf and clutched the rail. "How the hell did you get here?" he demanded, swallowing hard.

"I'm like the wind, fatman. You never see me."

"Exactly what I need: a fuckin' Indian mystic."

Simon slid his right hand off the rail and into his pocket. Even as his fingers tickled the Beretta, his nerves were screaming. A sudden realization hit: seeing the Indian in the flesh was much different than seeing him in a dream. Having him standing directly in front of you wasn't like seeing his fleeting image in a nighttime vision. Simon leaned back against the rail, his body trembling, the desire for another drink almost overwhelming.

"I understand you have a message for me," Seneca said. "Let's hear it."

Simon pulled out the small piece of paper and started to hand it to the Indian.

"Read it," Seneca ordered.

Fuck you. Simon's fingers gripped the Beretta's handle.

His mind screamed, barking out the order. Now is the time to kill this crazy Indian. Now is the time to erase him forever from my dreams.

"Read it," Seneca repeated, his voice harsh, cold.

Simon's trembling fingers uncurled from the gun. Now was not the right time. That would come later, when the Indian was ready to leave. That's when the situation would be most favorable. He'd put a bullet in his brain, take the yacht out in the Bay, weigh the body down, and dump it overboard. No one would have to know, not even Karl.

Seneca stepped forward, grabbed Simon by the throat. "I'm tired of waiting," he hissed. "Read the message."

Simon brought the paper up into the light and read the message, enunciating every word clearly and precisely. Karl would have been pleased.

Seneca nodded, like a satisfied elementary school teacher. He released his grip on Simon's throat, stepped to the rail, and looked out at the sea.

"Very good, fatman." Seneca continued to stare at the calm Gulf waters for nearly a minute, then abruptly turned and started to walk away.

"There's more," Simon said, his right hand again dropping into his pocket.

Seneca turned back around. "Read it."

"*Tuez le messager.*" Simon wadded the paper into a ball and clutched it in his fist. "I hope you know what that mumbo-jumbo means, because Karl didn't clue me in."

Seneca moved forward, that quicksilver smile on his face. "Just keep your eyes on me," he whispered into Simon's ear, "and I'll show you what it means."

Seneca took Simon's arm, lifted it up, and removed the Beretta from his hand. He stared at Simon, shook his head, and laughed softly.

"There are dreamers, and there are men of action," Seneca said, tossing the gun overboard. "You, fatman, are a dreamer."

Anger and hatred rose like white-hot lava within Simon. His lips curled back like an angry pit bull's. He silently cursed himself for not taking out the Indian earlier, for ignoring his basic instincts. It was too late now. He'd missed his chance. All he could do now was wait for another time, another opportunity. And there would be another time. He'd make sure of that.

"You have your message," Simon said. "So, unless you want to tell me what those words mean, why don't you scat?"

"I said I would show you."

"Okay, so fuckin' show me."

The Indian delivered a hard kick to Simon's groin, an on-target blow that sent the big man crashing to the deck. Simon groaned loudly, rolling from side to side, his meaty hands covering his injured genitals.

Seneca knelt beside him, held up the knife, and

smiled. The moonlight danced along the side of the blade. Simon's wide eyes, filled with fear, followed the knife until it came to rest directly below his sternum.

"No, Seneca, please! Dear God, why?"

"Just following orders," Seneca answered.

"Karl's? Let me talk to him. I can work things out."

"Not Karl's. Yours."

"Mine?" Simon said.

"*Tuez le messager*. Know what that means?"

"What?"

"Kill the messenger. And you, fatman, are the messenger."

Simon began to whimper. "I'm begging you, Seneca, have some mercy."

"Don't worry; you won't feel any pain."

Seneca placed the tip of the blade right under Simon's sternum, angled the knife downward slightly, then drove it upward with a fierce thrust. The strike was made with surgical precision, narrowly bypassing the rib cage and puncturing the heart.

Simon died instantly. As promised, he felt no pain.

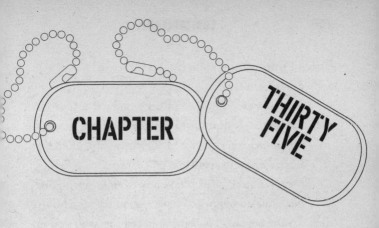

CHAPTER THIRTY FIVE

Midnight.

Cain lay on the bed, eyes closed, listening to the mixture of Manhattan sounds—car horns blaring, a Hispanic man exchanging obscenities with a black woman, police sirens, jazz from a club across the street. The sounds drifted in and out like a movie soundtrack being played for a blind man.

He was dressed in Levis, a white Polo shirt, and Nikes. Sleep edged into the picture, but he quickly shunted it aside. He had to stay awake, be alert. He thought of phoning Lucas, dismissed the idea as dumb. Then he thought of checking in with Kate but quickly assessed that notion as being even dumber. His only play: do nothing until hearing from Andy Waltz.

At 12:30, the phone rang. He reached for it, cleared his throat, and said, "Houdini?"

"I have an address for you," Waltz told him. "Five

fifteen Fifth Avenue, suite ten."

"Lush territory."

"Very pricey. You won't find much riff-raff around there. Apparently our friend has done well for himself."

"Or for others," Cain said. "Does he live alone?"

"I can't know everything, pal. Sorry."

"I forgive you. Will I have any trouble getting in?"

"No. Just so happens I have a good friend who lives there. Suite seven. You buzz her, tell her who you are. She's expecting you."

"You're still a magician, Houdini."

"The best, Cain. Just like you."

The woman, her voice husky but warm, answered the buzzer immediately, made an off-color remark about Waltz, then opened the door to the building. An un-smiling security guard lowered *The Racing Form* and shot Cain a nasty look. Cain walked briskly past the guard, who lit a cigar, then returned to his handicapping.

As always, Cain rejected the elevator in favor of the steps. Elevators were death traps; too confining, no means of escape. An upright coffin. A smart assassin avoided them if possible.

Suite ten was on the third floor, so Cain walked up to the fourth floor, waited five minutes, then walked down one flight. Seneca's suite was at the end of the hallway, on the left.

Standing outside the door, Cain closed his eyes and visualized what he was about to do. This was blood time at its most dangerous. This was Seneca, a worthy, deadly, vicious opponent. The most lethal opponent he would ever go up against.

This was no time for mistakes.

But Cain immediately sensed something was off. The scene had a bad smell, a too-easy feel to it. What he might expect from a lesser foe. For one thing, the door wasn't locked. Seneca would never leave himself that vulnerable. Also, the music coming from inside was too loud. No way Seneca, or anybody else inside, could possibly hear an intruder. Seneca would never be that careless.

Slowly, Cain turned the knob and nudged the door open. He dropped into a crouch and eased inside. In front of him Seneca sat on the sofa, locked in a tight embrace with a dark-haired woman. Their backs were to him, so he crept closer, his mind racing, his thoughts telling him that this was too easy, that a novice could successfully execute this take out. Mixed in was a feeling of disappointment. This wasn't how it was supposed to play out, not when two giants collided. This wouldn't be a kill worthy of a legend.

He carefully circled behind the sofa, stopping at the position that gave him his best angle from which to launch his attack. Seneca would go first, quickly, a judo chop to the Adam's apple, followed by a savage blow to the bridge of his nose. In three seconds, his deadliest rival would be history.

The girl? He would have to kill her as well. She was an innocent victim, a loose end, and loose ends can't be left dangling. Eliminating her was ugly, but necessary. He would do it swiftly, humanely.

In a move that took less than a heartbeat Cain grabbed Seneca by the neck, rolled him onto the floor, and prepared to deliver a blow to the throat. He drew back his right hand, fingers extended, ready to inflict the fatal blow.

Only, it wasn't Seneca.

The face staring up at him, though registering total fear, was an almost-identical version of Seneca—twenty-five years ago. Identical down to the most minute detail. The black eyes, square jaw, high cheekbones, dark skin, movie star looks. A remarkable resemblance in every critical detail. With the exception of the age difference, this was Seneca.

Cain stood, looked at the terrified woman, then helped the young man to his feet.

"Please," the Seneca clone said, shaking with fear, "I have no money, but whatever else you want, you can have. Just don't hurt us."

"Who are you?"

"Joey . . . Joey Rainwater."

Cain motioned toward the woman. "Who's she?"

"Emily. My girlfriend."

"Where's Seneca?"

"Who?"

"David Rainwater."

"Florida, I think. At least, that's where he said he was going." Joey looked at Emily, then at Cain. "You're not going to hurt her, are you?"

Cain tilted his head toward the sofa. "Have a seat and relax," he instructed, softly. Emily, terror still etched on her face, followed his command. "What's your connection to David Rainwater?" he asked Joey.

"He's my brother. Half-brother, actually."

"I didn't know he had a brother."

"That's not surprising. You see, David's mom died and his father married my mother. My mom was only eighteen or nineteen at the time, much younger than my father. When I came along, David was already in his mid-twenties and in the Army. So we haven't been close like typical brothers. Fact is, I hardly even know him."

Cain scoped the suite. "Who picks up the tab for this place? You?"

"Are you kidding? I'm studying film at NYU. I couldn't afford a room at the YMCA, much less this place. Nothing in here is mine except for some clothes and the video equipment. No, my brother pays."

"Place like this . . . David must be doing okay."

"Yeah, I guess so."

"What's his line of work these days?"

"He's a consultant for some big oil companies. Halliburton, Exxon, companies like that. Works overseas, mostly. I think he does, anyway. Me, I don't ask too many questions." Joey looked at Emily, forced a smile, whispered, "I love you," then looked at Cain. "How do you know my brother?"

"Army."

"A friend from the old days, huh?"

"Something like that."

"Throwing someone to the floor is a strange way to greet a friend," Joey said.

"We play rough." Cain shifted his gaze to Emily. "Still scared?"

"Yes."

"Don't be. You're in no danger."

She smiled weakly. Joey moved around and sat down next to her. He leaned over and kissed her on the cheek. After a long silence he turned to Cain and said, "Why are you looking for my brother?"

"What makes you think I'm looking for him?"

"I don't buy the story that you're some long-lost Army pal who just happened to drop by for a visit."

"You're a smart kid, Joey. No, you're right. That story's bullshit. Truth is, I need to give him something.

It's extremely important. That's why I need you to help me find him."

Joey put his arm around Emily and pulled her closer. "I don't know how I can help."

"Did your brother say where in Florida he was going?"

"No, he didn't."

"Ever hear him mention the name Simon Buckman?"

Joey shook his head. "Not that I recall."

"What about a phone number, an address? How do you reach him in case of an emergency?"

"I couldn't, unless he just happened to call here. He never gave me a number where I can contact him. Like I told you, my brother is seldom here, and when he is, he never talks about his business or his travels. Sorry."

"When was the last time you did see him?"

"About a week ago. He came by to pick up some stuff. Stayed about thirty minutes, then booked."

"Any idea when he might be coming back?"

"No."

Cain walked to the door. "Sorry about the rough stuff, but you do bear a striking resemblance to your brother."

"Physical resemblance is about the only thing we have in common," Joey said. "From what my father tells me, David and I are as different as good and evil."

"I'd say your father is absolutely right."

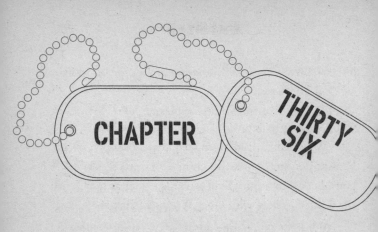

CHAPTER THIRTY SIX

The past three days had been troubling and unsettling for Hannah Buckman. She had spent them in virtual seclusion, staying in Simon's condo on Siesta Key, not once venturing outside. Friends had called, asking her to go out, but she declined, feigning illness. When Simon asked why she was so banged up, she told him she'd slipped and fallen. Hannah deplored lying and liars, but until her battered body healed she would do or say whatever was necessary to keep out of sight.

By the fourth day, most of the marks covering her body had begun to fade and she felt comfortable enough to make the trip into downtown Sarasota. Slacks and a light, long sleeve cotton turtleneck sweater hid the damage done to her body; sunglasses covered the purple bruises around the eyes. She could attribute the visible scratches on her cheeks and chin to an accidental fall. Her friends, knowing she was something of a klutz, wouldn't give it a second thought.

Psychologically, she was much less certain about the time it would take to recover. Those scars were slower to heal, to fade away. Questions kept bombarding her. Why had the Indian treated her so brutally? What had she done to provoke his outrage? Hadn't she willingly given herself to him? Hadn't she made it clear how much she wanted to sleep with him? What had she done wrong?

And most of all, after what happened, why couldn't she get the Indian out of her mind? She thought of him constantly. Saw his eyes, felt his touch, heard his voice. Wanted to be with him again. By all rights, this was a man she should hate. She should tell Simon, let him handle it. Or go to the authorities, get the law involved. Goodness knows, what the Indian had done was a crime punishable by law. Plenty of men had been prosecuted for much less. But Hannah knew she wouldn't tell Simon, or the police, or anybody for that matter. Those conflicting feelings had been at war for four days, and now the war had ended. Only one truth was left standing.

She had to be with him again.

Hannah put the convertible top down and inserted a Norah Jones CD. She turned up the volume and began to sing along. It was a good song, happy and upbeat, and it helped take her mind off the Indian. The song also reminded her of why she was going into town tonight, two days sooner than she had intended.

She was on her way to see a man.

His name was Roger Shaw. A writer for *Sports Illustrated*, he was a Connecticut native on assignment in Florida to do a story on a hot young rookie with the Tampa Bay Devil Rays. Hannah had bumped into him on the dance floor at Downing's Pub two weeks ago. After they exchanged apologies and quips about their clumsiness, he offered to buy her a drink and she accepted. They spent the next two hours dancing, drinking, and laughing.

He wasn't at all her type, and she realized it immediately. He was too educated, too cosmopolitan, too intellectual for her. But he was kind and he was funny. He made her laugh, and these days with Simon, laughs came about as often as snowstorms in the Everglades. Most of all, though, she liked Roger's honesty. He told her right off he was married but would like very much to spend the night with her. She declined, even though she was sorely tempted to say yes. She told him that given her husband's temper, and his network of snitches, their getting together wasn't worth the risk.

But after what had happened to her in the past two weeks, she changed her mind and decided to give Roger a call. After all, she reasoned, I deserve to have some fun. To be treated like something other than a ditzy second-class citizen or a punching bag. She remembered the motel where Roger was staying, and on the chance that he still might be in town, she gave him a call. He had eagerly accepted her invitation.

Roger was standing at the bar when she walked in. His eyes came alive when he saw her.

"It's good to see you again," he said, kissing her on the cheek. "I was hoping you'd call, even though I really didn't think there was much chance you would."

"I almost didn't."

"Well, believe me, I'm glad you did." He squeezed her hand. "The bar okay, or do you prefer a table?"

Hannah pointed to an empty booth in the corner. "How about over there? It'll give us more privacy."

"That's great." Roger picked up his beer mug, wrapped an arm around Hannah, and led her to the booth.

"This is dangerous, you do understand that?" she said, sliding into the booth. "I mean, like, really dangerous."

"We can go someplace else if you'd like. Or we can go to the motel. If we leave separately, it won't look suspicious to anyone."

"You're pretty sure of yourself, aren't you?"

"Why else would you have called?" He finished his beer and waved to the waitress. "Why else would you take the risk if you weren't interested in going to bed with me? Let's face it—we were attracted to each other from the beginning. We both felt it right away. It happens sometimes. What are you drinking?"

"Fuzzy navel."

"A fuzzy navel for the lady and another pint of Harp for me," Roger said to the waitress.

"Maybe I'll surprise you," Hannah said. "Maybe I'm only here for a drink and a few laughs."

He reached across the table and took her hands in his. "Look, I'm really a very nice guy and I'll abide by whatever rules you set. If you want to sleep with me, that's terrific. If you don't, that's okay, too. Just being with you is a lot better than not being with you. But I hope you do want to sleep with me, because I know it would be an exquisite experience for both of us."

"I was buying that until you got to the 'exquisite experience' part." Hannah paused as the waitress set their drinks on the table and then left. Hannah continued, "Then I think you kinda eased over into the bullshit category."

He laughed. "Revealed as a fraud. I confess, I confess. Please forgive me, Madam."

"I'll take it under advisement."

"Be lenient in your punishment." Again, he gently squeezed her hands. "I really do believe making love to you would be nice."

"What happened to exquisite?"

"I don't want to promise a home run, then strike out."

"We'd better leave separately," Hannah whispered. "Most of the people in here wouldn't care. They know what an asshole my husband is. But for safety's sake, we shouldn't leave together. You never know. My husband has friends, too, most of whom can be bought for the price of a drink."

"I'll leave first and go to the motel. You hang around here as long as you think is necessary."

"You know nothing can come of this, don't you?" she asked.

"I understand that."

"And you're okay with it?"

"Yes."

After Roger left, Hannah relaxed, settling into the booth, even smiling for the first time in weeks. She had come here knowing that she would sleep with this man, that she would accept and welcome his kindness, perhaps even his love, and that it would be as close to wonderful as she'd had in years. It was risky, yes. She knew that as well. Anything that could trigger Simon's temper was always risky. But just maybe, for one night at least, she could cast out those doubts and allow herself a moment of sweet peace.

Sweet.

And fleeting.

Because two precise and detailed visions combined to jolt her out of her dreamscape and back into the harsh world of reality: the vision of the Indian flashing in her head, and the sight of him coming through the door and walking toward her booth.

CHAPTER THIRTY SEVEN

Cain caught the first available flight to Sarasota: Delta departing at midnight. He was exhausted and ill-tempered. Twice before leaving La Guardia, he phoned Lucas and Kate. He connected with neither. Kate was attending a faculty meeting, and Lucas simply didn't answer. His failure to make contact only added to his already foul mood. No matter. He would try again during the layover in Atlanta.

Cain dozed off twice during the flight. His periods of sleep were brief and unsatisfying, more turbulent than the bumpy ride. On both occasions, upon waking he noticed the woman sitting in the opposite aisle seat staring intently at his hands, with great concentration, like a sculptor committing to memory her next project.

She was tall and thin, mid- to late-thirties, her black hair sprinkled liberally with gray. She had high cheekbones, full lips, and large green eyes. There was an air of supreme intelligence about her, a look combining dignity and culture. A young Susan Sontag, maybe, mixed in with a bit of ex-hippie.

"You seem to be very interested in my hands," Cain remarked.

"More intrigue than interest," she answered. There was the trace of an accent, almost lost, that Cain couldn't quite place.

"You an artist?" he asked.

"No. I'm a palm reader and fortune teller."

"Ah, a sorceress and a mystic."

He laughed; she didn't.

"What's so intriguing about my hands?"

"I suspect they hold many dark secrets," she said, looking away.

"Wouldn't that be true for most people?"

She smiled but didn't answer.

Cain dozed off again and was on the verge of dreaming when he was awakened by a Nazi-like pronouncement informing the drowsy passengers they would be landing in Atlanta in ten minutes. A second order followed immediately, this one demanding that all seats be returned to a locked and upright position and all seat belts fastened.

Cain shook the grogginess from his eyes and looked at the woman across from him. She was drawing a pair of hands on a sketch pad. When she finished, she lifted her head and let her eyes meet his. There was no hint of emotion or recognition.

During the ninety-minute layover in Atlanta, Cain ate for the first time in sixteen hours. He wolfed down a burger, fries, a slice of pizza, and a Pepsi. Then he found a bank of phones and called Lucas. He needed Simon Buckman's address, and if he didn't get it from Lucas he would be at the mercy of the phone book or the local authorities. Either way, a bummer. Phone books were always iffy, especially when the number belonged to a cheap hustler like Simon. Now with so many cell phones being used, more and more people were opting not to have their numbers listed in city directories. As for the locals, approaching them was always a last-ditch option. The fewer people involved, the better.

Ten rings, no answer.

Cain hung up, silently cursed Lucas, turned, and saw the black-haired woman moving briskly in his direction. She had a large bag on one shoulder and two hardback books in her left hand. The lines on her face were deep. She looked resolute.

"Pardon me, but I was wondering if I might read your palm. That is, if you have the time." She extended her right hand. "My name is Ariel."

"Cain."

"Cain? First name or last?"

"Just Cain."

"Man of mystery; is that it?" Her lips drew back in

a near-smile. Cain immediately assessed her as a woman who did not smile easily or often. "It'll only take a few minutes. Promise."

"Sure. Where?"

She looked around. "How about in there?" She nodded toward the snack area.

They found a table near the back. She ordered hot tea with lemon; he ordered a Diet Pepsi.

"Which hand?" Cain said.

"Right."

She took his hand and gently ran her forefinger across the palm. Her touch was soft, sensual, almost erotic. He was especially struck by the different look on her face. The hard edge had been replaced by a tender, gentle look. He wondered if perhaps this was her way of making love.

"What do the lines tell you?" Cain asked.

"That you're a terribly impatient man." She made another attempt at a smile, almost pulling it off. "Your hands are unlike any I've ever touched. They're very distant, very . . . it's as if they aren't your hands. And they're so hard, so rough."

"I work out a lot."

"You have a very divided personality," she said. "I suspect you're a Gemini."

Her fingers traced his palm, delicately, sensuously. She closed her eyes, tilted her head back slightly, and began rocking slowly back and forth, as if she were in a religious trance. After several seconds, she let out a deep sigh, leaned back and opened her eyes.

"See anything interesting?" Cain asked.

"Your life is in danger," she said, solemnly.

"It always has been."

"Imminent danger."

"Let's hope it isn't too imminent."

"Aren't you concerned?"

"If I weren't, I wouldn't be alive today."

"I don't know what that means."

"It means I'm aware of the danger."

She gently squeezed his hands. "Be careful. Matters such as these are not to be taken lightly."

"I never take danger lightly."

"No, you don't strike me as a man who would."

Cain nodded, then stood. "Thanks, I think, for a unique experience."

He turned to leave.

"When is your birthday?" she asked.

"May 27."

"A Gemini."

Turning away, he thought he detected a smile on her face.

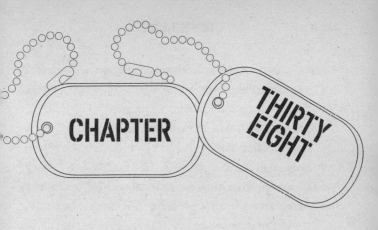

CHAPTER THIRTY EIGHT

Ask any athlete which he would rather have, luck or talent, and he is likely to say either will do in any given situation. Ask an assassin the same question, and he'll tell you talent is everything. Nothing beats skill in the killing business. But that same assassin will add this proviso: if talent has somehow been neutralized or rendered ineffective, luck is better than nothing.

Cain had always been as lucky as he was talented.

Simon Buckman's name and address were in the Sarasota phone book. Cain jotted down the number, then asked a cabby for directions to Jack's Marina.

"Twenty minutes from the airport," the cabby said. "A straight shot down Tamiami Trail, on the right, you can't miss it."

Cain found his rental, hopped in, and headed south.

After taking one look at the fleet of boats and yachts ringing Sarasota Bay, Cain didn't like his odds of finding

Simon's anytime soon. With this many boats, and without directions or the name of the yacht, it could take hours. Hours he didn't have.

He parked near the main building, a combination restaurant-office, got out of the car, and went straight to the marina office. A sign on the door said, "Closed: Back in an Hour." A waitress in the restaurant informed him that "something terrible has happened" and that Kevin, the marina manager, was "over there with the cops."

Cain walked back out to his car. Straight ahead, across from the yacht *Rebel Rouser,* sat three police cruisers and an ambulance. The lights on the middle cruiser were flashing, and the back doors of the ambulance were open. Onlookers began to crowd, necks craning, heads bobbing like a flock of curious geese.

Cain knew it was Simon's boat. He also knew this particular hustler wouldn't be brokering any more deals.

After winding his way through the geese, Cain quickly climbed onto the yacht. A female police officer rushed toward him, holding both hands high, signaling for him to stop.

"I'm sorry, sir, but I cannot allow you on this boat."

"Are you in charge here?"

"No. But that makes no difference. There's a police investigation being conducted, and no one who isn't part of the investigation will be allowed on board."

"Who is in charge?"

"Captain Finley is heading the investigation."

Cain glanced at her name tag. "Officer Melendez, it's urgent that I speak with Captain Finley."

"Regarding the investigation?"

"Yes."

"Are you a newspaper reporter?"

"No."

"Do you have information pertaining to what took place here?"

"Quite possibly."

"Well, I guess . . ." She paused, an anxious look on her face. "Just a moment while I confer with Captain Finley."

A few seconds later she reappeared, followed by a man Cain presumed to be Finley. The man was stocky and well-muscled, with the ruddy, tanned skin of a native Floridian. The dark tan stood in sharp contrast to his white hair, which was thick but cut short. He was dressed casually in checkered slacks, white cotton shirt, loafers, no socks. More a golfer's look than a homicide detective's. An insurance salesman with a six handicap.

"You have something for me?" he barked, his voice scratchy and gruff.

"We need to speak in private," Cain said. His tone, more order than request, seemed to throw Finley off stride. Sensing his control, Cain took Finley by the elbow and led him to the railing.

"Captain, you don't know me, but you're going to

have to trust me."

"Trust you? In what way?"

"By letting me search this boat."

"You with the FBI?"

Cain shook his head. "Are they involved?"

"Sure are. Agent Williams just called. He should be here any minute now. I'm not sure Simon Buckman is worth all this trouble, but the Feds apparently do."

"That makes it all the more essential that I begin my search ASAP," Cain said.

Finley stepped back and held up both hands. "Put the brakes on for a second, okay? Exactly who are you, what agency are you with, and what's your relationship with Simon Buckman?"

"My name is Cain. I'm with Army intelligence."

"Are you tellin' me Simon Buckman is—was— being investigated by Army intelligence?"

"Yes."

"That's rather hard to believe."

"Believe it."

"You got any ID that might prove who you are? A phone number, maybe?"

"I can give you a hundred phone numbers, Captain. But I don't have the time to wait while you're checking me out."

"I dunno. I think I'd best get some proof before I let you go sniffin' around a crime scene. Especially with the Feds involved. They'll hang my ass if I screw up.

They're a bunch of hard-core pricks."

"Simon Buckman is dead, right?" Cain said.

"Colder than a frozen popsicle."

"Killed by a knife. Single entry wound directly below the sternum. The blade penetrated his heart. He died instantly. Am I right?"

"You're so right you just became my number one suspect," Finley said. "How'd you know all that?"

"Time, Captain Finley. I'm running short on time. I'll gladly answer any question you have, but not until we're inside."

"Let's go," Finley said without hesitation.

"Is Simon's body still down below?" Cain asked.

"Nah. The big bastard was killed up top. Lucky for us, too. Be a bitch tryin' to haul that lard ass up those steps."

"Let me see the body first."

Simon's body, guarded by two local cops, had already been bagged and tagged. Cain knelt beside the body and unzipped the bag. One of the cops started to protest but went silent when Finley raised his arm.

Cain looked up at Finley. "What items were found on the body?"

"Everything we found is right there." Finley pointed to a small bag next to the body. Cain opened it and inspected the contents. A wallet, two diamond rings, a buckeye, and a silver flask.

"You're positive this is everything?" Cain asked.

One of the uniformed officers nodded. "That's all we found, sir."

Cain stood without closing the bag. "Let's go below," he said to Finley.

"You know who did this joker in, don't you?" Finley asked, trailing Cain down the steps.

"Yeah."

"Who?"

"An Indian."

"Why the hell would an Indian, or a cowboy, or a French queer, or an Eskimo, or anybody for that matter, punch Simon's ticket?" Finley asked.

"Because he's an assassin."

"But . . . Simon Buckman? Why him?"

"He was a danger to someone. A liability. He had to be done away with."

"What the hell is this all about?"

Cain's eyes scanned the cabin, finally coming to rest on a framed photograph behind the bar. An 8x10 color of a woman, early twenties, movie star beautiful, standing next to a red Jaguar. Cain went behind the bar, took the photograph, and showed it to Finley.

"Simon's daughter?" he asked.

"Wife."

"Where is she?"

"Dunno. We're still trying to locate her."

Cain set the picture down. "I wouldn't count on

finding her alive."

"Why? She on this Indian assassin's hit list, too?"

"No. He just has a thing for beautiful young women."

Finley snickered. "Hell, don't we all?"

Cain's ten-minute search yielded nothing of importance. No names, dates, places—nothing providing anything more than what he already knew. Cain had to give the big man his due. Whatever else Simon might have been, he was secretive and careful.

The female officer, Melendez, entered the cabin. "Sir, we just got word that Hannah Buckman was found dead in a motel across town. They say she was sliced up pretty bad."

Finley stared at Cain. "Looks like you called another one right on the money." He shifted his attention to Melendez. "Tell them I'll be there in half an hour. And tell them they'd better not destroy my crime scene."

"Yes, sir," she said.

Finley said, "Now, Mr. Cain, I'm caught on the horns of a terrible dilemma. Should I hold you for further questioning? Maybe even let the Feds have a go at you? Let's face it. You do seem to be in possession of considerable information. Or should I just let you walk out of here?"

Cain smiled. "I think you know the answer, Captain."

Cain left the yacht and walked to his car. He watched to his right as Melendez helped three attendants load Simon's body into the ambulance. She saw him and waved. He motioned for her.

"Officer Melendez," he said, scribbling his name and phone number on a scrap of paper. "This is a number where I can be reached. If you find anything that might be important—anything at all—please give me a call. It's terribly urgent."

She looked at the card. "Yes, sir, Mr. Collins. You can count on me."

CHAPTER THIRTY NINE

All in all, the Indian concluded, it had been a good day.

Three kills in twelve hours. Simon Buckman, beautiful Hannah, and a young college student who just happened to be in the wrong place at the wrong time.

The Indian sat at a booth in an all-night diner, a half-empty bowl of cold soup in front of him. He thought about the day's events, arranging them, as he always did, in reverse order of importance. Seneca always saved the best for last.

Victim number three was the unfortunate college student he met in a restaurant outside of Bradenton. The young man lived in Boston and was on his way to visit friends in Miami. He had a great gift for gab and an intense interest in a "real Native American." He also had something the Indian needed—an ugly yellow '81 Nova. The perfect vehicle for the next leg of his journey.

Seneca cut the young man's throat, wrapped the

body in an old rug, put it in a large dumpster behind a local high school, and covered it with wide strips of roofing he found lying on the ground. After closing the dumpster lid, he checked the surrounding area thoroughly, made certain he left nothing incriminating, then got into the Nova and drove away.

His thoughts shifted to Sarasota and his second victim.

Simon Buckman's death had deserved no more thought than the killing of a cockroach. His only regret: he hadn't made the fat bastard suffer enough. Simon should have experienced the same terror, felt the same pain, as—

Beautiful, sexy, delicious Hannah.

In the final moments of her life, she had come face to face with absolute horror. She experienced a level of terror few would ever know. Or could imagine.

The scenes flashed in his mind, clear, vivid, detailed. Hannah on the bed, covered with perspiration, her breasts heaving, nipples erect. Hannah with her mouth on his blood-engorged penis. Hannah on top of him, her tongue exploring his mouth, moaning softly as the first waves of orgasm closed in. Hannah whispering in his ear, urging him to join her in a tidal wave of pleasure, feeling him explode inside her, his semen pouring deep into her. Hannah lying on her back, tucking a pillow beneath her, legs ensnaring him, pulling him close, inviting him to enter her again.

Then another series of scenes flashed into his head.

The dark ones, the ones he remembered even more vividly. Hannah registering confusion when he rolled her onto her stomach and bound her hands and feet. Hannah's soft tears falling onto his hands when he tied the scarf around her mouth. Hannah paralyzed by fear when she saw the knife. Hannah's muffled cry when he extended her nipple, then severed it with one quick swing of the knife. Hannah recoiling when the blade touched her throat. Hannah trying to comprehend what was happening when the knife raked across her throat, then was driven deep into her chest, her belly, her pubic area. Hannah's eyes going blank.

Hannah dead, fear forever frozen on her face.

The Indian smiled. Three kills in less than twelve hours. All in all, a pretty good day.

Then his mind flashed on Karl's message. On the time, date, and place. His smiled widened. Those kills would make for a great day, perhaps his greatest ever. He didn't know who the intended victims were, but that didn't matter. The place said it all.

Camp David.

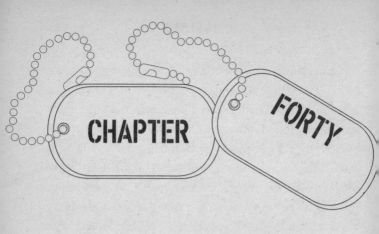

CHAPTER FORTY

General David Nichols couldn't believe it when an aide informed him of the call. "From someone named Cain. Said it was confidential, that you would want to take it in private."

Nichols shook with excitement. *Cain. Holy Jesus! Cain!* Nichols was in a fourth-floor briefing room, a full two minutes away from his office. He made it back to his desk in thirty seconds. Hand trembling, he picked up the phone. A call from Cain was enough to make anyone tremble.

He tried to control his voice. "Yes, sir, Major. How can I be of help?"

"General, I need a favor," Cain said.

Nichols turned crimson with excitement. "Anything, Major. Just name it."

"I want you to secure Simon Buckman's phone records for the past six months. I'm especially interested in any calls to New York, Chicago, or Washington."

"What about overseas calls?" Nichols asked.

There was a moment of silence. "Don't worry about them," Cain answered. "I'm trying to locate Seneca, and all evidence points to him being in the country. Stick with those three cities for now. If we need to widen our search area, we can do it later."

"I'll get to it immediately," Nichols said.

"One more thing, General. This is strictly between you and me. No one, and I mean no one, is to know that I've made this request. If anyone should ask, tell them you're doing it as a favor for the Sarasota police. Is that clear?"

"Yes, but what about—?"

"No one, General."

"Yes, sir."

"Here's a number where I can be reached. I'll expect to hear from you by noon tomorrow." Cain slowly read the numbers to Nichols. "Please read that back to me."

Nichols repeated the numbers.

"Good."

"Anything else, sir?"

"No. Remember: no one is to know I've made this request."

Nichols was slightly dizzy when he placed the phone on the cradle. His thoughts were racing at the speed of light. He replayed the entire conversation in his head several times, concentrating not only on Cain's words, but on his tone, inflections, points of emphasis—everything—not letting a single syllable pass without being studied, analyzed, broken down. It was as if he were trying to find and decipher a hidden code.

Nichols breathed deeply, sucking air into his lungs. His heart continued to pound. The exhilaration he felt was nearly overwhelming. During his entire military career he had never felt more important than he did at this moment. Or more necessary. An operation of great secrecy was under way, and he was now one of the select few involved. He had been brought into the inner circle. A wave of fear swept through him. That old nagging fear of failure.

He quickly wiped the intruding thoughts away. No way was he going to fail, to let anyone down. He would perform his duties, and he would perform them well.

He had to please the legend.

At the very moment General David Nichols was ending his conversation with Cain, another phone conversation was beginning. Although it lacked excitement or the presence of a legend, it was of equal importance and urgency to the caller.

The man placing the call tapped the tip of a pencil against his teeth as he listened to the phone ringing.

Twice, three times, four times, still no answer. By the fifth ring he was getting worried. By the seventh he was steaming with anger. Finally, after two more rings, just as he was about to slam the cell phone shut, someone picked up.

"Yes."

"Is this Dr. Nastasia Ivanovna?"

"Yes. Who is this?" Her voice was deep, full, heavy with a Russian accent.

"Karl."

"I do not know anyone named Karl."

"I have a message for Seneca," Karl said. "An extremely important message. Can I trust you to give it to him?"

Silence.

Karl could hear movement, followed by the sound of paper being shuffled.

"The message?"

"Tell Seneca there has been a change in the schedule. Tell him the new date is July 28, ten hundred hours, at a private estate on Long Island. He'll know what that means."

Silence.

"Also, tell him there will be another message informing him of the exact address and the number of principals involved. He should receive it within the next forty-eight hours."

"Is that all?"

"Yes."

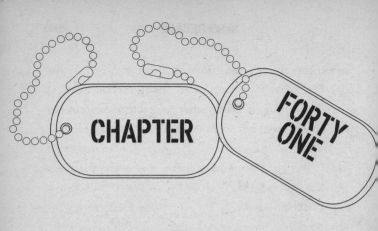

CHAPTER FORTY ONE

Cain arrived back in Manhattan a little before sunset and went straight to Andy Waltz's office. Unlit cigar in mouth, Waltz sat at his desk reading *Sports Illustrated*. Cain walked in without knocking.

Waltz closed the magazine, smiled, and shook his head. "You look like shit."

"Smell like it, too." Cain fell like a lump into a chair. He pulled out a package of Juicy Fruit gum and crammed two pieces into his mouth. "Got anything for me, Houdini?"

Waltz shook his head. "Not yet. But the way those bastards in Washington like to talk, it's only a matter of time before I do."

"Time is the one thing we don't have."

"Listen, Cain. I—"

"What?"

"I'm honored you came to me, and you know I'll do

whatever you want. But—"

"But what?"

"Look, a guy with your reputation, your connections—you could get this information in five minutes. From a dozen different sources. Why do you need me?"

"Because I trust you. And right now trust is as important as speed."

Waltz nodded. "I'll go to D.C. tomorrow. Dig around there. Shouldn't take me long."

"You have my number, right?"

"Yeah."

Cain forced himself out of the chair, rubbed his eyes with the back of his hands, then slowly walked to the door. He looked at Waltz, a thin smile on his face. "This is a shitty business we're in, Houdini. There's something evil about it."

"Evil has been with us from the beginning."

"Not like this."

Waltz put his hand on Cain's shoulder. "Get some rest, my friend. You look like you haven't slept in decades."

Cain opened the door. "I don't know, Houdini. Maybe I've been asleep too long."

Unable to sleep, Cain prowled his hotel room like an angry, agitated tiger. He felt trapped, caged. Morning

had arrived, yet there was still no word from Nichols.
These were the times Cain hated most—being at the
mercy of others. He thrived on action, calling the shots,
setting his own agenda.

Waiting. Relying on help from outside sources,
whose talent and skill levels varied, turned him into a
madman. *I travel best when I travel alone.* That had always been his way of operating.

At six, he ordered up breakfast from room service.
He was famished, yet he ate nothing. He was too wired
to sleep or eat. At eight, he looked down from his tenth
floor window onto the Manhattan streets. Already the
streets were alive with joggers, dog walkers, and Sunday morning churchgoers on a pilgrimage to find God.
Lucky them, he thought. Finding God was easier than
finding Seneca.

He circled the room, waited, looked at the clock. Started
pacing again, stopped. Frustration ate at his insides. Time
seemed to stand still.

At 11:58 the phone rang.

"Yes."

"Major, I have something for you." It was Nichols.
"Sorry it took so long, but I had to do an end-around to
avoid questions. The FBI. Nosy bastards."

"What did you find out?"

"Simon called two numbers in Chicago. One to
a blues joint called Butterfield's. The other to a woman

named Trish Underwood. He called both numbers twice."

"What about New York?"

"Now, that's a little more interesting. Simon called two numbers there as well. One was to an apartment belonging to George Armstrong. The second to a Dr. Nastasia Ivanovna."

"The professor of Russian literature?"

"One and the same," Nichols said. "Are you familiar with her?"

"I heard her give a lecture once. Must have been twelve, fifteen years ago. If my memory is correct, she was teaching in Berlin at the time."

"Very good, Major. She was living in Berlin then. Prior to that, she taught at the University in Moscow. For the past seven years, she's been at Columbia University."

"Simon Buckman called her? You're positive of that?"

"Yes. And get this. He called her five times." Nichols paused. "What do you make of that?"

"Well, it's for sure Simon wasn't discussing Tolstoy with her."

"I've already begun a background check on her. I should have some concrete information for you later this afternoon."

"Quash your investigation of Ivanovna, General."

"You sure?"

"Right now she may be our best hope of locating Seneca. If either of them gets even the slightest hint of our presence, Seneca will go so deep underground we'll never find him. I don't want to run that risk."

"As you wish, Major."

"Does anyone in intelligence know you checked Simon Buckman's phone records?"

"No, sir."

"Anyone at the Pentagon?"

"No, sir."

"Let's keep it that way."

"Yes, sir."

"You've done a helluva job, General."

"Thank you, sir."

Nichols' eyes were filled with tears when he hung up the phone.

CHAPTER FORTY TWO

At first glance Mariah's appeared to be empty. No customers, no one tending bar, no waitresses. The only person Seneca saw upon entering was the janitor, a small black man with stooped shoulders, watery yellow eyes, and a crown of snow white hair. The old-timer glanced up indifferently at Seneca, then continued mopping the floor.

It wasn't until Seneca heard music coming from behind him that he realized the janitor wasn't alone. He turned and saw a petite brunette sitting at the piano. Her brown eyes stared straight ahead, trancelike, as her long fingers played a slow and melancholy song.

Seneca listened to the music for nearly a minute before approaching her. When she saw him coming toward her, she stopped playing briefly, then began again.

"We don't open until four," she said. Her voice was soft, completely without emotion. "If you want a drink, try Butterfield's around the corner. It's open."

"I'm not here for a drink," Seneca said.

"Then what are you here for?"

"I'm trying to find a guy who hangs around this neighborhood. Perhaps you might know him."

"It's a big neighborhood."

Seneca pulled up a chair and sat down. "Maybe you know him; maybe you don't. All I can do is ask."

"Then ask."

"Derek Jefferson. You may know him as Deke."

Seneca knew by her reaction that he'd struck gold. She turned away, eyes quickly filling with tears.

He leaned forward. "You know him, don't you?"

She stopped playing and wiped the tears from her cheeks. After a few seconds, she removed a tissue from her purse and blew her nose.

"Deke . . . where is he?" Seneca asked. He started to say something else, then paused. "You're Trish, aren't you?"

She turned away without answering.

"Deke used to talk about you all the time. 'My little songbird,' he'd say. You . . . you're Trish, right?"

She nodded and whispered, "I'm Trish. And you are?"

"Seneca."

"The Indian. Derek's hero. He talked about you all the time."

"Where is Deke?" Seneca asked. "I need to find him, fast."

She laughed softly. "You really don't know, do you?"

"Look, little lady. I just hit town. I don't know anything. That's why I'm here."

"Derek is dead."

"Dead?"

She nodded, more tears running down her face. "I'm sorry, but it's difficult for me to talk about Derek. I mean, I loved him. Love him."

"How did he die? When?"

"A week or so ago. He was beaten to death."

"The cops find his killer?"

"Are you kidding? They'll never find Derek's killer. They won't because they don't give a damn. To them he's just one less black man they have to worry about."

"You have any idea who might have done it?"

"I'm sure Derek had his share of enemies."

"Any particular enemy who might've had an extra-strong reason for killing him?"

"Not really. But—"

"What?"

"There was a man who came around asking questions about Derek on the day he was murdered. I find that to be a curious coincidence."

"You mention this to the cops?"

"They never asked."

"This man—you get a name?"

Trish blew her nose again, wadded the tissue, and dropped it into a wastebasket. "He told me his name, but I wasn't really paying attention. I'm terribly sorry. I've tried like hell to remember, but I can't."

"Describe him."

"White. Brown hair, rather on the longish side. He was probably a couple of inches taller than you. Close to your age, I'd guess. Ruggedly handsome."

"Did he say why he was looking for Deke?"

"Not really. Only that they were Army buddies and he needed to find Derek. That's about it."

"Tell me exactly how Deke was killed. You said he was beaten to death. Beaten with what? Baseball bat, fists, a club?"

"I don't know all the details. But from what I've heard, he was just beaten. You know, someone used his hands to beat Derek to death."

"Take a helluva man to kill Deke using only his hands. This man you spoke with—did he look like he could handle someone as big and powerful as Deke?"

"I don't recall anything particularly noteworthy about his physical appearance. He certainly wasn't the pumped-up bodybuilder type. He was in good shape. Like you." She paused, eyes narrowing. "But he did have these incredible hands."

"What about his hands?"

"They were exceptionally large. Very strong look-ing. Almost to the point of being intimidating."

Seneca stood. "Was his name Cain?"

"Cain? No, it wasn't Cain."

"You're positive?"

"Yes, quite positive."

"Michael?"

"No, not Michael. But that does sound similar."

"Mickey?"

"Yes, that's it. His name was Mickey . . . Mickey Collins."

Seneca streaked for the door.

CHAPTER FORTY THREE

The desk clerk waved when he saw Cain walk through the front lobby.

"A gentleman phoned for you about twenty minutes ago," the clerk said. "He didn't give a name, but he did leave this message."

Cain thanked the clerk, took the note, and moved away several paces before reading it.

Rico's. 7 p.m. Urgent.

Houdini

Cain looked at the clock above the front desk: 6:32. Rico's was on Mulberry Street in Little Italy. He could make it by seven if he hurried.

At two minutes past seven, he walked into Rico's and was met by a heavy-set, smiling, middle-aged woman— a dead ringer for the old Italian actress Anna Magnani. She asked in halting English if he had a reservation.

"I'm here to meet Andy Waltz," Cain replied.

"Chances are he's already here."

"You're Mr. Collins, correct?" she asked.

"Yes."

"Please follow me."

She led Cain through the main dining area and into a smaller section off to the right. This section, which was separated from the main hall by a beaded curtain, had two tables and three booths lining the brick wall. A waitress nodded and smiled when they entered the smaller area.

Andy Waltz sat alone in the booth farthest from the curtain, sipping a glass of red wine. He waved when he saw Cain.

"Three past seven. Not bad." He lifted his glass. "Care for some vino? Merlot. Quite tasty."

"I'll pass," Cain said, sliding into the booth.

"Don't dismiss it so soon," Waltz said. "When you hear what I have to say, you might change your mind. Might even want something stronger than Merlot."

"That sounds ominous."

"Oh, we left ominous behind in the starting gate."

"Let's hear it."

"My source at the State Department tells me the prez is going to sit down with—are you ready for this?— the Israeli prime minister, the Palestinian president, and one of Hamas's top honchos. A one-day meet, super top secret. Has to do with a deal involving Gaza, the West Bank, and an exchange of prisoners."

"Hamas? Here? In the states? Almost impossible to believe."

"*Almost*? It's fuckin' unbelievable."

Cain plucked a breadstick from the basket and tapped it against his hand. "That's it. That's perfect for Seneca. Big, highly visible, difficult odds for success. Exactly what he likes."

"Who do you think gave him the green light?" Waltz asked.

"With that cast of characters, take your pick. It could be one of a dozen or more factions. I doubt if Seneca knows who's signing his paycheck."

"Boychick, let me hit you with a bit more bad news. The meeting is this Saturday."

"Saturday? You're positive?"

"As sure as I'm a Hebrew."

"What else are you sure of?"

"Saturday. That's about all I know for sure."

"Where?"

"Don't know."

"A meeting that big. How can you not know the location?"

"Nobody seems to know much, and those who do aren't talking."

"Doesn't matter where it is. We have to see that it's called off."

"I'm not sure that's possible."

"Why?"

Waltz shrugged his shoulders. "My State Department guy says this deal is so hush-hush you wouldn't believe it. Says there aren't five people on Capitol Hill who know it's happening. Even the prez's closest advisers are under the assumption that he's checking into Walter Reed on Thursday for minor surgery. The lid on this one is tight as hell."

"It's not that fuckin' tight. Seneca knows about it. Whoever hired him knows about it. Your State Department pal knows about it. I'd say this tight-as-hell lid has sprung a few leaks."

"Okay, point taken. I'll talk to my guy again, see if he can fill in some blanks."

"Work him hard," Cain said. "While you're at it, find out how much security is planned for the meeting, wherever the hell it is."

"Jesus Christ, anything else? Like what's on the menu, maybe?"

"Just get what you can as fast as you can."

"What about you? Where do you go from here?"

Cain shook his head. "I have a couple of ideas brewing, but whether or not I have enough time to implement them is a big question mark. Four days—that's short notice. And until we know the exact time and location, my options are somewhat limited."

"What about Lucas? If anyone can pull a few strings,

get the meeting called off or postponed, it's him."

"Yeah, he may be our best shot."

"You can't go wrong with that wily old bastard on your side." Waltz chuckled. "Lucas calling the shots, you doing the headhunting, me scrounging—man, this is just like the old days."

"Somehow the old days seemed easier." Cain paused, a faraway look in his eyes. "And awfully long ago."

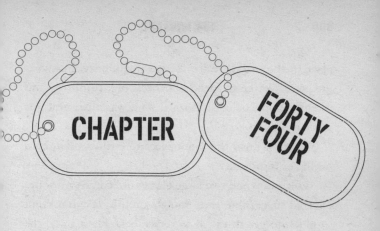

CHAPTER FORTY FOUR

Lucas White lived alone in a two-story white wooden house in Falls Church, Virginia. He was immensely proud of the house, the only one he'd ever owned. The house, which sat on a quiet, secluded corner across from the city park, had been built prior to the Civil War by a Virginia senator named Richard Wingate, and had remained in the Wingate family until 1988, when Lucas bought it two months prior to retiring from the Army.

A lifelong bachelor—who needs a bride when you have the Army as your mistress?—Lucas enlisted the wife of a former staff aide to help with the interior decorating. Under his watchful eye, and with enormous amounts of his money, she transformed the place into a miniature Southern mansion and a small but impressive museum to his long and rewarding military career. It was a house with character, taste, and history.

The den was Lucas's favorite room. His favorite

place in the world, really. It was small, cozy, intimate, the perfect place to spend hours reading, thinking, and listening to his beloved Mozart. This was his retreat, his safe haven.

That is, until this latest piece of business shattered his life of tranquility.

Lucas downed two large glasses of Scotch and water in rapid succession, then poured a refill. He drank not so much to get drunk as to remember. He wanted the alcohol to guide his thoughts back into the past.

Nostalgia was the tonic he used to fight off depression and melancholy. A moment of agony today could best be soothed by recalling a moment of glory from yesterday. An empty hole in his life at the present could best be filled by chiseling out a piece of the past.

His glorious past.

No matter what happened, regardless of what anyone said or did, they could never take away his past.

Tears came to his eyes as he gazed around the den. He fought against them, but it was a losing battle. They dripped from his eyes to his chin to the floor.

He brushed the tears away, downed another shot of Scotch, and thought about his past. His history was in this room, on these walls. His life. What it told him was this: he had been a good soldier, perhaps even a great one.

They could never take that history away from him.

Not the pistol given to him by Churchill, the Japanese

sword of surrender by his old colleague Doug MacArthur, or the set of golf clubs by Ike.

Lucas felt the Scotch take hold, drawing him deeper into a past that could never be stolen from him. He was now a traveler in his own land of memories, a land he cherished, a land growing more distant with each passing hour.

He took another drink, felt the fire roaring inside him, and let his eyes scan the room.

On the wall to his left were twenty-seven framed correspondences, personal letters, and memos addressed to him—four-star General Lucas K. White, by God, a fuckin' soldier's soldier—and no one could take that away, ever, and fuck 'em if they tried.

That bottom row of letters said it all: praise and congratulations and appreciation from seven presidents. They knew. They understood how great a warrior he had been. They appreciated what he had done for his country. How could anyone dare to doubt or question his contributions? His patriotism or his service to America's many causes? His absolute belief in duty, honor, country?

No one could doubt it—ever.

No matter what happened.

Then there were the photographs. Eighty-nine in all, covering virtually every inch of three walls. A pictorial history of General Lucas White's life, from his childhood through retirement. It was all there, for everyone to see, a man's life on full display. Snapshots taken in dozens of hot spots around the globe, during times of war, during times of peace, him with high-ranking officers and lowly enlisted grunts, all with one thing in common—respect for him, for what he'd done while in uniform. They knew. His men knew.

General Lucas White was a soldier.

And, of course, no historical gallery would be complete without pictures from his private life. From that outside world where celebrities, stargazers, and other notables worshipped the successful, and who, regardless of their own degree of fame, felt the need to reach out and make a connection.

A connection with him, General Lucas White, soldier.

There was Lucas pictured with Rocky Marciano. With Sinatra and Dean Martin and Sammy Davis Jr. on a movie set in Vegas. Getting a kiss from Angie Dickinson at a Palm Springs charity golf event. Pictures of him with Murrow and Bogart and Bobby Kennedy. There was one—his favorite—of him sitting at a poker table with Churchill, Hemingway, and a very young Norman Mailer. Yet another showing him with JFK and Pierre Salinger in the Oval Office during the Cuban Missile Crisis.

He had been there. Stood shoulder to shoulder with the great men of the twentieth century. Served them, advised them, elevated them.

They knew. They understood. More than understood. They bore witness to his past.

His glorious past.

He swiveled his chair and looked at the wall directly behind the desk. Hanging there was his most cherished possession, his greatest treasure: an original Picasso presented to him by the master himself shortly after the end of the Korean conflict.

Yes, he, Lucas White, had truly walked with giants.

He sipped more Scotch, eased back into the leather chair and scanned the room. So many memories, so much history. His life. Without his realizing it, his eyes came to rest on a framed 5x7 black and white photo on his desk. It showed him standing with another great soldier, perhaps the greatest he'd ever known.

Cain.

God, how he loved that kid.

Lucas closed his eyes, shutting out the present, keeping it at a distance as if he were trying to fight off some insidious disease.

He had no use for the present.

Now, at this moment, more than ever, he needed the past. His glorious past.

Precious memories swirled inside his head, tossed by wave after wave of uncertainty and confusion. The present, he knew, was rapidly encroaching, threatening to erase his past like footprints in a desert sandstorm. His past was in danger of being blown into the void of nothingness.

Lucas quickly opened his eyes and looked around

the room. The photos, letters, gifts, mementos—they were still there. Reassurances that his past was real.

It was . . . had been.

And they could never take it away.

Nor could they ever fathom his deepest secrets.

By the mid-1960s, rogue elements within the CIA were conducting a secret war inside the borders of Laos, which was in the middle of bloody civil unrest. This off-the-books operation, unauthorized by CIA officials, and far removed from any hint of military or Congressional oversight, was undertaken for the purpose of helping warlords like General Vang Pao fight against the North Vietnamese and the local Communist Pathet Lao. It was a fight the CIA believed in wholeheartedly.

This secret war was funded by the opium poppy, thanks primarily to a financial crop planted by the CIA a decade earlier. Top CIA officials, going back to the days of Allen Dulles, had long dreamt of finding the means to finance covert operations without having to beg for Congressional funding and support. In Laos, Cambodia, and later Vietnam, illegal drug production, distribution, and sales provided the answer to this problem. The war, now essentially privatized, paid for itself, thus eliminating the necessity of dealing with Washington red tape bureaucracy.

Lucas White, with Ted Shackley's blessings, trust, and confidence, was the point man for the operation's disinformation campaign. Lucas, highly respected within the Pentagon and the halls of Congress, had one simple goal: to convince those in Washington that we were winning the war against the Pathet Lao.

"When you testify before Congress, use the terms Communist and Communism as many times as you can," Shackley advised Lucas. "Toss in dominoes while you're at it. Same thing when you're talking to the media. They eat that shit up like it was pudding. No politician in Washington will dare withhold support if they think we are keeping the reds away."

What the decision makers in Washington were not aware of was Lucas's deep involvement with covert operations, or that he had been a valuable CIA operative since the Agency's earliest days, having been recruited by Allen Dulles immediately after the Korean War ended. Lucas was so deep undercover that his Army superiors had no clue to his covert involvement. Even Richard Collins, his closest friend, didn't know.

Lucas served lengthy assignments in London and Berlin prior to being sent to the Far East. Being in the military provided him the perfect cover to perform his covert duties. From the beginning of his career, he demonstrated a special talent for making friends in high places, earning their trust, then recruiting them into the

Agency. Within the Agency's inner circle, Lucas was
known as "Little Caesar."

This special talent enabled Lucas to recruit Quane
Rattikone, the Laotian General who, with CIA backing
and funding, was responsible for constructing a series of
large-scale heroin-processing refineries in the "Golden
Triangle," the area where Laos, Burma, and Thailand
converge. Landing Rattikone was considered a coup for
Lucas and an important "get" for the Agency.

Rattikone proved to be immensely valuable, both as
a warrior against enemy forces and as a drug producer.
He was instrumental in beating back the Communist
insurgents, while at the same time adding millions of
dollars to the CIA coffers. His involvement was a dou-
ble-sided victory for Lucas.

It was perhaps inevitable that such enormous profits would draw the attention of others in the worldwide
drug business. Among those who took a keen interest
was Lucas's close friend Santos Trafficante, the Mafia
boss who had often been linked to JFK's assassination.
Trafficante, already doing business through Hong Kong,
took control of several Saigon bars and immediately
began selling heroin to American soldiers at cut-rate pric-
es. The result was inevitable—more and more American
G.I.'s returned home hooked on drugs.

Large quantities of high-grade heroin were also
shipped back to the United States, oftentimes in body

bags containing dead soldiers. Dover Air Force Base, which served as a mortuary, was reputed to have been the primary Mafia drug pickup point on the East Coast.

By late 1970, Lucas and Shackley had become convinced that the "poppy problem" was spiraling out of control and that their drug operation was in danger of losing its secrecy. Prying eyes from the national media and the politicians in Washington were beginning to look long and hard at what was already a costly and unpopular war. Given the growing antiwar sentiment in the United States, Lucas and Shackley knew it was only a matter of time before an investigative light would be shone into the dark corners where the Agency operated. That was not acceptable. Something had to be done.

Trafficante's operation was ruled off-limits; neither Lucas nor Shackley had any interest in antagonizing the Mafia. There was another practical reason for leaving that partnership untouched—financial considerations. They didn't want to shut off the steady flow of money coming in. As Lucas once remarked, "Profits make for strange bedfellows."

There was, however, a second major drug operation—this one headed by a notorious Cambodian warlord who demanded to be called Hank—that was not considered to be sacrosanct. Though Hank's operation was equally lucrative financially, he was deemed to be expendable for two reasons: he sold poor heroin, and he supplied money and arms to the North Vietnamese.

"He needs to disappear from the world stage," Lucas said, adding, "and I will see that it gets done. Hank will trouble us no more."

Shackley grinned and nodded. "Once he's history, we will take over his operation. He has people begging us to move in and provide proper leadership."

One hour later, Lucas met with Cain. "Dispatch one of your men—Houdini would be best suited for the task—to meet with Hank in Prey Ling. Houdini will inform Hank that a high-level meeting is to take place at the Army base outside Tay Ninh. Hank is naturally wary, so Houdini will have to be especially persuasive. Hank also has a gigantic ego, which Houdini can use to—"

"Why not send me?" Cain asked. "Then there will be no need to worry about Hank's ego."

Lucas chuckled. "Hank has to vanish, not simply be eliminated. I understand you can make that happen. However, in this case, I have something special in mind for our friend Hank."

"What? Now you're telling me how to do my job?"

"My boy, only a fool would dare do that. And I'm no fool. But Hank is an especially loathsome creature, one I have disliked and distrusted for many years. Because of my disdain for him, and my desire to give him a unique sendoff, I plead for your indulgence in this matter. In short, humor me, my boy."

"Why Tay Ninh?" Cain asked.

"Because there is a wonderful yellow bridge overlooking a small pond," Lucas said, smiling. "You will understand what I'm hinting at once you get there."

"And I'm to take Hank out onto that bridge, right?"

"Oh, yeah."

"Who's my contact there?"

"Colonel Dunlap."

Cain stood. "I'll dispatch Houdini this afternoon," he said, opening the door.

"Let me know when it's done. And, my boy . . ."

"What?"

"Enjoy this one."

The yellow wooden bridge extended like a misplaced McDonald's arch across a circular, cement-bottom pond about two hundred feet from the main base camp. Running along either side of the walkway was a handrail fashioned from two long, steel pipes, gleaming now in the sun like a pair of silver snakes. At its apex, the bridge rose twenty feet above the water, which was fifteen feet at its deepest point. Draped to the east side of the bridge, the side facing the gate that allowed entrance to the pond area, was a large Confederate flag.

Concrete, bleached bone-white by the sun, extended

out around the pond like a priest's collar and ran half-way up a fifteen-foot embankment, eventually giving way to another ten feet of burnt-out grass, dirt, rubble, and weeds. Wrapped around the entire setting was an eight-foot-high wire-mesh fence, topped off by a thick, black wire that, according to Colonel Dunlap, had once provided the death current in "Old Sparky," the Kentucky state prison's electric chair.

The pond area had been excavated almost three years ago out of necessity after its two inhabitants—Samson and Hercules—had outgrown their previous home, an old washtub kept in the mess tent. No washtub could possibly house one full-grown alligator, much less two.

Cain and Dunlap spent much of the afternoon entertaining Hank, who was dressed in jeans, a denim shirt, and cowboy boots. Completing the Western ensemble was a red bandana tied around his neck. Hank's drink of choice was straight tequila, and he became louder and more boisterous with each downed shot.

After an hour of listening to Hank expound on the greatness of American movies, Dunlap suggested they take a walk. Hank reluctantly agreed, but only after being persuaded that the subject of their conversation was for his ears only. Cain helped Hank to his feet and led him out of the tent.

"What do you think of that pair down there, Hank?" Dunlap asked, as the three men reached the center of the bridge. "The one lounging on the cement, the larger one—that's Samson. The smaller one is Hercules. Pretty impressive, huh?"

Hank shrugged indifferently, then flicked ashes from a thick cigar. "They're just alligators," he mumbled. "I've seen gators before."

Cain pointed at Hank's pistol. "Nice six-shooter, Hank. What is it? A Colt .45?"

"Yes."

"You're a real cowboy, Hank."

"Exactly like John Wayne," Dunlap said.

"The Duke," Hank said, flipping his cigar into the water below. "I watch all his movies. He is great American."

"Amen, brother," Dunlap said.

Cain put both elbows on the railing and looked down at the water. "Colonel Dunlap, looks to me like Samson and Hercules need to be fed. They appear to be famished."

"Yeah, it's getting close to their chow time."

"What do you think, Hank?" Cain asked. "They look hungry to you?"

"I am not here to discuss alligators," Hank barked, his face beet red and dripping sweat. "You said we were meeting to discuss a different financial arrangement. Why is it going to be different?"

Cain shot a quick glance at Dunlap, giving a slight nod of the head. Dunlap nodded back, then eased closer to Hank's left side. Cain slid a foot closer to Hank on the right, pushed away from the railing, and looked down at the gators.

"Here's the difference, Hank," Cain said. "You're out."

"Out? What? I cannot be out."

"Out, Hank. For good."

Cain and Dunlap, in a perfectly coordinated attack, lunged at Hank, Cain going for the arms, Dunlap for the legs. Hank knew a fraction of a second before the attack that they were coming after him, yet despite his instincts and training, he was powerless to prevent it. Cain and Dunlap were on him in a flash, moving quicker than two NFL linebackers bent on destroying the opposing quarterback, their powerful arms like four pythons, encircling him, applying extreme pressure, squeezing the breath out of his lungs, freezing his arms and legs, pinning them together, rendering them useless.

Lifting him.

Over the railing, out into space, above the water.

Releasing him.

Hank hit the water butt first, went under, staying submerged long enough that Cain and Dunlap both thought he'd died in the fall. "Damn, I hope the bastard survived the plunge," Dunlap said, adding, "Samson and Hercules prefer live prey."

Samson, tail thrashing wildly, shot past Hercules, hitting the water before Hank did. Hercules quickly followed his partner, submerging completely within seconds, disappearing beneath the water like a nightmarish submarine. Moments later, Samson went under, and for an instant, the pond was serene, undisturbed, a postcard picture of bright sun reflecting on still, peaceful waters.

Hank was the first to disturb the calm, coming up, shooting half a body length out of the water, gulping for air, looking around, trying to get his bearings. Once he did, and once he refilled his lungs with oxygen, he began swimming frantically toward the bank opposite where the gators had been lounging.

He made it less than five feet before being pulled under, disappearing in the water like a rock dropped from the bridge. In a split second the pond became a whirlpool, water churning, whipped into a violent frenzy as the two gators bit into Hank's body, then began turning and turning in the classic gator death roll, ripping off huge chunks of flesh, swallowing, going back for more. The water quickly turned dark, bloody red, and small pieces of human tissue and bone soon began to appear on the surface.

"Bastard never screamed once," Dunlap said, admiringly. "Gotta give him credit for that. He handled it just the way John Wayne would have."

The two men watched as a denim-covered arm floated to the top, only to be swallowed whole by Samson. Seconds later, a cowboy boot with Hank's foot still inside, was gulped down by Hercules.

"Damn, I sure wish I'd taken that Colt .45 before we sent him over," Dunlap said, shaking his head. "That was a genuine classic, a collector's item."

"If you want it that bad, jump down there and get it," Cain said.

"I'm crazy but not insane."

Cain laughed. "You know, you just might make general yet."

"Well, my boy, fill me in on the details," Lucas said between sips of Chivas Regal. "Was it as deliciously gory as I imagine it?"

"Not really."

"What was your impression of Samson and Hercules? How did they behave?"

"They were efficient," Cain answered.

"I'm sure they were. And Hank. What did you think of him?"

"I killed him, Lucas. I didn't think about him."

"Did you enjoy yourself?"

"Not particularly. Feeding someone to alligators isn't my style. If he needed to be eliminated, I would have preferred to do it my way."

"My boy, sometimes one jungle predator must give way to another jungle predator. It was my intention for

Hank to suffer greatly and to experience extreme fear prior to his final breath. That would not have happened had I left his termination to you."

"Why Hank? Why take him out? He's not a player in this war."

"There are many wars, my boy."

"What are you into, Lucas?"

Lucas paused for a long time, then said, "Shadows that even you, the great Cain, can never penetrate."

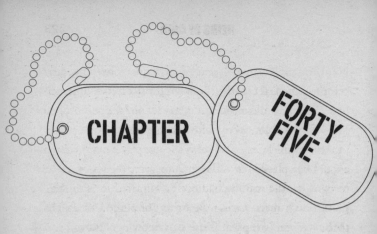

CHAPTER FORTY FIVE

Seneca found the package addressed to him when he arrived at Dr. Nastasia Ivanovna's West 54th Street apartment, along with a note from her saying she was having lunch with a friend from the Russian Embassy and wouldn't be back until after two.

He checked the clock in the study: 12:10. Perfect. Two uninterrupted hours to digest the contents of the package. More than enough time to memorize the details.

Seneca ripped it open and dumped the contents onto the kitchen table. Inside were photographs of five men and a note attached to a much thicker piece of quarter-folded paper. He removed the photos and shuffled through them.

Four of the faces were instantly recognizable; the fifth man was unknown to him. He put the four familiar faces on the table, keeping only the stranger's photo in his hands. He flipped it over. Written on the back was the man's name: Daniel Abraham Cohen. Seneca stared at the face, studied it hard, committed it to memory. Never would he forget what Daniel Cohen looked like. Never. Not even after he killed him.

But Daniel Cohen was only a fringe player in the drama about to be played out. The real stars were the four men he recognized, the men he had been contracted to eliminate. Four foolish men chasing the dream of peace and coexistence in a part of the world that had known only blood and hate for centuries. Men doomed to failure, doomed to learn that no amount of arrogance or perceived power can truly change the tide of history.

Doomed to die.

Seneca smiled, his heart pounding like a drum. When this business was finished, he would stand alone as the world's greatest assassin. There would be no room left for arguments or debate. All others, regardless of past accomplishments, would forever remain in his shadow.

Even the great Cain.

He replaced the photographs, picked up the type-written note, and quickly read its message:

Seneca:

Enclosed are photos of your targets, along with an architect's blueprint of the Cohen estate and two aerial photos of the grounds. Security will be tight but small in number . . . no more than 25 personnel.

Speed is essential. The meeting is set to begin at 10 a.m., Thursday. I've marked the site on the blueprint.

Good luck.

Karl

Seneca wadded the paper into a ball and angrily tossed it onto the tabletop. How dare Karl use the word *luck*. The misguided fool. Luck would play no part in this. Luck is fickle, like most of the women he'd known in his life. Luck cuts both ways, good and bad. Talent, however, is true, like the laws of physics. Talent isn't subject to the winds of caprice.

He smiled. No, Karl. Talent, not luck, is what guarantees success.

And he would be successful. No one could stop him. No one.

Not God, not Cain.

Cain had just finished speaking with Andy Waltz when the phone rang.

"Hello."

"Good morning, my boy. It's good to hear your voice again."

"Lucas."

"Considering how long it's been since we last spoke,

I'm surprised you remember my name."

"It hasn't been that long, Lucas. What . . . three, four days?"

"Given the grave importance of this mission, three or four days is an eternity. It's not like you to keep me in the dark during a crisis. Is there a reason why I've been kept incommunicado?"

"I haven't exactly been sitting on my ass, Lucas. When you get my expense report, you'll see I've been on the move."

Lucas snickered. "My boy, I'm all too familiar with your expense reports. I can hardly wait. So, tell me, what have you learned from your travels?"

"Not much. I'm afraid I've yet to earn my paycheck."

"Don't explode when I ask this. Have you thought of going outside? Maybe use the CIA, FBI, or Homeland Security?"

"Houdini is scrounging for me."

"Ah, yes, Houdini. I should have guessed. A smart move, my boy. He's resourceful and he's accurate."

"He'd better be fast, because my gut tells me the hourglass is about to run out of sand."

"Perhaps I can brighten your day a little," Lucas said. "Rumor has it that our mutual friend is in cahoots with a Russian lady. A rather notorious Russian lady, I might add."

"Dr. Nastasia Ivanovna."

"Well, well, as usual you have downplayed your accomplishments. Please put modesty aside and dazzle me with what you've learned."

"Not much, really. She lives on West 54th Street in Manhattan, and she teaches at Columbia University."

"What led you to her?"

"Simon Buckman made several phone calls to her number. Since Simon didn't impress me as the scholarly type, I could only assume he was calling Seneca."

"Your assumption is correct. Seneca has been staying with her for the better part of two months."

"Tell me about Ivanovna."

"What do you want to know?"

"Is she former KGB?"

"Highest level."

"I'll pay her a visit, see what information I can get out of her."

"Do not underestimate her, my boy. She's a dangerous, deadly lady."

"Wouldn't have it any other way."

"Of that I am sure."

"The grapevine says the president is meeting with Israeli, Palestinian, and Hamas leaders this Saturday," Cain said. "You heard anything about it?"

"No. Should I have?"

"Not really. I just thought you might."

"Come, come, my boy. You are withholding something

from me. Give."

"I heard that rumor, and I was wondering if you knew anything about it. That's all."

"My boy, I have been around you too long to believe that story. However, out of my respect for you, I will pursue it no further. I can only assume that in due time you will share the truth with me. The whole truth."

"The truth is simple, Lucas. If the grapevine is accurate and if we don't find Seneca, we're fucked."

"Crassly stated, but completely accurate, I'm afraid."

"Lucas."

"Yes, my boy."

"It might be wise for you to check the president's itinerary for Saturday. Get it altered, if you can."

"My ability to work miracles does have its limits."

"Make the effort."

"I'll see what I can do."

Seneca folded the architect's blueprint, lit the bottom corner with a cigarette lighter, then dropped it into the kitchen sink. He stood silently, watching the thick paper turn black as the blue-orange flames engulfed it. After two minutes, nothing remained but ashes. He turned on the faucet and washed the charred remains away.

The contents of the package were now stored in

his memory bank. Faces, names, the Cohen estate layout—everything. Nothing had been overlooked. He
memorized the dimensions of every room, including the
guest house and the beach house. Lawn shapes and sizes
were memorized, along with data relating to plumbing,
underground gas and water lines, electrical wiring, and
the height of the wall surrounding the estate.

A simple rule: it's better to know too much rather
than too little.

In this case, Seneca knew he had stored more data
in his memory bank than was necessary. He knew this
because of the red *X* marked on the blueprint. The room
where the meeting was to take place—in the library on
the east side of the house.

Where the large window opened to a picturesque
view of the Atlantic.

He smiled. *Idiots. Don't they know anything about
security? Don't they know to stay away from windows?* He
thought about changing his plan and launching his attack through that very window. It could easily be done.
A rocket-propelled grenade launcher would make hamburger meat out of everyone in the room. But . . . maybe
another time, another job. For this special occasion, he
had something else in mind.

A surprise.

One the whole world would remember.

Forever.

Cain entered his hotel room, sat on the bed, and opened his cell phone. There was one missed call and a message.

"This message is for Michael Collins. Mr. Collins, this is Emily Melendez. You said I should contact you if we found anything else. I know this sounds stupid, but we found a note crumpled up in Simon Buckman's hand. How we missed it, I'll never know. Anyway, the note said July 30, Camp David, 10 a.m. And it ended with these three words. French, I think. I can't pronounce them, so I'll spell it out for you: T-U-E-Z-L-E-M-E-S-S-A-G-E-R. Hope that helps."

CHAPTER FORTY SIX

The doorman was in his mid-twenties and had that familiar forget-this-monkey-costume-I'm-really-an-actor look about him. He was handsome, with a chiseled face, blond hair, a big smile, and sensitive blue eyes. A young, cut-rate version of Robert Redford. He flashed a mouthful of white when he saw Cain approaching.

"You look like a man seeking information," he said.

"As a matter of fact, I am," Cain answered.

"Know how I knew that?"

"How?"

"'Cause you've been eyein' the place since early this morning."

The kid was right. Cain had spent the morning in a coffee shop across from the West 54th Street apartment building. After four hours on his ass and half a dozen cups of coffee, there had been no sign of Nastasia Ivanovna or Seneca.

332

Cain checked the kid's name tag. "You should be a cop, Doug."

"Played one once. *The Sopranos*. Bit part, only a couple of lines. But, hey, I got a paycheck, just like James Gandolfini, only his had a few more zeroes." He opened the door for an elderly woman carrying a shopping bag from Gucci's. Turning back to Cain, he asked, "How can I help you?"

"You know David Rainwater?"

"Nah. Can't say that I do."

"George Armstrong?"

"Sure. Dr. Ivanovna's 'friend.' Lousy fuckin' tipper."

"Is he here now?"

"Nah. He left early this morning, right after I came on duty—7:10, maybe. Had me get his car for him. I heard him tell Dr. Ivanovna he'd be back around six."

"She's out, too?"

"Nah, she's here. She was just getting back from her morning walk when Mr. Armstrong was leaving. That's how I happened to hear him."

Doug stepped away and opened the door for a couple and their two small children. The oldest kid, a boy of about seven, grinned and exchanged a high-five with Doug. The boy's father nodded and handed Doug a crunched-up bill.

"Nice folks," Doug said, walking back toward Cain. "Unlike Mr. Armstrong. He's a sullen, tight-ass bastard, if you want my opinion. Dr. Ivanovna, she's okay. Kinda quiet, but usually pretty nice. For a Russian." He laughed. "That Mr. Armstrong. What is he, an Indian?"

"Cherokee. Listen, Doug, does he have any habits that you know of?"

"Who? Mr. Armstrong?"

"Yeah."

"Habits? You mean, like drugs or alcohol or kinky sex? Stuff like that?"

"No. Routines he follows, certain patterns—that kind of thing."

"Well, when he's here, he runs every night. Regular as clockwork. Up in Central Park. Leaves the building about eleven and usually gets back a couple of hours later. I used to work nights, so that's how I know. Personally, I think he's nuts for running up there at night. I mean, this city ain't that safe, regardless of what the mayor says. Dr. Ivanovna walks in the morning. I told you that already, didn't I?"

"I need to see her," Cain said, "but I don't want you to buzz her."

"I'm not supposed to do that. Could get me in a lot of trouble, you know. Maybe even cost me this gig. And, you know, this is perfect. I have lots of time off to make auditions."

Cain took out a roll of bills and peeled off five twenties. "Will a hundred help ease your conscience?"

Doug smiled and pocketed the cash. "What conscience?

She's on the fifth floor. Apartment 505."

Cain disregarded his old rule and took the elevator to the fifth floor. He found 505, knocked, and stepped back. Seconds later the door opened, a woman's left eye the only thing visible to him.

"Yes? What is it you want?" she said.

"To speak to you."

"Whatever you sell, I don't want. So, please, go away."

Cain pressed his right shoulder against the door and forced it open. Ivanovna backed away, stumbling slightly when she bumped into a small wooden table. Quickly regaining her balance, she gave Cain the coldest smile he'd ever seen. Her dark eyes burned with hatred, but lacked any sign of fear.

"Where's Seneca?" Cain asked.

"I am not familiar with anyone named Seneca."

"No games, please. I haven't the time." He walked past her, into the den. "I want to know where Seneca is and how he plans to take out his intended targets."

"I cannot help you on either count," she said.

"I don't believe you."

The reptilian smile again. "You must be Cain."

"What about it?"

"I've heard of you."

"That's nice. Tell me: where's Seneca?"

"I don't know. He left very early this morning in the car. Said he'd be back late this afternoon. That's all I can tell you. Now, please leave."

"How is he going to eliminate his target?"

"Target? I don't know what you're talking about."

"Sure you do."

"Leave. Now."

"I can make you talk. You know that."

"You Americans are so arrogant. I do not fear you or your threats of torture. I am Russian. We perfected torture."

"There's a big difference in perfecting it and withstanding it. How are you in that department?"

"I will say nothing."

"We'll see." He pointed to a chair. "Have a seat."

She remained standing, her dark eyes locked on his. "I do not take orders from you. Nor do I fear your threats."

He pushed her into the chair. "Where is Seneca?"

"I do not know where he is."

"Tell me all you know about his plan. His target."

"I know nothing of these targets you ask about. This plan."

"And you wouldn't tell me if you did, right?"

She smiled. "No. Under no circumstances would I tell you."

"Funny thing about circumstances. They can be most unpleasant."

"I do not fear you."

"You will."

She rose and moved directly in front of him. "You

are going to kill me, yes?"

"Yes."

"How?"

"Does it matter?"

"Not really."

"Then don't worry about it."

"You are eager to kill me, yes?"

"When will Seneca be back?"

"Will you enjoy killing me?"

"Almost as much as I'll enjoy making you tell me where Seneca is and who his targets are."

"I will tell you nothing."

"You'll tell; then you'll die."

"No. I think I will deny you that pleasure."

Reaching into her pants pocket, she removed a white capsule, put it into her mouth, and swallowed hard. Within seconds her face contorted into a mask of pain and her skin turned an ashen, almost bluish color. Her body shook violently, she slammed against the wall, then slumped forward onto the floor, her eyes still open.

Cain felt for a pulse; there was none. Ivanovna had checked herself out. Kneeling next to the body, he caught a familiar odor. Cyanide. The coward's number one alternative to prolonged pain.

After giving the apartment a perfunctory going-over, which yielded nothing, Cain locked the door and hurried to the elevator.

Outside, Doug was helping a woman load her luggage into the trunk of her Lexus. He saw Cain, looked at his watch, and frowned. "That didn't take long."

"She didn't answer," Cain said. "You sure she's there?"

"I never saw her leave, so, yeah, she should be there. Unless something's wrong."

"Maybe you ought to have someone look in on her. Make sure everything's okay."

"I'll do that."

CHAPTER FORTY SEVEN

The Daniel Cohen estate was located three miles outside of East Hampton on Long Island. It was more of a
compound than an estate, surrounded on three sides by
a ten-foot-high brick wall and by the Atlantic Ocean on
the east side. The extreme security measures had been
deemed necessary by the estate's previous owner, fabled
mobster Meyer Lansky.

Daniel Cohen's father, Isaac, purchased the estate
from Lansky in the mid-1960s. The elder Cohen, a
noted criminal defense attorney, knew Lansky well and
had, on several occasions, successfully represented him
in court. Lansky was that rarest of mob creatures. He
never spent a day behind bars, and he died of old age,
worth a reported half-billion dollars. Isaac Cohen's re-
ward for keeping his celebrated client from behind bars
was this estate. Lansky sold it to Cohen for one thousand dollars.

Daniel Cohen had not followed in his father's footsteps, nor had he remained in contact with the old man's business associates. Despite his father's considerable wealth and influence, Daniel was a self-made man. He graduated from Columbia University, then spent many years living and working in Israel. There he met and married his wife, fought in the Six Day War, and was elected to the Israeli Knesset. After returning to the states in the late '70s he bought a small clothing store from an uncle, eventually turning it into a highly profitable national chain. He also bought several run-down warehouses in Brooklyn, which he converted into luxury apartment buildings and business offices. Both endeavors had made him a very wealthy man.

Daniel Cohen's way of life demanded neither a ten-foot brick wall with electric wiring across the top nor an on-duty guard in the shack at the main entrance. Despite his vast wealth, his life was simple, safe, without controversy or conflict.

But Daniel Cohen hadn't left Israel without learning some important lessons. There were certain times, special moments in history, when security was all that stood between freedom and slavery. If four thousand years of history had taught the Jews anything, it was this: the line between survival and annihilation is often thinner than a blade of grass.

This was, he knew, one of those special moments.

Daniel Cohen smiled when he saw the handsome, dark-haired man drive onto the estate and exit his car. He waved and began walking briskly toward the visitor.

"Hello," Daniel said. "I didn't expect any security personnel until Wednesday morning."

"How do you know I'm part of the security detail?" the man asked.

"Well . . . I'm assuming you are."

"Never assume anything." The dark-haired man removed his sunglasses and extended his right hand. "But your assumption is correct—this time. I'm George Armstrong. From the FBI."

"Well, don't I feel like a complete idiot?" Daniel said. "Being a Jew, I should know better than to take anything for granted."

"Don't beat yourself up. To the average person, security means bolting the front door."

"But with my experience, I should be more aware." Daniel Cohen shook his head. "However, that is another matter and not your concern, is it? Now, young man, how can I be of help?"

George Armstrong pointed toward the main house. "My only concern is the room where the meeting is to take place. That's my sole responsibility. I'll give the room a preliminary going-over today and a more thorough one tomorrow. On Wednesday, when the rest of the security detachment arrives, the entire estate will be covered. Every inch of this estate will be inspected."

"Right this way." Daniel spun on his heels and began marching toward the house.

Daniel Cohen led George Armstrong into the main house, down the front hall, and into the library. Once inside he switched on the light, waved his arm in a grand gesture, and said, "There are more than two thousand books in here, many of which are quite rare. As you can imagine, I'm immensely proud of this collection."

George Armstrong's eyes traveled slowly around the room, photographing images, burning them into his memory bank. The bookshelves, which rose from floor to ceiling, covered three walls. Directly ahead, at the entrance to the room, was a large window that opened to the Atlantic Ocean. In the middle of the room was a long oak table surrounded by eight chairs.

"An impressive room," he said. "But not a good choice from a security standpoint."

"Why not?" Daniel Cohen asked.

"Too much exposure to the outside." George Armstrong pointed to the window. "Easy access for an outside attack."

"It's my understanding that several helicopters will be in use while the meeting is in process."

"There are good helicopters, and there are bad helicopters, if you know what I mean. An open window like this makes sitting ducks of everyone inside."

"Can anything be done?"

"We'll simply have to be extra alert; that's all. And, hopefully, the meeting won't last too long."

Daniel Cohen's face brightened. "I've been informed that if all goes well, the meeting will last less than two hours. The negotiations have been ongoing for many months, so all that remains is for the papers to be signed."

"How did you earn the honor of hosting such an event?"

"The Israeli prime minister and I are old friends," Daniel said, smiling. "We fought together in two wars. Having the meeting here was his idea. I was only too happy to oblige."

"Do you mind telling me the purpose of this meeting?"

"Peace, God willing. An end to the senseless killing. An exchange of prisoners."

George Armstrong barely heard Daniel Cohen's words. His eyes were on one of the bookshelves, which he now realized was lined not with books but with movies. Hundreds of them. He counted the rows. There were ten. Each row was lined with at least fifty movies, all encased in identical dark brown plastic jackets.

George Armstrong turned, smiling. "You must like movies."

"I'm the world's number one movie buff," Daniel

proudly proclaimed. "They're my absolute passion. I spend hours each day watching them. In my humble opinion, the VCR is the single greatest invention in the history of mankind. My only regret is that I didn't invent it."

"All of these are yours?"

"Bought 'em all. That way I don't have to bother taping them off the TV, with all those dreadful commercials."

"Very impressive," George Armstrong said, turning toward the door. "Well, I should be on my way."

"Have you seen everything you need to see? I'll be more than happy to give you the complete tour."

"That won't be necessary. I know exactly what needs to be done."

The two men walked out into the sunlight. Neither man spoke until they were at George Armstrong's car.

"I would imagine a man of your experience can glance at a particular location and see a hundred danger zones," Daniel said. "You probably saw things the rest of us wouldn't see in a million years."

George Armstrong opened his car door and slid into the front seat. He put on his sunglasses, looked up at Daniel Cohen, and smiled.

"Know what's scary?" he said.

"What?"

"A good assassin only needs one danger zone."

"Camp David is the meeting site." Cain pressed the phone close to his ear. "At least, that's the message I got."

"Is that so?" Andy Waltz asked. "And where exactly did you come up with this bit of information?"

"A note found on Simon Buckman." Cain sipped water from a glass. "Wasn't found until they got him to the morgue. We got lucky."

"Think so? Boychick, let me clue you to something. You need to find yourself better sources."

"What do you mean?"

"The location has been changed. It's not going to take place at Camp David. Either Simon got it wrong or he was purposefully misinformed. No way I can know that. What I can tell you for certain is that it ain't happening at Camp David."

Cain set the empty glass on the table. "Okay, so enlighten me. Where is it taking place?"

"A private estate on Long Island."

"Whose estate?"

"Daniel Cohen's," Waltz said.

"You trust your source?"

"Pentagon guy, four stars. He's gold."

"Why the change? Why this Cohen guy's place?"

"Only guessing, but probably for security purposes. Or to better elude the press." Waltz waited several beats, then said, "Are you ready for the really bad news?"

"What?"

"July twenty-eight, not the thirtieth."

"Ah, shit."

"Still consider yourself lucky?"

"What do you know about Daniel Cohen?" Cain asked.

"Owns a chain of clothing stores and about half of Brooklyn. Has more money than Bill Gates."

"What's his story?"

"Don't know much, except that he's clean. My hunch is he's one of those Jews who has finally grown tired of the bloodshed in the Middle East and wants to do something about it. Could be he thinks he's the Messiah. Or maybe he's *meshugge*. Who knows? Your guess is as good as mine."

"I want to know everything about this Cohen guy's estate. I need a map, layout of the house, architect's rendering, aerial photos, anything that might be beneficial. And I need it by tonight."

"You'll have it," Waltz said.

Seneca was ten minutes outside of Manhattan when his cell phone went off.

"Yes?" He immediately recognized the caller's voice. "Karl? Why this call?"

"To warn you to stay away from Ivanovna's place."

"Why?"

"She's dead."

"How?"

"Cyanide."

There was almost a minute of silence before Seneca finally said, "She wouldn't have gone out like that unless she knew she was going to be tortured. Did—?"

"She had a visitor. A man. He came down a few minutes after arriving, said no one answered the door. The manager checked, found her dead."

"This man—did he give his name?"

"No."

"Doesn't matter. I know who he is."

CHAPTER FORTY EIGHT

Cain opened the large brown envelope and pulled out the picture. Attached to the front was a note that said,

Hope this helps. It's not much, but it's the best I could do on short notice.

Houdini

The 8x10 picture was an aerial view of the Cohen estate. At the center of the estate, on the left side of a circular driveway, was the main house. To the north there was a black-bottom swimming pool and a putting green. Approximately thirty yards from the pool were two tennis courts. Another twenty yards or so from the tennis courts was a smaller visitor's cottage. The beach house was nearest to the ocean and separated from the main house by a clump of trees.

Of particular interest to Cain was the snakelike brick wall curling from the top of the picture to the bottom. What caught his attention was a part of the wall on the east side between the beach house and the ocean that had been badly damaged by years of wind and water. A section had crumbled, leaving a gap large enough for a man to climb through.

That would be his point of entry.

Luck. Take it when it comes your way.

He put the picture down, picked up a towel, wrapped it around his eyes, and tied it tightly in the back. Reaching out with his right hand, he switched off the light. He wanted darkness.

Total darkness.

The unyielding darkness a blind man knows.

For it was in absolute darkness, in the strange black world where the ability to move within shadows separated him from all others, that he could find that muddy river again. Where he could hear the voices of men afraid to speak, yet unable to remain silent.

Men awed by the wonder of what they had just witnessed.

By what the great Cain had done.

He sat still in the darkness, feeling his heart beat, and listened.

They were nearing now, closing in on his shadow world, eyes wide and fearful and disbelieving.

He listened.

And listened.

"*Jesus God, did you see that?*"

"*Yeah, I saw.*"

"*The look. Did you see the look in his eyes?*"

"*I saw, I saw. The little dink bastard never knew what was happening.*"

"*No, not him, not the dink. The captain. Did you see his eyes while he was wasting the little motherfucker?*"

"*No, I wasn't watching his eyes.*"

"*I've never seen anything like that before. Scary. Really scary. And cold, like a cobra or something. Like a hungry animal. I'm tellin' you, it was spooky.*"

"*Forget his eyes, man. Did you see that dink's head tumble into the river? It hit the water so hard it bounced.*"

"*Look at the captain now.*"

"*Yeah, he's out there, man. Out there in that killer's zone.*"

"*First kill, sir?*"

"*Forget it, man, he's too far out there to hear you.*"

"*First kill, sir?*"

"*I'm tellin' you to forget it. He's not hearing you.*"

"*First kill, sir?*"

An hour later, Cain loosened the towel and let it fall into his lap. Slowly, he stood, eyes still closed, and walked into the bathroom. Without hesitation, he switched on the light.

And didn't blink.

With the flick of a switch, he had gone from absolute darkness to glaring brightness, yet he had not so much as blinked. Others would have. Others would have shielded their faces, covered their eyes, been forced by the abrupt change to wait until their eyes made the adjustment.

But he was Cain, and for him the darkness, that shadowy world where he thrived, contained more light than a hundred suns.

He stared at his reflection in the mirror. At his eyes. They were steel gray.

He switched off the light and stood once again in the familiar darkness.

Seneca was close.

So was blood time.

Cain smiled.

He was ready.

CHAPTER FORTY NINE

Carrying two large paper sacks, one under each arm, Seneca entered the tiny apartment. He moved swiftly to the kitchen, setting the cumbersome bags on a small wooden table. He went back to the door, checking to make sure it was locked. After filling a glass with water and drinking it, he turned on the kitchen light, took off his shirt, yanked a chair away from the table, and sat down.

Now ready to prepare his surprise, he picked up the heavier of the two sacks, then dumped its contents onto the table. Five movies purchased from a Blockbuster on 42nd Street. He quickly opened the large protective jackets, removed the cassettes, and tossed them into a trash can. Taking a ruler, he measured one of the five identical jackets: nine and a half inches by six and a half inches by one and a half inches.

Absolutely perfect for what he had in mind.

Next, he emptied the second sack. It contained a common size D battery, a wristwatch, and a smaller sack filled with ball bearings and nails.

The other two items, the ones at the heart of his plan, he already had: the plastic explosive Composition C-4 and a blasting cap.

He took a block of the light brown puttylike C-4 and began molding it into one of the movie cassette jackets. When the jacket was half full, he took ten ball bearings and three razor blades, carefully placing them into the smoothed-down layer of C-4. Still not completely satisfied, he grabbed his empty glass and went to the sink. Using a hammer, he tapped the glass until it shattered. He sifted out the five largest slivers and placed them on top of the plastic. Satisfied with this added touch, he filled the remainder of the jacket with C-4 and closed it.

Following the same routine, he filled three more jackets. In one he used several large nails rather than glass. In another he used the rusty tips taken from some darts he found in one of the kitchen drawers. Variation always made things more interesting.

When the four jackets met his approval, he took a cloth and carefully wiped them clean. He picked them up, two in each hand, and lined them against the wall. Time now for a memory check.

He looked at the four white identifying labels on the edge of each jacket, then without hesitation arranged them in the proper order, from left to right.

All About Eve, Anatomy of a Murder, Animal House,

Annie Hall.

Reaching into his pants pocket he took out a small piece of paper and read the words he had written on it. His memory had served him well. The movies were in the same order as the ones in Daniel Cohen's library. Third row, numbers thirteen through sixteen.

Head-high and close to those seated at the table.

He couldn't have asked for more.

Except to be there when it happened.

That's why explosives weren't his preferred method of killing. Too distant, too impersonal. Also, the risk of failure was too high, although at this close range that wasn't likely. Unlike Arlington, where too much distance separated the bomb from the victims. Where a lucky bitch just happened to be in the walk-in freezer when the blast went off.

No, given the choice, he would be in the room, Uzi in one hand, knife in the other, waiting for the distinguished guests to arrive. That way there would be no risk of failure. They would die, up close, looking him squarely in the eye. Exactly the way he liked it.

He opened the fifth jacket, the one appropriately marked *Apocalypse Now*, and filled it half full with C-4. Taking the battery, he taped it to the left side of the top half. On the right side he taped the wristwatch, which had been pre-set for 10:30 a.m. on Thursday, July 28. All that remained was to place the blasting cap securely into the C-4, then run the small piece of wire from the watch to the battery to the blasting cap.

When he finished, he closed the jacket, cleaned it with the rag, and placed it in its proper place. To the right. Number seventeen.

He then took a piece of thin wire and twice wrapped it around the five movie jackets, binding them together. This procedure troubled him—none of Cohen's movies were bound into groups—but he had no other choice. The five jackets needed to be secured in order to ensure detonation and to provide maximum killing effect.

He stood, backed away, and looked at the containers lined against the wall. From a distance of less than five feet, the thin black wire was virtually invisible. For the wire to be seen, someone would have to be looking for it.

No one would be.

Seneca arrived at the Cohen estate a few minutes before 7:00 a.m. He parked at the end of the street and observed the area around the front gate. After fifteen minutes, he concluded that no military personnel were present. Confident the area was safe, he drove Dr. Ivanovna's Honda Civic past the vacant guard shack and onto the estate grounds.

Daniel Cohen and a slender white-haired woman

emerged from the main house and walked toward the tennis courts. He carried two rackets under his left arm and a Prince tennis bag in his right hand. He grinned and waved when he saw Seneca approaching.

"I was wondering when you'd be back," Daniel said, putting the bag down. He turned to the woman and put his hand on her shoulder. "Honey, this is the fella I was telling you about. He's just about the most observant man I've ever met."

She smiled and extended her hand. "I'm Anna Cohen, Daniel's wife. It's a pleasure to meet you. It seems you made quite an impression on my husband. Believe me, Daniel isn't easily impressed. However, the impression you made wasn't sufficient enough for him to remember your name."

"George Armstrong."

Anna studied him closely. "Do you mind if I ask you your heritage?"

"American Indian. Cherokee."

"An original American. That's quite a rarity these days. I hope you're not offended by my inquisitiveness. It's only that I have a great interest in different nationalities. Probably stems from being Jewish."

"I'm not offended."

"You are, I'm sure, aware of the great irony attached to your name," Anna said. "George Armstrong Custer. Not a particular favorite among American Indians, I wouldn't think."

"If every U.S. Army general was like Custer, we'd still have our land," Seneca said.

Anna laughed out loud. "Yes, I suppose you would."

Daniel Cohen gave his wife a hug. "In case you haven't guessed, my wife taught American history in high school for thirty years. And like every history teacher I ever knew, she'll wear you out with boring facts."

"Just like I'm gonna wear you out on the tennis court," Anna said. She smiled at Seneca. "He hasn't taken a set from me in two years."

"I absolutely detest a braggart, don't you?" Daniel said to Seneca. "Even when what she says is the truth. Young man, you go ahead and do what you have to do. The front door is unlocked. If you need me for anything at all, don't be afraid to give a yell. The way she roughs me up, chances are I'll need a break."

Seneca waited until the couple was out of sight before opening the car trunk and removing the small leather bag. He opened it quickly, double-checked the contents, and closed it. Inside were five movie jackets and a large knife. Just in case.

The library was dark, but not unoccupied. A black woman was on her knees washing the baseboard in front of the big window. She jumped when he entered the room.

"Lordy, lordy, child, you scared me," she said, her hand over her heart. "I wasn't expecting anyone."

"I'm from security," he answered. "I'm here to check the library."

"Yes, sir, you go right ahead. I can come back and finish this later." She walked to the door. "How long before I should come back?"

"About an hour."

Seneca waited ten minutes before locking the door. He pulled the curtains and flicked on the light. Without hesitating, he located the five movies that were to be replaced. He opened the bag and removed the five plastic containers. Time for one last check, one final comparison to make sure his five were in the exact order of the original five. He took his five and held them directly beneath the five lined up on the shelf. Slowly, his eyes went from top to bottom, checking the order.

All About Eve, Anatomy of a Murder, Animal House, Annie Hall, Apocalypse Now.

Perfect.

He removed the five from the shelf and dumped them into the bag. Carefully, he filled the empty spaces with his five. Stepping back, he looked at the shelf. Nothing was different. He moved closer and looked for the wire binding the bomb together. It was invisible to the naked eye.

Satisfied, he turned and paced off the distance between the bomb and the table where the principals would be sitting. Just over five feet.

They would never know what hit them.

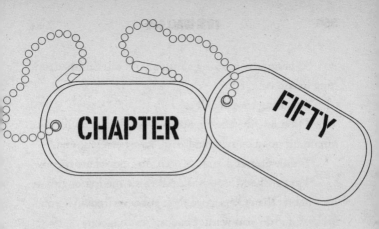

CHAPTER FIFTY

Andy Waltz entered his Bank Street apartment shortly before 11 p.m. He switched on the light, tossed a handful of magazines onto the sofa, loosened his tie, and went into the kitchen to mix a drink. Jameson and Diet Coke, his drink of choice following an exceptionally rough day at work. And today had been one of the roughest.

He stirred and sipped. The Jameson was smooth as silk and hit the spot. After dropping in another ice cube, he turned off the light and went back into the den.

Where he found himself staring into a pair of dark, familiar eyes.

Seneca.

"How'd you get in?" Waltz asked, backing away.

"That's a rather lame question coming from a gifted orator like you."

"Considering my surprise, it's the best I could come up with."

"What's so surprising about an old war buddy dropping in to visit a fellow vet?"

"Breaking in, I'd call it."

"Dropping in, breaking in—call it what you will. The important point is, two old friends have been reunited."

"We were never friends, Seneca. You didn't have friends."

"I'm crushed, Houdini. All this time I thought we were tighter than O.J.'s glove. You just never know, do you?"

"What do you want, Seneca?"

"Why are you shaking?"

"Because you're a scary fuck; that's why. I repeat: what do you want?"

"You know the answer to that one."

"No, I don't."

"Where's Cain?"

"Cain? How would I know? I haven't seen or heard from him in ten years."

"Is that right? Then, why is it that I don't believe you?" Seneca reached behind him and pulled out his knife. He pointed toward the sofa, motioning for Waltz to sit. "One more time, Houdini. Where's Cain? And don't insult my intelligence by saying you don't know."

"One of the hotels uptown. I'm not certain which one."

"Not good enough."

Seneca grabbed Waltz's hair, pulled his head back, and placed the tip of the knife against his throat.

"Ask yourself this: is Cain worth dying for?"

"You'll kill me either way," Waltz managed to whisper. "So why should I tell you?"

"Because maybe I've become a nice guy over the years."

"You? Nice? Don't insult my intelligence."

"You've got guts, Houdini. I'll give you that. An admirable trait."

Seneca picked up a cell phone from the table and handed it to Waltz. "Call Cain," he ordered. "Tell him to meet you in Central Park in an hour. By the carousel."

"Cain's not stupid. He'd know something's wrong."

Seneca pressed the knife harder against Waltz's throat, drawing blood. He pulled the knife away and flashed the bloody blade in front of Waltz's eyes.

"Convince him, and maybe I'll let you live."

CHAPTER FIFTY ONE

Waltz's eyes scanned right to left. He listened. Nothing. Only darkness and silence.

And the thumping of his own heart.

Seneca's knife pressed against his back. Waltz fought hard to keep from wetting his pants.

"It's 12:50. He's not gonna show."

"He's already here, Houdini. Out there, somewhere in that darkness. He only needs a little incentive to join us."

"Incentive? What incentive?"

Seneca grabbed Waltz and put the knife against his neck. "Watching me kill your sorry Jew ass."

"Come on, Seneca, cut me a break."

"Don't beg, Houdini. It's beneath you."

Seneca slammed Waltz to the ground, pressed a knee hard against his chest, and drew the knife back. "Looks like your big hero let you down this time, Houdini. Sorry about that."

"Seneca." A voice—*his* voice—coming from the trees.

Seneca jumped to his feet, took two steps forward, and let his eyes search the darkness. For nearly a minute there was total silence and no movement. Even the wind had vanished. Waltz would later say it was as if time stopped.

After a few more seconds, the outline of a man began to take shape within the shadows. The figure moved forward several steps, stopping at the line dividing darkness from light, his face still hidden from view.

The silence seemed to last forever.

Finally, it was broken by the man in the shadows.

"Been a long time, Seneca."

"Is that you, Cain?" Seneca laughed. "Well, kiss my Cherokee ass. Cain. The great Cain. The big man himself. I knew you'd show up."

"How could I disappoint a wonderful guy like you?"

"No flattery, please, Cain. It's not you." Seneca took a step forward. "I've been expecting you for quite a while."

"Is that so?"

"Ever since I heard what you did to Deke. Not a very nice thing for you to do, Cain."

"What you did to Cardinal wasn't nice either."

"*Had* done to Cardinal. I would never have fucked things up like Deke did. Sloppy bastard."

"You're sloppy, too, Seneca. Leaving a survivor in

Arlington. Terribly amateurish for someone with your reputation."

"Horseshit explosives. Never did like them."

"Is that what you're using tomorrow? Explosives?"

"Don't have a clue what you're talking about."

"Playing dumb isn't your style, Seneca."

"Okay, if you're so smart, Cain, you fill me in."

"Long Island. Cohen estate. How'd I do?"

"You've done your homework. I'm impressed, Cain. But what else should I expect from a legend? Explosives it will be; C-4 to be exact. Not my preference, but under the circumstances, the best I could come up with."

"It won't happen."

"Who's gonna stop it? You?"

"Yeah, me."

Seneca laughed. "You've been away too long. Things change; legends fade. Your time has passed."

"You trying to scare me or convince yourself? Because I'm catching a drift of fear coming my way."

"Save the psychology, Cain. That shit won't work on me."

"I don't need psychology to take you out, Seneca. I don't need anything. Just these hands."

Seneca reached out, hooked his arm around Waltz's neck, and placed the tip of the blade against his throat. "First, I'm gonna make you watch your friend die, then I'm gonna take care of you and your fucking legend."

"Kill him. He means nothing to me," Cain said.

"You'd give up your little buddy that easily? What's that say about friendship?"

"Be done with him, Seneca. Then you can come for me."

"I'll give you credit, Cain. You've never given a damn about who gets sacrificed during a mission. That's one of the few qualities I admire about you."

Cain stepped out of the shadows and into the light.

Upon seeing Cain, Seneca pushed Waltz to the ground and moved forward, holding the knife in front of him. "To hell with Houdini. It's you I want."

"Here I am."

"You have one of those death cards with you?" Seneca asked. "The ace of spades?"

Cain smiled. He knew. Seneca was afraid.

"My last one. Just for you."

Seneca gripped the knife tightly and began to creep toward the shadows.

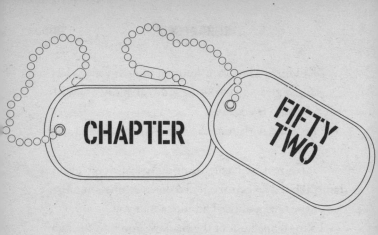

CHAPTER FIFTY TWO

Cain seldom considered a man with a knife to be a serious threat. Unless the opponent launched a surprise attack from behind, in which case the situation could get dicey, the knife wielder had little chance of success. Even an opponent with Seneca's experience and gift for killing.

A man with a knife invariably makes two fatal mistakes. First, he concentrates totally on the use of his weapon, thus forgetting completely his other killing tools—hands, feet, fingers, head, teeth. Second, by assuming his opponent's concentration is focused only on defending against the knife, he underestimates his opponent's offensive abilities. Those two miscalculations usually spell death for the man whose weapon of choice is the knife.

In all his years in this business, Cain couldn't recall one blade-happy assassin who lived to retirement age.

Cain had suspected from the beginning that Seneca would ultimately prove to be no better than ordinary.

The Indian was deadly but only on his own terms. He was a classic bully, one who lacked the ability to improvise or ad-lib. His weakness: not being able to vary his game when the script demanded sudden change. In the final analysis, Seneca's greatest gift was selectivity: the ability to choose the right opponent and the right moment.

Unlike now, when the opponent and the moment chose him.

Seneca made his first move when he was still ten feet away. He came at Cain quickly, slashing right to left. It was, Cain thought, a weak and poorly executed opening gambit, certainly not one worthy of an assassin of Seneca's repute. Or one Cain had taught.

Cain crouched, pivoted slightly to his left to avoid the knife, parried the weapon downward, and sent his elbow deep into Seneca's kidney.

The blow achieved two critical results. It drove the air from Seneca's lungs and momentarily cost the Indian his balance.

In that tiny fraction of a second, Cain established a huge—perhaps an insurmountable—advantage: he gained immediate control of the situation. With such an early edge, only the biggest error of his career could cost him his life.

And the great Cain didn't make errors.

Not during blood time.

Moving slightly to his left, he squared his body, then snapped a kick that found Seneca's ribs. Cain followed with a blow aimed at the neck, and although it missed its intended mark, the carotid artery, by less than an inch, it had enough force to send Seneca crashing to the ground.

The Indian grunted loudly, rolled over several times, spit up a mouthful of blood, then began a desperate life-and-death struggle to get to his feet.

He never made it.

In rapid succession, Cain executed four moves with deadly precision.

First, he drove his foot into Seneca's groin.

Second, he grabbed the knife arm just above the wrist with his left hand, hooked his right forearm behind Seneca's elbow, and then in a single, powerful move, snapped the Indian's once-deadly arm like plastic. Seneca's screams pierced the night.

Third, he took Seneca by the shoulders and pulled him up into a standing position. With all the force he could muster, Cain smashed his open right palm into Seneca's chest, sending vibrating shock waves through the chest cavity that in all probability stopped the Indian's heart.

Fourth, he drew his right hand back, then slammed a judo chop onto the bridge of Seneca's nose, driving bone and cartilage into brain.

Seneca slumped to the ground, dead. Cain knelt behind him and felt for a pulse. He couldn't find one.

Although Cain was certain the Indian was dead, there was yet one final move to be executed.

For insurance.

He rolled Seneca over onto his stomach, placed a knee in the middle of his back, cupped him under the chin, and gave a quick, strong backward pull. The crunching sound of breaking bone echoed in the still night air.

Never leave an opponent breathing.

Cain stood and walked quickly toward Waltz. "Hey, Houdini, thanks for the help. I appreciate it."

"You kidding? I'm a hustler, not a fighter. No way I was about to get involved in that brawl."

"Let's go before someone shows up."

Waltz stared down at Seneca's lifeless body. "The fucking bastard made me set this up. I had no other choice."

"I know. Don't worry about it."

"Hey, Cain, you didn't really mean it when you told Seneca to kill me, that I meant nothing to you, did you?"

Cain laughed. "Every word."

"Serious?"

"If I hadn't said it, he would have killed you," Cain answered. "But when I said I didn't care, he didn't care."

"Forgive me, but it was somewhat disconcerting to have a crazy fucking Indian holding a knife to my throat and hear a good friend tell him to go ahead and use it. You can understand why I almost crapped my pants."

"Perfectly."

"Where to now?" Waltz asked.

"You're going home. I'm heading to Long Island."

CHAPTER FIFTY THREE

Sunrise was less than an hour away when Cain parked his car a short distance from the Cohen estate. He shut off the motor and got out. Through the misty night, he saw the helicopter circling above the compound. The chopper, with its powerful searchlight, could be a problem. To reach his final destination would require an exposed fifty-yard sprint from the wall to the wooded area near the main house. He had to hold off making that dash until the light was aimed out over the ocean.

There were, he knew, simpler, safer options than the one he had in mind. Why not choose one of them? Why not drive to the front gate now, alert security, tell them about the bomb, and let them handle it? Or wait until full daylight, then approach the estate and inform security?

Safer choices, perhaps, but not necessarily wise ones. For starters, personnel deployed for this mission had surely been ordered to shoot first, identify later. This was a take-no-chances situation. A no-mistakes-allowed situation. The men would have been warned to not let any unidentified vehicle get close as it might contain explosives: death coming at you on four wheels in the form of a deadly, improvised explosive device. That was one of the hard lessons learned in Iraq. Everything, and everyone, was a potential IED.

Then there was the issue of trust, a factor he never overlooked or discounted during any mission. How could he be certain all security personnel were righteous? What guarantee did he have that one trigger-happy traitor hadn't been planted within the group guarding the estate, ready to silence any dissenting voice? It's not something Seneca would have done, but Seneca was only the executioner, not the mastermind behind the plan. Whoever had orchestrated this assassination would have put in place several contingencies, and the first would be to take out any unknown interloper.

No, Cain would do it the hard way. *His* way. As always. Alone and coming out of the shadows.

He cut through to the beach and headed north. The helicopter, which was now well out over the ocean, was not a factor at this point and wouldn't be for several minutes. Walking briskly, he reached his point of entry in less than five minutes. The decayed section was wide enough for him to slip through. The only danger was noise. To enter meant climbing over a caved-in section, almost certainly sending loose stones falling to the ground. But behind him was the ocean, which should provide enough background noise to drown out the sound of falling rubble.

At this stage, it didn't matter. Risks were a non-factor. He had to move.

Cain lifted himself up and looked over the wall. He saw nothing, heard plenty. Footsteps, two men, thirty to forty yards to his right. An animal, most likely a squirrel, in a tree no more than twenty yards away. The static of a walkie-talkie closer to the house.

After scaling the wall, he eased himself down to the ground and listened again. No new sounds. Next, he looked up at the sky and found the helicopter. It was moving in the direction of the estate, with the searchlight aimed away from him. He took a deep breath, let it out slowly, then began his sprint toward the big house.

Reaching the wooded area, he knelt behind a tree and surveyed the scene. There were at least eight men wandering around the back part of the estate. Six were standing within a few feet of each other at a safe distance to his right. The remaining two were approximately twenty yards apart, one walking toward him, the other at the back door.

The approaching man posed no problem. Cain could easily avoid him. However, that might not be the case with the man at the door. That situation was much trickier.

Although Cain had no taste for killing one of his own, if it came to that, he would.

It wouldn't be the first time.

Cain moved to within ten feet of the approaching soldier, stopped, and waited until the man passed. He continued creeping forward until he came to the edge of the wooded area. The G.I. guarding the door paced nervously back and forth, stopped, yawned a couple of times, shook his head in an effort to stay awake, and then began pacing again. He wore an automatic pistol on his hip and carried an M16 in his right hand.

Cain had no choice but to kill the young soldier. It was his only option if he hoped to gain entrance into the house. And he had to do it now, in a one-on-one situation. The lone soldier would be no match, but that situation could change if he delayed. The others were sure to return within minutes, and he wasn't keen on a one-against-eight confrontation.

A second factor brought on a sense of urgency—the sun. It was beginning to edge its way over the rim of the horizon. In less than fifteen minutes, his cloak of darkness would be completely swallowed up by daylight.

Cain reminded himself to take out the young soldier as painlessly as possible. A sudden snap of the neck, and it would be over for the young man in a fraction of a second. An unfortunate casualty in a war he played no part in.

Cain picked several pebbles from the ground, found one he liked, then quietly dropped the others. He smiled. For all his greatness, for all his cunning, he was resorting to the oldest trick in the book—tossing a rock against a wall to draw the opponent's attention, then moving in for the kill.

But the soldier got lucky.

Nature called.

He looked around, rested his M16 against the house, walked toward the wall, and disappeared into the darkness.

When Cain heard the unmistakable sound of a man urinating, he dashed toward the back door, turned the knob, and went inside. The downstairs area, where the library was located, was dark and empty. Security, such as it was, consisted of the eight men out back, an equal number at the front, and the helicopter. The main security force wouldn't begin arriving until an hour or so after sunrise. By then he'd be long gone, provided all went well.

One look inside the library, and he knew this was where the meeting would be conducted. This conclusion was based on the arrangement of the furniture, the recording equipment, and the lights. There was a long oak table in the middle of the room, eight chairs, four television cameras set to record the occasion. This was the place, all right.

Which also meant the explosives had to be here.

He needed light. Without it, finding the bomb

quickly would be extremely difficult. But that wasn't possible. Light would draw the soldiers like fireflies. He played with the idea of opening the curtain covering the big window. But that, too, was a flawed and dangerous notion. Ultimately, he knew, this mission, like so many others, would have to be played out in his dark, shadowy world.

In a very real sense, it would also be played out in Seneca's mind. For there, Cain knew, he would find the clues to where the explosives were hidden. He had to think like the Indian, put himself in the Indian's shoes, become the Indian.

Cain always felt like he knew his men better than they knew themselves. That included Seneca. Now was the time to prove it. He would enter Seneca's mind, track his thought process by asking basic questions.

What explosives were being used?

Composition C-4.

Why C-4?

It's a putty-like substance that can be molded to fit any container.

How many primary targets?

Four.

Where would they be located?

Sitting at the table.

Which end?

Judging from the position of the cameras, the end nearest the big window.

What part of the body is most vulnerable to a mortal wound?
The head.
When a man is seated, how far is his head from the floor?
Approximately four to four and a half feet.

Cain sat in the chair at the head of the table, where, most likely, the president would be seated. In the stillness, he listened, hoping to hear the sound of a timer ticking. All he heard was the silence.

He turned and looked to his right.

Movies.

He looked to his left.

Books.

Straight ahead.

More books.

Eyes to the right again.

The movies.

The realization exploded like a mortar shell inside him.

He knew.

The explosives were in the movie jackets. Had to be. It was Seneca. It was perfect. And a man sitting in this chair, at this table, had no chance of surviving a blast at this range.

The C-4 was in the movie jackets. But which ones? And how to find them in the darkness? Cain weighed his options. Should he turn on a light and take his chances? No. Without question, security had been told to shoot first and check IDs later. As haphazard as those young guys outside were, one of them would probably get lucky and score a hit.

Should he lose himself inside the house, wait until the president and the others arrived, and then make an appearance? On the surface, that wasn't a bad idea. He and the president had met on several occasions, so they weren't strangers. But the plan had a major flaw: he'd probably be riddled with bullets before the president recognized him.

The only alternative was to locate the explosives now. But how? For once, he cursed the darkness.

What he needed was a break, a piece of luck—anything that swayed things in his favor.

Then it happened. Just like that.

Anna Cohen came into the library.

Cain had been aware of her every movement from the time she got out of bed until she entered the library. He'd heard her open the bedroom door, use the toilet, and then come down the stairs. He was behind the door when she walked in.

Even before she was anywhere close to flicking on the small table lamp, Cain grabbed her from behind with his left arm and covered her mouth with his right hand. He held her as securely as he could without causing pain.

"You must listen to me, and you must believe what I tell you," Cain whispered into her left ear. "If you don't, everyone at the meeting will be killed. Do you understand?"

Anna Cohen, eyes wide with fear and confusion,

nodded her head.

"I'm going to remove my hand. If you elect to scream, several things will happen. First, I will break your neck. Second, those bozos outside will race in here and kill me. Third, the president and your husband and everyone else in this house will be blown to tiny bits. Understand?"

Anna Cohen nodded her head again.

Cain lifted his hand away from her mouth and turned her toward him. "My name is Cain. I'm with military intelligence. There is a bomb in this room, and we have less than two hours to find and defuse it."

"A bomb? How could a bomb have been placed in this room? By whom?"

"An Indian who probably told you his name was George Armstrong."

"Yes, a man with that name was here. Twice, in fact. He also said he was from security."

"He was a paid assassin. He's dead now."

"Dead? How do you know this?"

"I killed him."

Anna Cohen's body shuddered. "And how do I know you won't kill me?"

"If I wanted to kill you, you'd already be dead."

"And you're positive there's a bomb in this room?"

"Yes."

"All right. What can I do to help?"

"Who's the movie buff?"

"What?"

"The movies. Who collects them?"

"My husband. Why?"

"Is he here?"

"Yes, he's upstairs, sleeping."

"Go wake him. Get him down here as fast as possible."

"What shall I tell him?"

"Whatever it takes to get him down here without alerting the men outside."

"Wouldn't it be better to tell them? To use them as a resource? That way, we'd have a better chance of finding the bomb."

"It would only create chaos and confusion. It's better if I do it alone. If that doesn't work, we'll consider other options. Now, hurry and get your husband."

Anna Cohen left the room and scampered up the stairs. Cain went to the big window and peeked through the curtains. The eight men outside, oblivious to the fact that their wall of security had been penetrated, silently went about their business.

Five minutes later Anna Cohen returned, followed closely by her husband.

"What's this nonsense about a bomb?" Daniel Cohen growled, tightening the sash on his bathrobe. "That's a ludicrous notion."

"I believe him," Anna said, firmly. "And I think you should, too."

"Where is the Indian? Why isn't he here?"

"He was an assassin, dear. He planted the bomb."

"He—Are you certain?"

"Yes." Anna nodded toward Cain. "We should do what this gentleman says."

Cohen looked at his wife, then at Cain. His expression was one of fear and concern and disbelief. "Okay, young man, if my wife believes you, that's good enough for me. Tell me what you need."

Cain walked to the far end of the table and pointed to the section of the wall where the movies were located. "I'm convinced the explosives are here. I want you to tell me if anything looks different."

"This is a huge house. What makes you think the bomb is in this particular room?" Cohen asked.

"Why not? The president will be seated here, with the others in those three chairs. The best position for the explosives is here." Cain pointed to the wall of movies. "And the protective jackets are perfect for housing a plastic explosive like C-4."

"Plastic explosives?" Anna muttered. "*Oy vey.*"

"The bomb is here, in this room," Cain said. "Seneca wouldn't have placed it anywhere else."

"Wait a second," Daniel Cohen said. He started to open a desk drawer, hesitated and looked at Cain. "Is it safe to open this drawer?"

"Yes. The bomb is in one of the movies."

Daniel opened the drawer, took out a small penlight and handed it to Cain. "This might help."

After climbing onto a small metal ladder, Daniel began his search at the top shelf, moving slowly from left to right, occasionally stopping, tilting his head slightly as he studied each movie jacket. He worked his way down the shelf, repeating the procedure for all ten rows. Then he went through it a second time. And a third.

"I can't find anything," Daniel said, shaking his head. "My eyes aren't what they used to be, so you might want to take a look. Maybe you can spot something I missed."

Cain had no reason to look. His eyes, from several feet away, had discovered the bomb two minutes earlier.

Taking the penlight from Daniel, Cain shone it on the third row up from the floor. "Here's your bomb," he said.

"Where?" Daniel asked, climbing down the ladder. His wife moved between the two men.

"See this thin piece of wire?"

Daniel shook his head. "No, I'm afraid I don't."

Cain held the penlight at eye level and angled the beam downward. "Now can you see it?"

"Yes, I do. Clear as day. How did I miss it?" Daniel stepped back, only now realizing the gravity of the situation. Hugging his wife, he repeated, "How did I miss it?"

"It's almost impossible to see head-on. I merely

happened to see it when the light hit it from an angle."

Daniel said, "We would have been killed, and the dream of peace would have died with us."

"Peace is just that, Daniel—a dream," Anna said, her tone angry and bitter. "I doubt the Messiah can end the hatred and the killing."

"There *must* be peace," Daniel said, tears filling his eyes. "And we cannot wait for the Messiah. We have already waited too long for him."

Anna gently touched her husband's arm, then turned to Cain. "Is the wire some sort of fuse?"

"No, it's simply there to connect the jackets. To make sure they all ignite when the timer goes off. My guess is that the timer, battery, and dynamite cap are in this one."

Cain pointed to the jacket marked *Apocalypse Now*.

"My God! What kind of a world do we live in?" Anna Cohen exclaimed, anger rising in her voice. "What are we becoming?"

"Will it be difficult to defuse?" asked Daniel.

"No. This bomb is efficient, but very simple. Explosives weren't Seneca's forte."

"Seneca?" Anna asked. "That was his name?"

"Code name."

"Code name," she repeated. "And you . . . do you have . . ." She shook her head. "Cain. Of course. The first assassin."

Cain carefully removed the five movies from the shelf and set them on the table. He unwound the piece of wire, separated them, picked up the one marked *Apocalypse Now,* and held it to his ear. After listening for several seconds, he put the jacket against Daniel's ear. "Hear that?"

"Yes, yes, I do," Daniel answered. "Sounds like a watch."

"It is."

Cain opened the jacket and removed the dynamite cap from the plastic. Next, he pulled the wire from the tip of the dynamite cap. Finally, he unwound the length of wire that connected the battery and the wristwatch. It took him less than thirty seconds to render the bomb harmless.

"It's hard to believe something like this could be so deadly," Daniel Cohen said, shaking his head. His body shuddered with fear as he stared at the bomb. "Such destructive force in so small a package."

"It can be terribly nasty," Cain said. "Knowing Seneca, I imagine he added a few extra touches."

Cain opened the jacket marked *Animal House.* Buried in the plastic were ball bearings and slivers of glass.

"In the name of . . ." Anna Cohen's voice trailed off, leaving her thoughts unfinished.

Cain opened the curtains six inches and looked outside. The sun had not yet fulfilled its early promise, leaving the morning dark and gloomy. That would make his escape much easier. So would the placement of the eight soldiers, who were now standing together near the beach house, talking, laughing.

He was thankful they weren't assigned to protect him.

"Do you have a pen and a piece of paper?" he asked, closing the curtains.

"Yes, just a second." Anna moved quickly to the desk, took a sheet of paper and a ballpoint pen from the top drawer, and handed it to him.

Cain leaned over the table and scribbled a brief message. When he finished, he folded the paper and handed it to Daniel.

"Tell the president what happened here," Cain said. "And give him that note."

"Why can't you tell him yourself?" Daniel asked.

"I won't be here."

"Why?'

"Because I have one more stop to make."

CHAPTER FIFTY FOUR

It was 8:00 p.m. when Cain steered his car into Lucas White's driveway.

A teenage boy dressed in red Nike sweats listened to his iPod as he walked crisply down the street. His movements, in time with the music he was hearing, were spirited, almost dancelike. He smiled and waved as he passed by the car.

Cain sat still, feeling very weary, very alone. He laid his head back and rubbed his eyes. Only now did he realize it had been days since he'd last slept.

At moments like this, when severe melancholy and fatigue held sway, he relied on nature's beauty to elevate his sagging spirits. The ocean, a chirping bird, the wind, a soft rain. They were his usual weapons against despair.

But in those truly dark moments, like now, when his inner pain reached its maximum level, he always counted on the sunset to restore his soul. That was his ultimate

385

defense in the fight against despair. There was nothing he loved more than the sunset. Climbing out of the car, he looked to the west, where the fading bright orange sun dominated a fiery crimson sky.

He felt nothing.

No relief, no uplifting of his spirit, no hint of joy.

Nothing except a deep, overwhelming sadness.

Slowly, almost reluctantly, he forced his heavy legs to climb the steps to Lucas's porch. Before reaching for the door, he hesitated, turned, and took another look at the sunset. Nothing. Inner peace continued to elude him.

He opened the unlocked door, stood briefly in the darkened hallway, then went into the empty den. Standing there, listening, he could hear the sound of running water coming from the bathroom. Looking around, he suddenly realized he hadn't been in this room in nearly ten years, yet it hadn't changed much since he was last here. It was old, familiar.

Like Lucas.

Being in this room, in this shrine, seeing the evidence of a military man's great career, did little to lift his trashed spirits. As he surveyed the wall of photos, the weight of despair grew heavier; his spirit sank deeper into depression. He wanted to run, disappear, lose himself in shadows.

But . . .

"Have a seat, my boy. I'll be finished in here shortly,"

Lucas shouted from the bathroom.

Cain walked behind the desk and looked closely at the Picasso painting. It was a work he adored, even though Picasso wasn't his favorite artist. Then he looked down at the picture of himself standing next to Lucas, a photograph taken only months before he left Vietnam forever.

So many years ago.

The bathroom door opened and Lucas emerged wearing a silk bathrobe, blue pajamas, and brown slippers. He smelled of talcum powder and after-shave lotion. His eyes, red and swollen, found Cain's and held them while he filled a large glass with Chivas Regal and ice. When the glass was full, he took a drink, eased behind the desk, and sat in the big leather chair.

Neither man spoke for what seemed an eternity.

"What made you so sure it was me and not Seneca?" Cain finally asked.

"Because you were always the better man. I never doubted it for an instant."

"Disappointed?"

"Not in the least," Lucas said quickly. He sipped at the Scotch. "Regardless of what has transpired, I am genuinely fond of you. Always have been, for that matter."

"You have a peculiar way of showing it."

"Fate sometimes sends us in strange directions."

"It's over, Lucas."

"So I gathered. I watched the news with great interest

this morning and when I heard nothing out of the ordinary, when none of those lovely CNN anchor women informed me that my president had been slain, I could only conclude that the mission had not succeeded. I must admit I was left with mixed emotions."

Lucas picked up a pencil and began doodling. Just as quickly, he put the pencil down and looked at Cain. "I am curious. How did you find out?"

"*Tuez le messager*. It was on a note found in Simon Buckman's hand."

"Brought down by a bottom feeder like Simon Buckman. I don't know whether to laugh or cry."

"Why, Lucas?"

"My boy, I could spend hours trying to explain the *why*s to you, but I'm afraid you would never understand. Not with that rigid sense of right and wrong of yours."

Cain sat in the chair across the desk. "Try me."

"Cutting straight to the heart of the matter, the answer is that I had no other option."

"There are always options, Lucas. Especially for a man with your connections."

"My boy, you don't understand. It's precisely because of those connections that I was left without options. Without choices."

"Who, Lucas? Who could put a man like you in that position? And why?"

"I don't know who."

"Come on, Lucas. You can do better than that. You're behind a plan to kill the president of the United States, and you expect me to believe you don't know who ordered it? That's asking a lot, don't you think?"

"Maybe so, but it's the truth. I don't know. Faceless men; that's all I can tell you."

"Then let's skip to the *why*."

"Why do you think?"

"I have no idea."

"Come, come, my boy, put that wonderful deductive mind of yours to work. Think. I am not a greedy man, nor am I unpatriotic. When you eliminate the obvious, what are you left with?"

"Blackmail."

"Bingo."

"Who?"

"My answer remains unchanged. I don't know who."

"Okay, Lucas, let's forget the *who* and stick with the *why*. What reason would anyone have to blackmail you?"

"Old markers." Lucas emptied his glass in a single swallow, then poured a refill. "Outstanding debts."

"What old markers? What debts? Come on, Lucas, tell me. I want to know. I *need* to know."

"The assassination of Sadat. The shipment of arms to Iran. Selling secrets to Russia. Dealing in the heroin trade. Giving money and supplies to the Taliban. Take your pick. My sins are many."

"You were involved in Sadat's death?"

Lucas nodded. "Sheik Abdel-Rahman ordered the fatwa. I arranged for the assassins to be brought in."

"Why?"

"I'm a soldier. Soldiers take orders."

"Are you telling me someone in our government ordered Sadat's death?"

"Not directly in the government, but closely aligned."

"This 'someone' had the juice to get you involved?"

"That surprises you?"

"Yes."

"My boy, with your track record, you should be well beyond being surprised."

"Who, Lucas? Who ordered it?"

"Who? How can I possibly answer that? A plan of that magnitude starts somewhere near the top, then like slime it works its way downhill. No one ever says the words 'Let's kill Sadat.' There's no paper trail, no taped conversations. It's never like that. It's communicated with a nod of the head, the lifting of an eyebrow, a wink. There's a tacit understanding that 'this must be done, so make it happen.' And it happens."

Lucas sipped more Scotch. "A sordid world we live in; don't you agree?"

"What about the arms shipment to Iran?"

"I had a hand in it. Not a big hand, mind you, but

enough to make me accountable. I had connections on both sides, so it was only natural for me to bring all interested parties together. Once that was accomplished, I performed a few minor functions, then dropped out and left it in the hands of others. Only one or two people knew of my participation. Or so I thought. Then, about six months ago, I received a call from a member of one of those extremist jihadist's factions. He demanded that I meet with him. At first I wasn't overly concerned—I figured him for a crackpot, a hot head. But when I met him, I learned otherwise. He had names, places, dates, my signature on a letter directly linking me to the operation. When I saw that, I knew my neck was in the noose. From then on, I did what I've done my entire life. I followed orders. Only this time, I served a different master."

Cain slumped forward, letting Lucas's words sink in. "And their orders were to kill the president? How could you, a lifelong soldier, even begin to consider such an act?"

"My boy, you haven't been listening. I had no choice. If they had ordered me to kill Jesus Christ, I would have stood shoulder to shoulder with Judas."

Cain's head throbbed; his pulse raced. He felt dizzy, on the verge of throwing up. He leaned back, closed his eyes, took three slow, deep breaths.

Lucas continued. "Although I'm sure this isn't going to mean much in the way of a defense, I'll tell you anyway.

The president was strictly a secondary player in this little drama. The main targets were the other three. You must understand: there are people in the Middle East who prefer war—the killing, the turmoil. Naturally, they don't think much of the peace efforts. There is very little money in peace. They would like nothing better than to see any leader seeking peaceful solutions join Sadat in the grave. War keeps the money flowing in."

"So you called in Seneca?"

"My only hope of avoiding the noose."

"I'm afraid that bit of logic escapes me."

"Elementary, my boy. You see, you and Seneca have always been different sides of the same coin. All I had to do was flip the coin. Either way it was bound to come up 'killer.' I couldn't go wrong. Once Seneca was involved, it would only be a matter of time before you entered the picture. I made sure of that. Of course, I needed a reason for bringing you in, which Deke so kindly supplied when he failed to finish off Cardinal. Then I basically got out of the way and let you do your thing."

"And you were covered either way."

"Absolutely. If Seneca succeeded, I was off the hook with my Arab friends. If you stopped Seneca, I could hardly be faulted for the mission's failure. I'd be safe. At least, until they hatched another plan."

"Which they would have."

"That's the trouble with blackmailers. They tend to

be very persistent."

"You should have come forward, Lucas. You should have told someone, trusted some people."

"Why? So I could watch everything I worked for turn to shit?" Lucas stood and pointed a finger at the wall. "So all of this would be reduced to nothing? So my past would be stripped away like so much dirty wallpaper? No, my boy; that was too steep a price to pay."

"So you sold your soul to a bunch of terrorist thugs? Seems to me that's a pretty high price."

"My boy, I had no choice. I couldn't fight it. The men who brought me on board for Sadat's execution are dead, leaving me to face the music alone. Hell, Carter made Sadat a hero in this country. I had no desire to be the lone figure standing there answering for the death of a martyr. And the Iran thing? I wasn't about to go through the same ordeal MacFarland and Poindexter went through. Or that asshole North. Those Congressmen would have thrown me to the wolves, hung me out to dry. Look what they put North through. He waved the flag, cried, ate apple pie—everything—and he damn near still got crucified. What chance do you think I would've had? And in today's post-9/11 world, how do you think it would have looked when my dealings with the Taliban were uncovered? I would have been portrayed as an old fart trying to make a few extra bucks under the table. Believe me, it wasn't that way at all."

"I believe you, Lucas."

"But you're still going to turn me in."

"Like you, Lucas, I have no other choice. You've committed sins you have to atone for. This. Cardinal's death." Cain paused, waited, then sent out an arrow that drove deep into Lucas's heart. "Treason."

"Ah, yes," Lucas said softly. "You always were big on that one. Good and evil. America now and always. No middle ground. Not for you. Oddly enough, I take great comfort in that. You see, at my deepest core, I share those same sentiments."

Lucas turned and looked at the Picasso painting. After several moments, his back still to Cain, he said, "Giants once roamed the earth. Men of talent, courage, vision. Men who dared to dream, who sought to create splendor and magnificence. They don't exist anymore. They've been replaced by animals who seek nothing more than to prey upon the weak."

"But you aren't weak, Lucas."

"Nor am I as strong as you believe me to be." Lucas turned to face Cain. "You understand, of course, I can't let you take me in."

"Don't make this any harder than it has to be. For either of us."

Lucas reached into the pocket of his bathrobe, took out a .45 automatic, and aimed it at Cain. Tears streamed down his face.

"I've loved you as if you were my own son," he said, his voice choking. "Indeed, in some ways, you are my creation. I don't want to do this, my boy, but there is no way I can allow you to take me in."

Cain eased around the side of the desk, his right hand extended. "You won't shoot me, Lucas. Your hands could never be that bloody."

"I must. Don't you see? I simply cannot allow them to strip me of my honor. Of all that's in this room. On these walls."

"Give me the gun, Lucas."

Lucas backed up until he was directly against the wall, beneath the Picasso painting. Shaking his head, he whispered, "I can't. I simply can't."

"Give it to me, Lucas. It's finished."

Lucas smiled, nodded slightly, put the barrel of the gun against his temple and squeezed the trigger. The force of the bullet drove him violently to the left, slamming him hard against a file cabinet. Blood spattered onto the Picasso. His limp body bounced off the cabinet and dropped to the floor. He blinked twice, let out a final breath, then stared straight ahead. A steady stream of thick, red blood spouted from the wound like water from a spigot.

Cain knelt beside the lifeless body of his old friend, a man he loved like a father. He felt for a pulse, although he knew he wouldn't find one. Lucas was dead. Cain stood and leaned against the wall. Emotions charged within him like rampaging electrons. Sadness. Shock. Relief.

Ultimately, his sense of relief won the race. Relief that Lucas found a way to avoid the humiliation and public disgrace he so feared. That he found a way to keep his past unspoiled. Lucas was free. No one would ever know.

His secrets would go to the grave with him.

The memory of a giant would be left untarnished.

An hour later, Cain pulled his car into a deserted shopping center parking lot and cut the engine. Leaning his head back and closing his eyes, he thought about all he had learned from Lucas. What surprised him most was his lack of surprise. Or outrage. Cain had long suspected Lucas of playing both sides. Many men in Lucas's position did, oftentimes without realizing it. They were ghostly figures operating in a strange parallel world where the line between right and wrong was easily blurred, easily crossed. What he hadn't suspected was the extent of Lucas's activities, the depth of his double-dipping. Somewhere along the way, Lucas had taken a wrong turn, colluded with the wrong devils. How much damage had he caused? How many lives had been lost because of his actions? Those questions could never be answered.

Cain opened his eyes and picked up the envelope he had taken from Lucas's desk. With trembling hands, he opened the envelope, removed the letter, and began reading.

CHAPTER FIFTY FIVE

Gen. Richard L. Collins (Ret.)
525 Ocean Road
St. Augustine, FL 32085
Aug. 15, 1987

Dear Lucas:

As you have no doubt heard by now, your old comrade in arms has recently been given a death sentence. It's the Big C, pancreatic, inoperable, so far advanced that neither chemo nor radiation is a viable option. My doctor says I have maybe three months, but that's being optimistic. Right now I feel fine. I do tend to get a little weak as the day wears on, but overall I'm coping. However, my doctor says when it kicks in for real, I will go downhill rather fast and the end will come quickly.

I have lived now eighty years, more than

three-quarters of a century, a full, rich and rewarding life in every way. I have been blessed with a
wonderful family, a wife who has endured both me
and my military career with graciousness, tolerance,
love, and understanding, and two daughters who are
so gentle and loving that I sometimes question if they
are truly mine. Those three have been the anchor in
my nomadic life, the ones who held things together
when I was circling the globe fighting big wars or putting out small fires. You and I were together on many
of those excursions, so you know what I'm talking
about. A career soldier's family does not have it easy.

The prospect of imminent death does not fright-
en me, Lucas. It angers me. I am simply not ready
to die, and the thought of having to do so at this time
does not make me happy. Is it selfish for a man who
has been given so much to want more time? Yes, but
I couldn't care less. When my time does come, if the
Almighty greets me with open arms, I am likely to
respond with a punch to his cheek. And if he's foolish enough to turn that cheek, I'll punch the other
one as well.

I will not, under any circumstances, go gently
into that good night. The Angel of Death will have a
fight on his hands when he comes for me.

Yesterday, while looking through an old trunk
in the garage, I happened across a photo of you, me,

and Michael that was taken at Arlington Cemetery on July 4, 1960. Michael couldn't have been more than 10 or 11 at the time, yet he was already as tall as either of us. Funny, but I can't recall him being small. Odd, isn't it, for a father to have no memories of his only son as a baby or a small child? I remember the girls as infants, but not Michael. He was always a man.

There have been many times when I envied your relationship with Michael. Oftentimes, I was downright jealous. In many ways, you have been more of a father figure for him than I have. You've certainly spent more time with him, and now that I am at the end of my rope, having not spent more time with my son may be my biggest single regret in life.

Our relationship, as you well know, has always been difficult and stormy. Michael and I seldom seemed to be on the same page about anything. Perhaps that was inevitable, given his extraordinarily high level of intelligence, which far exceeded mine. Goodness knows, he is a sharp lad and always has been. Whatever the reason or cause, we simply never clicked. We may as well have resided in different galaxies. I don't think I was a bad father, and he certainly never was a bad son: a judgment, if accurate, that only adds yet another layer of mystery to the strangeness of our relationship.

Oddly enough, I fear this extreme assessment is more mine than Michael's. Whereas I saw us as separated, he saw us as different. There was, for me at least, a gap that could never be bridged. I don't think Michael ever saw our relationship in those terms. He maintained a hope I could never muster. You would, I suspect, take his side in this matter and you may not be wrong in so doing. The outsider looking in often has the more accurate perspective on such affairs.

You once told me Michael was the greatest soldier you'd ever been privileged to know. Coming from you, that is high praise indeed. As his father, and as a lifelong soldier, I can't begin to express the pride I have for Michael. No father could want or expect more from a son.

However, I can't deny a certain trepidation mixed in with that pride. I am not deaf—I have heard the stories. I know what they say about Michael, and I don't doubt the veracity of those reports. I'm well aware of the myth surrounding him. I'm also certain he likely did more than has been shared with me. As his father, I am positive many of his "deeds" were kept from me. That was probably for the best. I have no yearning to know everything.

Yet, as I close in on the final page of my life, I am continually haunted by a series of questions: The Michael you know, the supreme warrior—where did he come from? Where did he obtain the strength, the will, to perform such deadly deeds? Where did that confidence, that fearlessness, come from? And, finally, what price did he pay for such actions? I can't imagine anyone doing the things he did, then walking away unscathed.

The biblical Cain received a mark for his actions. I have searched my son for such a mark and have not found it. I have looked deep into his eyes, hoping they might reveal answers to my many questions. But those answers are not there, or if they are, then they are far beyond my ability to grasp.

Therefore, I am left to wonder, Is my son a monster? Is he a ruthless creature lacking the quality of mercy? Is that my curse, going to the grave wondering if my own flesh and blood was capable of committing brutal and savage acts without displaying any emotion or regret? If so, I fear I'm in for an unsettling stay in eternity.

I can see you now, Lucas, ramrod straight with Scotch in hand. I can hear your familiar chuckle as you say, "There you go again, Richard, being overly dramatic. No, Michael was not a monster. He was Cain."

Maybe that's the answer, Lucas: sleight-of-hand wordplay to bring me peace before I die. Never confuse Michael for Cain. Isn't that what you advised so many years ago, back when Michael was still in

Vietnam? "Michael is your son, Richard. Cain is an aberration." Wasn't that how you worded it? Yes, I believe it was.

Once again you have the luxury of standing on the outside looking in. You can watch this aberration with awe and amazement, with a certain sense of detachment and always from a safe distance. I cannot. For me, he can never be an aberration. He is my son, always my son. Therefore, the ghosts of his past will follow me to my grave.

I am tired, Lucas. Far too weary to continue this pursuit of answers I will never find. Questions concerning the nature of good and evil, the mystery of faith, the very existence of a supreme deity, whether or not my son is a monster—they have tormented me all my life, and they torment me still. Sadly, I now must confess that those answers continue to elude me.

My days of tilting at windmills have passed, I'm sorry to announce. Father Time has won the race. He gets the big trophy. As for me, I ready myself for the final battle, one I know I'm destined to lose.

Take care, my dear friend, and be well. My ride may have ended, but the many fond memories remain. Know I have treasured our friendship, the adventures we shared, our lengthy discussions, and the vast quantities of Scotch we consumed.

Know this as well: I love Michael more than he

can possibly begin to comprehend. He is my beloved son, in whom I am well pleased.

As for Cain—let him dwell forever in dark places.

Farewell,
Richard

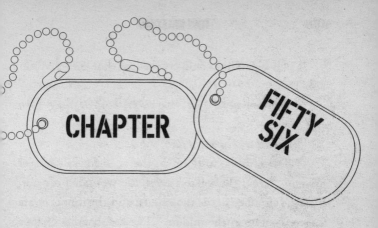

CHAPTER FIFTY SIX

Cain sat on a wooden bench in the small park three blocks from his house. Above him, the trees swayed to a gentle evening breeze. A cardinal circled toward the heavens, writing a silent poem against the star-filled sky.

Cardinal.

Cain's thoughts drifted to his men, magnificent warriors, soldiers who had operated in a dark and bloody world most Americans never knew existed. Men who had done the dirtiest deeds, known the blackest evil. Men who fought a secret war, answering to no one, responsible only to each other.

So many were dead now. Cardinal, Rafe, Deke, Moon, Seneca, Lucas. All history. And Snake. It was only a matter of time before he took his final breath. Cain wanted to cry, to let his tears wash away the blood and grief. But he couldn't. Pity and tears are for the weak. And weakness leads to failure, failure to the grave.

Michael Collins could cry; he had that luxury. Cain didn't.

The killing never ends, does it, my boy? It just goes on and on.

You nailed that one, Lucas.

Wars continue to flourish, the need for killers ever present. Blood flows like a river, the wounded cry out, the dead number in the thousands, and the innocent are forever caught in the middle. The combatants change with the swiftness of the seasons, but the hate and greed and lust for power never cease. If history's cruel lessons have taught us anything, it is this: those better angels Lincoln spoke of have long since flown away.

Cain, and those like him, will never lack for employment. Men in power will see to that. From their high places, their dark rooms, they will send out the call: *assassins wanted.*

And men like Cain will emerge from the shadows.

Always.

Cain opened the letter he had taken from Lucas's desk and read it again. It was, he knew, his father's confession. Not until this moment, not until he had digested his father's words, did Cain realize how heavy was the burden of guilt his father carried deep in his soul. Cain saw this not in the many questions his father asked, but rather in the words unwritten. What had been omitted said more than what was on the page. Richard Collins felt trepidation, questioned his son's "deeds," even asked if his own flesh and blood was a monster. Those questions, Cain knew, were little more than diversionary tactics. Richard Collins was a soldier; as such, while he may not have understood Cain, he did understand the necessity for Cain's existence. He could live with his son being an assassin.

What he couldn't live with, however, and what lay at the heart of his guilt, was his failure to make a greater attempt to bridge the vast chasm between father and son. For Richard Collins, that failure to connect was a far greater sin than any committed by his son. Killing could be forgiven, but distance between father and son could not.

Cain recalled something he overheard during a long-ago conversation between his father and Lucas. "Call him Mickey," Lucas suggested. "Do it one time, Richard, only once. Who knows? Maybe that's all it will take to bring the wall crashing down."

Not once did his father ever call him Mickey.

Cain folded the letter, rose from the bench, and walked back to his house. Kate Marshall sat on the steps, a manila folder in her hands. Her eyes were red and puffy.

"Is it over?" she asked as he sat beside her.

"Yes."

"Will you tell me what it was about?"

"No."

"Why?"

Cain was silent.

"Don't you think I have a right to know, Michael?"

"Let it go, Kate."

"Just like that?"

"Yes, just like that."

"Why should I?"

"It's my world, Kate. You don't belong in it."

"Don't I have a say in that?"

"No."

"I love you, Michael. Maybe more than I've ever loved anybody. And I want a future for us, a life together. But . . ." She opened the folder and removed the letters and photos. "Please, Michael, tell me the truth. That's all I ask. Do that, and I'll deal with wherever it takes me. Wherever it takes us."

"The truth?"

"Yes, the truth. All of it."

"The truth can be tricky."

"It's a risk I'm willing to take."

"Leave it alone, Kate. Close that folder; forget about what you've read; forget about me—about us."

Kate began to cry. She laid the folder down, stood, and faced Cain. "Forget?" she said, wiping her eyes. "Why should I forget? And why is it wrong to want to know about you? About your life?"

"Because my life is off-limits."

"To me?"

"To everyone."

"Why?"

"Because there are rules."

"Rules? That's your answer? Whose rules? Please, Michael, tell me what this was all about?"

"Retribution."

"What does that mean?"

"Debts were paid. Old markers collected."

"You aren't going to be straightforward with me, are you?"

"You wanted the truth—there it is."

Kate pointed to the folder. "Okay, Michael, answer this. Who is Cain? Simple question. Please answer."

Silence.

"One last time, Michael. Who is Cain?"

Silence.

Choking back a sob, Kate handed the folder to Cain, turned, walked to her car, and got in. She started the motor, backed out of the driveway, and drove off into the night.

As her car was swallowed up by the darkness, Cain scooped up the folder and stood on the steps. The hint of a smile crossed his lips. Kate's last words echoed in his head.

"Who is Cain?"

I am.

One More Moment

Check it out! There is a new section on the Medallion Press Web site called "One More Moment." Have you ever gotten to the end of a book and just been crushed that it's over? Aching to know if the star-crossed lovers ever got married? Had kids? With this new section of our Web site, you won't have to wonder anymore! "One More Moment" provides an extension of your favorite book so you can discover what happens after the story.

medallionpress.com

STRESS
FRACTURE

Consultant to the writers of *CSI: Miami*, *Law and Order*, and *House*

D.P. LYLE

Dub Walker, expert in evidence evaluation, crime scene analysis, and criminal psychology, has seen everything throughout his career—over a hundred cases of foul play and countless bloody remains of victims of rape, torture, and unthinkable mutilation. He's sure he's seen it all . . . until now.

When Dub's close friend Sheriff Mike Savage falls victim to a brutal serial killer terrorizing the county, he is dragged into the investigation. The killer—at times calm, cold, and calculating and at others maniacal and out of control—is like no other Dub has encountered. With widely divergent personalities, the killer taunts, threatens, and outmaneuvers Dub at every turn.

While hunting this maniacal predator, Dub uncovers a deadly conspiracy—one driven by unrestrained greed and corruption. Will he be able to stop the conspirators—and the killer—in their bloody tracks?

ISBN# 978-160542134-6
Hardcover / Thriller
US $24.95 / CDN $27.95
AVAILABLE NOW

THE ROAD THROUGH WONDERLAND

Surviving John Holmes

Dawn Schiller

The Road Through Wonderland is Dawn Schiller's chilling account of the childhood that molded her so perfectly to fall for the seduction of "the king of porn," John Holmes, and the bizarre twist of fate that brought them together. With painstaking honesty, Dawn uncovers the truth of her relationship with John, her father figure-turned-forbidden lover who hid her away from his porn movie world and welcomed her into his family along with his wife.

Within these pages, Dawn reveals the perilous road John led her down—from drugs and addiction to beatings, arrests, forced prostitution, and being sold to the drug underworld. Surviving the horrific Wonderland murders, this young innocent entered protective custody, ran from the FBI, endured a heart-wrenching escape from John, and ultimately turned him in to the police.

This is the true story of one of the most infamous of public figures and a young girl's struggle to survive unthinkable abuse. Readers will be left shaken but clutching to real hope at the end of this dark journey on *The Road Through Wonderland*.

Also check out the movie Wonderland (Lions Gate Entertainment, 2003) for a look into the past of Dawn Schiller and the Wonderland Murders.

ISBN# 978-160542083-7
Trade Paperback / Autobiography
US $15.95 / CDN $17.95
AUGUST 2010
www.dawn-schiller.com

A CATCH IN TIME

DALIA RODDY

In one moment, with no explanation, six billion humans fall unconscious. For three minutes, minds collide with truths hidden beyond the physical realm.

During those decisive minutes, every conceivable accident transpires. People reawaken to a world that has changed, drastically and horrifically, with decimated populations and gutted social order. And no one seems to remember the truth that has been revealed.

But Laura remembers—most of it, anyway. Yet even she doesn't know why all post-Blackout births are mutations, and what is so wrong with some of the survivors.

ISBN# 978-160542103-2
Mass Market Paperback / Horror
US $7.95 / CDN $8.95
AVAILABLE NOW

THE FRENZY WAY

GREGORY LAMBERSON

In every hardened cop's worst dreams there lurks a nightmare waiting to become reality. Captain Mace has encountered his. When a string of raped and dismembered corpses appears throughout New York, the investigation draws Mace into an interactive plot that plays like a horror movie. Taking the lead role in this chilling story may be the challenge of his career, testing his skills and his stamina, but even a superhero would find the series of terrifying crime scenarios daunting.

Unlike anything Mace has experienced, every blood-spattered scene filled with body parts and partially eaten human remains looks like an animal's dining room strewn with rotting leftovers. Only Satanic legends and tales from the dark side of spiritual oblivion resemble the mayhem this beast has created in his frenzy. In the wake of each attack is the haunting premonition of another murdering onslaught.

As Mace follows this crimson trail of madness, he must accept the inevitable conclusion. Whoever—or whatever—is responsible for this terror does not intend to stop, and it's up to him to put an end to the chaotic reign of a perpetrator whom, until now, he's met only in the annals of mythology. The mere mention of the word would send New York into a panic: *werewolf.*

ISBN# 978-160542099-8
Mass Market Paperback / Horror
US $7.95 / CDN $8.95
JUNE 2010

www.slimeguy.com

MEDALLION
P R E S S

Want to know what's going on with
your favorite author or what new releases
are coming from Medallion Press?

Now you can receive breaking news,
updates, and more from Medallion Press
straight to your cell phone, e-mail, instant
messenger, or Facebook!

Sign up now at www.twitter.com/MedallionPress
to stay on top of all the happenings in and
around Medallion Press.

For more information
about other great titles from
Medallion Press, visit

m e d a l l i o n p r e s s . c o m